A
Void
the Size
of
the World

A

Void

the Size

of

the World

RACHELE ALPINE

Simon Pulse

New York   London   Toronto   Sydney   New Delhi

For my sister, Amanda . . . your kindness and compassion
for others is inspiring. The world is so lucky to have you.

SIMON PULSE

An imprint of Simon & Schuster Children's Publishing Division

1230 Avenue of the Americas, New York, New York 10020

First Simon Pulse hardcover edition July 2017

Text copyright © 2017 by Rachele Alpine

Jacket photographs copyright © 2017 by Chev Wilkinson (people);

copyright © 2017 by Thinkstock (clouds)

All rights reserved, including the right of reproduction in whole or in part in any form.

SIMON PULSE and colophon are registered trademarks of Simon & Schuster, Inc.

For information about special discounts for bulk purchases, please contact

Simon & Schuster Special Sales at 1-866-506-1949 or business@simonandschuster.com.

The Simon & Schuster Speakers Bureau can bring authors to your live event. For more

information or to book an event contact the Simon & Schuster Speakers Bureau

at 1-866-248-3049 or visit our website at www.simonspeakers.com.

Jacket designed by Regina Flath

Interior designed by Steve Scott

The text of this book was set in Goudy Oldstyle.

Manufactured in the United States of America

2 4 6 8 10 9 7 5 3 1

This book has been cataloged with the Library of Congress.

ISBN 978-1-4814-8571-5 (hc)

ISBN 978-1-4814-8573-9 (eBook)

08 17

Here

These violent delights have violent ends
and in their triumph die, like fire and powder
which, as they kiss, consume.
                    —William Shakespeare

1

I didn't mean to kiss my sister's boyfriend.

At least, not the first time.

The day it happened, thick gray clouds sagged and hung so low that it made you think you could reach out and brush your hand along the bottoms. The air blew fast and forced trees to bend toward the ground as their branches stretched for invisible objects. I kept an eye on the darkening sky as I headed home from my job where I scooped ice cream for sunburned kids, tired parents, and classmates. I snuck free cones even though my manager strictly forbade handouts. It wasn't the most glamorous job, but it was a paycheck. And a paycheck meant money that would get me out of this town one day.

I felt the rain on my back before I saw it; large blobs of water fell on my neck and covered the sidewalk in polka-dotted specks around me.

I was still a ways from my house, but only a block from

Morton Park. I ran and hoped I could make it there before it poured, because the only thing worse than being covered in ice cream was being soaking wet and covered in ice cream.

Most of the park wasn't anything special; it had the usual swings, slide, climbing gym, and seesaw. What made it different was that there was also a graveyard for half a dozen old construction tubes dumped in the grass by the city. They were pulled out of the street when it was repaved with asphalt. The tubes sat covered in graffiti and forgotten except as an alternative jungle gym for kids brave enough to scale their massive shapes.

My sister, Abby, and I used to beg Mom to take us here when we were little. Abby would quickly scurry to the top of some massive piece of equipment and I'd try to follow. I wanted to keep up with her, but instead, I'd slip back down and skin my knees. Abby would stand tall and proud, and the only way I could join her was when she reached out her hand to pull me up.

It was by those same tubes that I saw Tommy.

He had on the giant headphones he always wore, his head bobbing to the music. He moved farther and farther away from me, and I told myself to go over to him before he was gone. But I couldn't. These days it was impossible to be near him. Because he wasn't mine.

A crack of thunder rattled the earth, and Tommy looked up and noticed me. But if he was surprised that I was in the park, he didn't show it.

"Rhylee!" He gestured at me to come toward him, but I remained rooted to my spot.

and around in circles, finding myself back where I started.

Tommy stared outside the tunnel. The rain warped every-thing and made it feel as if we were hiding in some kind of fantasy world.

He reached into his pocket, pulled out a cigarette and a lighter, then waved the two at me. "Is this okay?"

I started to tell him it wasn't, smoking was disgusting, but stopped.

"If you share," I said instead.

"You smoke now?" Tommy asked and tilted his head, as if what I said surprised him. As if I wasn't allowed to change anything he knew about me.

Tommy smoked with some of the other boys at school. They hid behind the baseball dugout, slipping away during lunch. My sister would never dream of smoking, because of running; she said it messed up your lungs. So this, this smok-ing, was something I could do that Abby wouldn't.

I shrugged as if it was no big deal. "I haven't in a while," I lied.

"Since Gina and Joe's wedding?" Tommy asked with the goofy lopsided smile I loved.

I narrowed my eyes at him and stuck out my chin. "I've smoked since then," I told him, which wasn't true at all. In seventh grade when his sister got married in their backyard, the party went into the night, and as our parents celebrated with an endless supply of alcohol, Tommy and I had slipped away with a beer hidden under his jacket and a pack of cigarettes we found abandoned on a table. We drank the beer, passing it back and forth, the foreign taste making our heads foggy and light at the same time. We lit cigarettes and pretended we knew what to do as we coughed our way through tiny puffs that made our eyes water. After, we lay in the field and watched the stars sparkle and shine in the inky blackness around us.

Abby caught us as we headed back, the smell a dead give-away. She was hurt we left her behind. I felt bad and put an arm around her shoulder, pulling her into our group, but she shrugged it off and walked ahead of us. We tried to include her when she was around, but no matter what we did, it seemed that's how she always felt about Tommy's and my friendship. Left behind. Which was so different from what Abby was used to, because my sister was always the center of attention. Tommy had been the one thing that was mine and only mine, but Abby found a way to take him, too.

"We don't have anything better to do while we wait the storm out." Tommy interrupted my thoughts. He pressed on the lighter and held the cigarette against his lips. The end glowed bright as he took a breath in. He slowly blew the smoke out before he passed it to me.

I placed it in my mouth. I sucked in like he did, but the drag was too deep and my eyes watered. I fought the impulse to cough, even though my throat burned. Coughing was a sign of weakness.

"You haven't smoked again, have you." It wasn't a question but a statement. He knew me too well.

"There's a lot of things I haven't done," I told him. "But that doesn't mean I'm not good at them."

"Is that so?" Tommy asked in a slow, drawn-out way. He

reached for the cigarette and his fingers wrapped around mine, holding on for longer than a moment before he took the cigarette back.

"Something like that," I said, my voice caught in my throat. I stopped before I went too far. I was confused by what was going on. It sounded an awful lot like I was flirting with Tommy, and flirting definitely wasn't allowed with your sister's boyfriend. Especially when it felt as if he was flirting back.

The two of us sat so close our shoulders touched, the music from his headphones now a slow, sad song. He didn't mention Abby, and I wasn't about to bring her up. My sister had a way of taking over things. She'd gone with friends to a nearby lake earlier today. She had dropped me off at work on her way, her friends singing along to the radio, their hands trailing out the car windows as they drove away.

A flash illuminated the sky and the thunder that followed was so loud it seemed to shake the ground. I jumped and hit my head on the top of the tunnel.

"You okay?" Tommy touched the spot. His fingers wrapped around a piece of my hair and twirled it. We were so close I could feel the soft cotton of his shirt against my arm.

"I'm fine," I said, but I wasn't. I didn't feel fine at all. Instead, I was nervous and sad, but I definitely didn't want him to know any of that. I took the cigarette from his hand and placed it between my lips again. It was still wet from his mouth. I inhaled deeply, this time getting it right.

"Careful," Tommy said.

Thunder rumbled around us. I closed my eyes. My body hummed with electricity.

"I don't want to be careful," I said.

"Me either." He held my gaze, and I willed myself not to look away. His eyes revealed everything we weren't saying to each other, and I was dizzy with desire.

"I made a mistake," he said.

"I made a bigger one," I replied, and those words opened everything.

Because in this dark tunnel, with the rain pounding down around us, I felt different. Like I was the person Tommy was supposed to be with. I forgot about the night a few months ago when he tried to kiss me and I pushed him away, too scared of how things would change. I didn't think about the hurt on his face that changed to anger, because that wasn't the way he thought it would go. And I certainly didn't remember how I found him later that night, his arms wrapped around my sister as she kissed him in the way I should have.

Instead, I became the person I wish I'd been that night. The one who kissed Tommy back instead of running away scared.

I flicked the cigarette outside and watched it sizzle out in a puddle.

I couldn't wait any longer.

I made the first move, but Tommy didn't hesitate. We closed the space between us. I opened my mouth to let his air in. To let him in. His breath smelled sweet and smoky as his lips slid against mine and erased everything else in the world.

We didn't take things slow. There were no gentle kisses or hesitations. Instead, I kissed him with a furiousness that took my breath away. I pressed myself into him, trying to take everything that I could before I lost it all again.

And he let me.

He pulled me down so I was on top of him, and I would've traded my soul to the devil if we could've stayed like that forever. His skin burned against mine. I kissed him until my lips swelled and bruised, but still I wanted more more more.

Our kisses went beyond this moment. They held years of our friendship; scraped knees and mosquito bites we scratched until they bled, snowball fights on the way home from school, and Tommy crying next to me when a car hit his dog. It was him standing up to the boys who pushed me down in fifth grade, the two of us scaring ourselves silly over the horror movie we weren't supposed to watch, and me standing next to him and holding his hand at his grandma's wake when he was ten. It was the way things were always supposed to be.

He buried his face in my neck, my hair, against my mouth until it seemed as if neither of us could ever breathe again without the other. I don't know how much time went by; a minute, an hour, the entire night, our lifetime. It didn't matter.

Nothing mattered but us.

We kissed until his face was lit up in a flash of lightning. The thunder after was what shocked me back to reality and we paused to catch our breath.

"It was always supposed to be you and me," he said into my hair.

9

"Always," I answered back.

I put my hand on his chest and felt his heart racing through his shirt. He placed his hand on top of mine and this was us.

I thought about what he said. *You and me. You and me. You and me.* And what that would mean to my sister. His words took us to the edge of things that involved "deceit" and "destruction"—but for him, I was willing to jump.

2

I went straight to my room when I got home.

I walked past my eight-year-old brother, Collin, and Mom, who were making cookies in the kitchen, and crept past Abby's bedroom door, which was open enough for me to see that she was in there watching something on her laptop.

I searched through my music on my phone until I found the recording Tommy had made for me for my birthday last year. I'd asked him to record himself playing the piano, and he surprised me by sending a file of songs that sounded so good, you'd think you were sitting in one of those big fancy concert halls I've seen pictures of in New York City or Europe. But that was who Tommy was. He was music, and I had no doubt that one day he'd end up playing in those concert halls. We used to plan our future together. The two of us would go to college in New York City; Tommy would go to a fancy music school and I'd major in something artsy and creative. The two of us would page through old travel magazines and talk about exploring the world together. Tommy would wow audiences with his music, and I'd spend my days discovering places that tourists didn't know about, the hidden parts of the city that exist only for those willing to look.

I hadn't listened to his songs since he started dating Abby, but tonight, it was all I wanted to do. I put my headphones on and the notes poured over me. I thought about the two of us together in the concrete tube, about what didn't happen between us and now what had. I allowed myself once again to dream about a future that held the two of us.

I pulled out the shoe boxes I kept hidden in my closet. Three of them stacked on top of one another. When you opened each, a pair of shoes sat on top of tissue paper, but they were only a decoy. It was what was below that mattered.

They held stacks of papers full of the collages I made. My own secret worlds I had created since I was young. I held on to pieces of junk mail, scribbled doodles in notebook margins, and ripped pages out of magazines with places I longed to go, far off countries I fell asleep dreaming about. I used maps, newspaper articles, receipts, and other tossed-aside items to create backdrops for lives I wished to live. I pieced together letters and words to create poetry over my creations. And always, in the middle of every collage, I pasted an image of myself. Because here, I existed beyond my sister, outside of her shadow, and it seemed possible that if I created enough of these, I might be able to figure out exactly who that person was.

My fourth-grade teacher taught us that in China you go by

your last name first. Your family name is more important than your first name.

That's what life with my sister felt like. If you asked anyone in our town if they knew Abby, they'd tell you that they did. Even if they had never met her in person, they recognized her face. From the black-and-white grainy photos in the newspaper praising whatever race Abby had won that week or the highlights from the news during the sports segments. She was the track star. She was the pretty and smart one. She was the one Tommy was with. Abby was the chosen one.

And I was always Abby's sister, Rhylee. To teachers, friends of my parents, even classmates. Who I was, what I did, had never seemed important to anyone but Tommy, and then I'd lost that too.

But after today, that had all shifted. Tommy wanted me. Maybe I was a fool to believe it, but now that he had been mine for a moment, I didn't want to give him back.

Tonight, as Tommy's music washed over me and the burn of his kiss was still on my lips, I created a new collage. I layered pictures on top of one another to make a city landscape with an apartment in New York where the lights blazed against the ink black sky. And this time, it wasn't just me I placed in the center. I cut out a picture of Tommy so that we were together, and the line between fact and fiction blurred because maybe, just maybe, the images in front of me could be real.

3

I must have dozed off, because I woke up to a dark room and someone knocking on my door.

"Rhylee?" Abby called.

Shit.

I pushed my collages into the shoe boxes and shoved them under the bed. I'd put them away safely when I had the chance.

"Yeah?" I nervously answered, afraid she'd somehow found out. It was one thing to be with Tommy, it will be a completely different thing to admit to Abby what we've done.

"Mom wants to know if you're okay. We're having parmesan chicken for dinner; you never miss that."

I relaxed. She didn't know. She wouldn't be talking about dinner if she did.

"I'm okay, just tired from work," I replied. "Tell her I'll get some leftovers later if I'm hungry."

Abby left without saying anything more and the early

evening gave into night, and things remained the way they always had been. The TV turned on downstairs, and Dad and Collin cheered for the Cleveland Indians. Abby talked with her friends in the bedroom across from me, her laugh punctuated the air every once in a while, and Mom retreated to the bathroom to soak in the tub.

I hid in my room, not daring to come out for fear that everyone would notice I was different, because I sure felt different.

I fell asleep to Tommy's music on repeat; the familiar sound rushed over me and made it feel like everything was going to be okay.

I slept deeply until my phone beeped in the late hours of the night with a message from him. It was only five words, but five words was all it took to unhinge every last piece of me.

I'm breaking up with Abby.

I didn't respond right away. I understood what his words meant and what they'd do to Abby and me. We'd grown so far apart since she began to date Tommy. The cracks in our relationship were already there, and this, this would cause everything between us to crumble.

Was I ready for that?

I should write back and tell him that this couldn't happen. It was the right thing to do. But slowly, a tiny flash of hope began to unfurl.

I didn't want to leave Tommy to Abby anymore. I wanted that high-rise in NYC. I wanted to travel all over the world with him. I wanted to be a part of his life.

There was no way I could continue to pretend I didn't care that he and my sister were together. I'd lost him once; I wasn't going to make the same mistake a second time.

I want to be with you, I texted, and before I could stop myself, hit the send button.

I deleted both messages so Abby would never see them, the words burned into my heart. And in my ears, his music rose and fell in peaks and valleys, invading every part of me as if I was breathing in the sounds of him, absorbing them into my soul.

4

Three days passed and I didn't hear back from
Tommy. I caught glimpses of him at school, but it was only for
a quick moment and we never made contact. Our secret still
seemed to be just that, a secret.

All around me, life too was paused. Fall would be here
soon, and the world hung in a hazy suspension of denial. The
kind where you suddenly felt like you needed to do everything
you hadn't, but all you want to do is sit still and will the minutes not to rush forward.

I had grabbed the mail when I got home from school and
now sat at the kitchen table sorting through the newest stack
of college brochures. I saved the ones from the schools that
I could see myself at and ripped out images from the schools
that I wasn't interested in, to use in my collages.

These brochures had almost become an obsession. Ever
since our guidance counselor talked to our sophomore class

about "thinking ahead to our future" and told us how to request information, I couldn't get enough. The school had wanted to give all of us a push, try to boost their numbers of students who went to college, even though it was pointless; most of my classmates were fine with staying in Coffinberry their whole damn lives. But that wouldn't be me. I contacted all kinds of schools: big and small, universities in the middle of nowhere and others in big cities. It didn't matter. The only prerequisite was a school that didn't have a strong athletics program. My parents hadn't even gone to college, so it wasn't something they pushed on Abby and me, but the idea of living in a place that Abby didn't dominate was enough to motivate me to do whatever it took to get myself out of here.

Collin walked in and took a seat at the table. He waved his hands in front of the big fan that did nothing but stir the hot air around. It blew his blond hair straight back.

"Careful," I told him. "You'll chop your fingers off if they get stuck in there."

"They will not," Collin said.

I shrugged. "Maybe I'm wrong, but I sure wouldn't want to find out."

I handed a rolled-up piece of paper to him, and when he opened it, his eyes got huge.

"Another edition to your story," I told him. It was his own personal comic book. I'd been adding to it for months, ever since Collin wandered into my room one day when I was working on a collage.

18

"Can you create one of these for me?" he'd asked. "Something that gives me superpowers?"

And how could I say no? I made him a world where he was the hero. I created images where Collin leaped buildings, tamed tigers, and was cheered while up at bat by a baseball stadium packed with fans. I put him at the center of the universe in every picture, and he hung each one up over his bed. A quilt made from pictures where my brother ruled.

In today's collage, he soared through the solar system and raced alongside comets. I'd ripped pictures out of an old science textbook I'd found at the library's used book sale and created a sky peppered with stars.

"What do you think? Do you like it? I thought it was about time we got rid of you and sent you to the moon."

Collin stuck his tongue out at me but grinned. "I love it." He bent over and examined it up close.

"Good, I thought you would."

I grabbed a soda out of the fridge and headed outside to the porch to search for a breeze. The day was sweltering; even walking from room to room created a fine mist of sweat all over my body.

I sat on the old porch swing Dad had hung years ago and moved slowly back and forth, my bare feet scraping against the dusty wooden boards of our porch. In the distance, gray clouds sat lazily on the horizon and the sky flashed bright with lightning. In this heat, storms blew through daily, and today's would be here soon, stirring up the stale muggy air. My skin tingled as I remembered the park and the way

Tommy and I had kissed as if we couldn't get enough of each other.

The hum of a motor filled the air as Dad cut the field to the left of our house.

He sat on his old riding mower twice a week and followed the lines up and down in the early afternoon before he left for the night shift, attaching bumpers to the front of fancy cars we could never dream of affording. Bumpers that came in glossy colors with names like candy apple red and champagne bliss. He worked at the same car factory most of my classmates would end up at. The same one I'd end up at if I didn't get out of this town.

He mowed straight lines for Abby to run, and she ruled the field just as she ruled the cross-country team at our high school. Her long muscled legs raced the stretch along the woods, down the path Dad created, and up against the old wooden fence that separated our yard from Tommy's. Abby ran that trail every day. She never stopped moving, her blond hair shining in the sun, and I'd watch from the porch and wish I could be my sister.

I was born shortly after she turned a year old, and Mom would talk about how crazy those first two years were. We looked alike, but there wasn't anything twin-like about us. Her outgoing and confident personality was a foil to my quiet, introverted self. She was part of a team while I dreamed of leaving everyone behind and discovering a world that right now I was so small and insignificant in. She was the one teachers loved. They'd tell me over and over again that I was nothing like my sister. It was meant as a joke, but beneath, there was a sense of disappointment, exactly like the one I felt from my parents when I'd get a bad grade or they'd bug me to join a club at school, to get involved, as if it were so simple to find a place for myself when my world was so full of Abby.

Tommy was always the only thing I'd had that she didn't. And then she'd taken him, too.

But now I had him back.

And I liked that feeling.

My long hair stuck to the back of my neck in the heat. I twisted it around my hands and wished for a hair tie. Dad must be boiling out there without any shade. The rain would be welcomed, cooling us all.

The screen door creaked, and Abby came out and sat next to me. I stiffened. The ice in my glass clinked together as the swing moved back and forth from her weight.

"I swear, it's pretty much child abuse not to have air conditioning," Abby said and fanned her face with her hand. "It's cooler out here than it is inside."

"It feels like the whole world is on fire," I told her in a voice that didn't sound like my own. I was someone pretending everything was okay, and I was sure she could see through me, but she didn't.

"Your scrapbooking stuff is all over the table again," Abby said, and I relaxed a tiny bit. She wouldn't be complaining about that if Tommy had talked to her.

"It's not scrapbooking," I argued, even though it was pointless. Abby didn't get it. No one did. A few years ago I'd shown my family a collage that had taken me hours to complete. It was on a giant piece of butcher paper, and I'd pieced together images and items from a family vacation. Abby thought it was hilarious that I'd spend that much time "playing with a glue stick," Dad hardly glanced at it, and Mom told me she thought it was "cute." It was stupid, really, to think they'd care. If it didn't have Abby's name attached to it, then forget about it. So now I kept that stuff private. They'd probably laugh me out of the house if I told them I actually thought I might like to do something with art for a living.

"Right, those pictures you make," she said in a way that made them feel so stupid and dumb. "Anyways, that's not why I'm here. I'm bored."

She held out a bottle of nail polish. It was pale pink, like the inside of a seashell. The same color she had on her nails.

"Give me your feet. I need something to do and it's too hot to run."

"I was about to work on some homework," I lied.

"Oh, please, homework can wait. I need someone to talk to, so stay out here and let me paint your toes," Abby ordered.

I did as she said, because I didn't have a better excuse. I stuck out my legs and laid them in her lap. They were even paler against her sun-colored legs, browned from days of running with the cross-country team. She slapped the bottle against the side of her hand and then bent over to draw the brush across my first toe. Her hair fell against my legs and tickled my skin.

"Don't move," she instructed when I wiggled.

The air shifted slightly as the storm drew closer; the loose pieces of hair twirled around my face. I wanted to be anywhere but here, but maybe this was my punishment for what I'd done. I was forced to face my sister straight on, and it sucked.

Abby concentrated as she painted each nail, the tip of her tongue sticking out the side of her mouth. The only noise was the buzzing of Dad's mower across the field and the low voices from some TV show Mom was watching inside. I studied my sister's face. The summer had stamped a constellation of freckles across her nose. It was odd to be this close to her when we'd grown so far apart. Tommy had pulled us away from each other, and it made me anxious to think about the secret I held inside.

When she finished the first foot, she pulled back and inspected her work.

"It looks good," I told her, and she nodded. She moved on to my second foot, dipping the brush into the bottle after each toe.

"Do you ever feel like something bad is going to happen?" she asked.

I closed my eyes and remembered Tommy's lips against mine. How we had betrayed her. "Bad things happen all the time. The news is nothing but gloom and doom."

She gazed across the field to Tommy's house. You could see the second-floor windows and roof from this far away. When I was younger, Tommy and I sent coded messages with flashlights. But that was so long ago. Now his light switched on and off as he lived a life separate from my own.

"Things aren't right," Abby said, and paused. A drop of

23

polish fell off the brush onto the porch. It spread out in a small puddle and sank into the wood.

I tried to brush it away with my thumb. Mom would kill us if she found it, but Abby didn't seem to care. She went back to painting my toes.

"I think Tommy's going to break up with me," she continued.

I jerked my foot away and a streak of polish smeared across the top of my foot.

"Jesus, Rhylee, look at what you did," Abby complained.

Far off, the sky grumbled as the sound of thunder reached us.

Shit. Did she know about the text message? Had Tommy said something?

"Here, give me your foot back so I can fix it before the polish dries."

I stayed still so she could finish and tried not to act as completely freaked out as I felt. She didn't know anything. She couldn't. Abby wasn't the type of person to play games, so if Tommy had told her about the park and the text message, she'd say something.

"Why do you think something is wrong?" I asked cautiously.

"He's being really strange, and he hasn't been over here in a few days. He keeps coming up with excuses that I know aren't true, because Mary Grace told me she saw him this morning at Otis's Diner when he said he had to help his dad with his truck."

She put the brush back into the bottle and rolled the polish back and forth in her hands. I'd never seen my sister this nervous before; she was the confident one. Even before a race, she was strangely cool and unaffected. So this seemed odd. Off. In a world where Abby was usually in control and the chosen one, the roles were suddenly reversed. This fear was something different, and even though I was the cause, I had to admit that I kind of liked it.

"He's probably busy," I said. "It's the end of the summer. I'm sure he's spending a lot of time helping his family out with the farm."

"No, it's not that. Something is going on." She sat straight up and tilted her head as if inspecting me. "You don't think he's cheating on me, do you?"

The soda I was taking a sip from went down the wrong way, and I coughed. I couldn't catch my breath and my eyes watered.

"Geez, what's your problem?" Abby pounded on my back as if that would help.

"Nothing," I said when I caught my breath. "I drank too much at once."

"What do you think?"

"About what?" I asked, done with the conversation. I didn't want to be out here anymore.

"About Tommy cheating on me."

"Tommy would tell you if something was going on; that's the type of person he is," I said, and thought of the text he'd sent me about breaking up with her.

"Yeah, I'm being stupid. Tommy and I are fine, right?"

I paused before answering. I remembered back to the

morning after the party when I had pushed him away from me and found them kissing. Abby had knocked on my bedroom door and climbed into bed with me, like we used to do when we were kids.

"Promise you won't get mad," she'd whispered, the two of us under the covers.

"Promise," I'd said, because how can you be mad at something you caused?

"Tommy kissed me last night."

I didn't tell her I already knew. That I had seen the two of them tangled around each other, and it had broken my heart.

"It's okay, right?" she asked. "You and Tommy aren't like that. . . ."

"No, of course we're not," I interrupted her, because what else could I do? I'd never told Abby how I felt about Tommy. And I'd had my chance with him, but I'd pushed him away. How could I stake my claim when it wasn't mine to stake?

But now, here, outside on our porch, I wanted to say the words I didn't all those months ago when Abby told me about the kiss she didn't know I saw. I could tell her I was in love with Tommy and had been for years. I could tell her how much it hurt to see the two of them together. I could confess the truth and maybe she'd understand.

But what if she didn't? Abby always got what she wanted. So instead, I lied.

"I'm sure everything is fine." I looked off over our field

toward Tommy's house. The sky had darkened and the clouds raced in now. The storm would soon be here.

"You're right," Abby said. "I'm worrying about nothing."

"Exactly," I said. "Things will work out just the way they're supposed to."

5

Coffinberry, Ohio, is a pit. A town of about a thousand people, most of whom will never travel more than forty miles past its borders in their entire lives. A town so small we leave our back doors unlocked and if we aren't careful, we'll run out of people to kiss and have to start all over again at the beginning of the line. So when there isn't any fun to be had, we create our own. We walk through the fields and make fires deep enough in the woods that our parents turn a blind eye. The same woods they partied in when they were our age.

Saturday night began exactly like all the other nights where we hiked into the woods, carrying backpacks full of beer and scratchy wool blankets. It was the end of the summer. Fall loomed up behind us, and everyone was eager to let loose, ready to celebrate one of the last nights of warm weather.

I followed Abby and her friends across our field. It was

obvious our discussion yesterday hadn't worked. My sister was anxious and jumpy, talking and trailing off midsentence. I was anxious and jumpy too; I had no idea when Tommy was going to talk with her. I both dreaded and wanted it to happen.

Abby opened her purse and pulled out two of those miniature bottles of vodka. She dumped them into a water bottle of orange juice she'd poured in our kitchen while waiting for her friends Mary Grace and Erica to arrive.

"What are you doing?" I asked. This wasn't right. Abby never drank. Ever.

"Lighten up," she said and playfully tugged on the end of my ponytail. She pushed the cup at me. "I'm happy to share."

"I'm fine," I told her. Everything about this was off and made me uneasy.

"Suit yourself," she said.

We made our way through the woods to the bonfire. I soon fell a ways behind the girls, but it didn't matter because they pretty much acted as if I didn't even exist as they talked and joked with one another. I cursed myself for not agreeing to go with my best friend, Tessa, but she was getting a ride with her boyfriend, which pretty much meant being the third wheel to their nonstop PDA.

"We need to leave at eleven thirty," Abby reminded me. "Don't be late, or you can explain to Mom and Dad about why you missed curfew."

"I'll be here," I said, but Abby and her friends had already scattered, disappearing into the shadows as they made their way to the fire.

I followed behind. A mix of fear and excitement pulsed through my body as I thought about Tommy. Maybe tonight. Maybe it would happen tonight.

I spotted Tessa near the fire and waved.

"There you are, girl! I've been waiting forever for you to show up." She wrapped her arms around me and gave me a giant kiss on the cheek. One that probably left a bright red lipstick mark on me.

Leave it to Tessa to greet me in her usual dramatic fashion. Tessa was a hugger, and greeted everyone as if they were her long lost friend.

"Let me get a look at you." She put both hands on my shoulders and stepped back to inspect me. Her curly red hair was piled on top of her head in a messy bun and she had on jeans tucked into yellow rain boots. Ever since I'd met Tessa in kindergarten, when she'd colored her entire body in bright orange polka dots with a Sharpie marker from our teacher's desk, she did everything loud and big. She wanted to be on Broadway, and I had no doubt she'd make it there. Tessa had the confidence I wished I had and when she left a room, everyone remembered her.

I stood awkwardly as she took in my outfit of jeans and a tight black T-shirt that was cut just a little lower than I was comfortable with.

"You look hot!" she declared.

"You think?" I fiddled with the top of the shirt. She batted my hand away and pulled it even lower than before.

"I know so. Tommy will definitely notice you," she said and winked at me.

"Shhh," I hissed and looked around to see if anyone else heard. "Are you crazy?"

"Relax. Everyone here is either too drunk or too horny to care about you and your crush. Why don't you just tell him how you really feel already and get it on so I can stop listening to you moan about how in love you are with him?"

"Um, I think there's a little obstacle in the way called my sister," I said.

Tessa laughed. "Nah, your sister is a blip on the map. You're the one Tommy wants; you just have to let him know you're ready for him."

"The only thing I'm ready for is something to drink," I told her, so I wouldn't have to listen anymore. I was pretty sure Tessa's number one goal in life was to get Tommy and me together, regardless of what was in the way. I couldn't decide if I loved her optimism or wished she'd just let it go. One thing I did know was that she would go nuts when she found out that we'd kissed, and I hated keeping it from her, but I wanted to keep it to myself a little longer.

"And I'm going to get me some Jarrett." She pointed to where her boyfriend stood. She let out a wolf whistle and when he noticed, she blew a kiss his way.

"Keep it PG," I joked.

"I can't promise anything." She gave me a wave over her shoulder and skipped off toward him.

I stood near the fire for a moment and watched sticks pop and crackle in the flames. The night was loud and full of energy. Music played from a truck that had pioneered a road through the woods. Kids from school ran past, their voices rising and falling in the muggy air.

Abby stood in front of the flames with Mary Grace. They looked like day and night together; Abby with her long blond hair next to Mary Grace with her tangle of dark curls. The two had their arms outstretched and faces turned up to the sky, spinning in circles. Abby moved so close to the fire that I half expected her to come out the other side, ablaze and streaming trails of light behind her.

I headed away from the fire. I told myself I was going the long way to get a drink, but in reality, I wanted to go back to where everyone parked to see if Tommy's truck was there.

When I reached the clearing in the woods, it wasn't only Tommy's truck I found, but Tommy himself. He sat inside with the headlights off. A country song played on the radio, the singer crooning about love gone wrong.

"Hey," he said to me out the window, and I felt shy, as if Tommy and I were strangers. I didn't know how to act around him now.

"Hey," I said back.

"Is your sister here?"

I tried not to look upset, but it was hard when the first thing he asked was about Abby. "She's over by the fire."

He didn't say anything, so I felt the need to keep talking. To fill in the silence. "She's been drinking. She never drinks."

"It's because of me," he said.

It was dark here. Shadows moved around his face so his features went in and out of focus. It warped who he was, and

32

I wondered if I looked different to him, too, because I sure as hell felt different.

"She's worried about you," I offered. "She asked me if I had any idea what was wrong."

"I'm pretty sure she knows what I'm planning to do." He climbed out of his truck so he was directly in front of me. "I never should've been with her in the first place," he said, and I let his words slip through me, fragile and thin.

"Then why were you?" I asked, because I had to. It wasn't like it was a one-time hook-up. They'd been dating for months. If he liked me, then why stay with her?

"That night—when you pushed me away, I was confused and hurt. I thought . . . I thought I was wrong. About everything. When Abby found me and kissed me, I didn't stop her."

"You could've ended things."

"I didn't know how. I tried to ignore how I felt and let myself believe Abby was right for me, but you can only pretend for so long."

"And I pretended like it didn't bother me," I said.

"But it did."

"It did," I confirmed, and a tremor of nervous excitement raced through my body. What was happening between us was real. I hadn't imagined it and however wrong it might be, Tommy felt the same.

If I were a good sister, I'd stop this from happening. I wouldn't want my sister to get hurt. But I wasn't good anymore. Not even close. Because I wanted to be with Tommy. I wanted him to be mine.

I reached out and touched his cheek. It was warm and smooth as if he'd just shaved. He placed his hand on top of mine, never once taking his eyes off me.

"I don't want the summer to end," someone at the fire shouted. "Screw school; I'm staying right here."

People cheered, and above them all, Abby shouted, "Tonight we're free!"

I wanted to be free too.

I pulled Tommy to me. He fell into me and his touch consumed me. He kissed me again as if it was what he'd been waiting for his entire life. His lips pressed against mine, and I took from Tommy until the sounds around me melted away. We kissed and we kissed.

"What are you *doing?*" A voice screamed and the two of us broke apart.

It was Abby.

"How could you?" she cried, and the pain on her face made it feel as if someone had punched me in the stomach and knocked the air right out of me.

I tried to say something, but I opened and closed my mouth, words useless. This wasn't supposed to be how she found out. This wasn't supposed to happen.

She turned and disappeared into the woods.

"Shit, shit, shit," Tommy muttered and backed away. "I need a flashlight."

I reached out to touch him, to calm him down so we could figure out what to do, how to make this right, but he pushed me away from him.

I stumbled and fell back to the ground. Pain shot through my wrist as I broke my fall, but it didn't hurt nearly as much as knowing how much I just hurt my sister.

"I need a goddamn flashlight," he yelled and rummaged around in the truck bed until he found one. He turned it on, raced into the woods, and vanished into the trees.

6

I went after Tommy and Abby.

The branches slapped and tore at my skin as I raced into the woods with only the light from my phone to guide me.

The party raged behind me. My classmates whooped and laughed, and their world seemed so separate from mine.

I found Abby before I found Tommy.

Her own phone's light winked as she ran through the trees.

"Abby," I yelled, and she stopped and turned toward me. Her face was a mess of tears, and pieces of her hair blew in front of her and stuck to her wet cheeks.

"Get away from me," she sobbed.

I reached out to touch her, to get her to look at me. She flinched as if I'd burned her, and I felt like a monster.

"No," she moaned as she walked backward.

"You need to come with me, it's not safe out here," I said. "Please, let's go back to the fire."

"I always knew," she said through her tears.

"What?"

"How Tommy felt about you. I ignored it, but it was there. Always."

I didn't know what to say; what could I say? It was true.

For once in my life, I was the chosen one. Tommy had wanted me instead of Abby.

And tonight, he'd chosen me again—but at what cost?

"Please," Abby begged. "You've done enough tonight. Leave me alone. Tell Tommy to do the same. I can't look at the two of you right now."

"Abby, wait." I tried to reach out to her again, but she'd already turned away from me. I touched nothing but thin air.

I tried to follow her, and got turned around. Everything was dark and confusing, as if I were running in a maze.

I wandered through the woods with only the light of my phone to guide me. I should've been terrified to be here alone at night, but I wasn't. I needed to find my sister and make right what I'd done.

Finally, a flash of light bounced off the trees and Tommy appeared in front of me.

"You haven't found her?" he asked.

"I tried to talk to her a few minutes ago, but she wouldn't listen. She told me to leave her alone and ran off. We need to find her and talk to her. We have to make this right."

Tommy nodded, and together we moved through the woods calling out and hoping to catch a glimpse of her as we shined the flashlight through the trees. We searched for more than an hour, but there was no sign of her.

"Do you think she went back to the fire?" Tommy asked.

"She's probably with Mary Grace and her other friends, telling them what I did."

"This wasn't the way it was supposed to happen," he whispered.

The wind rushed through the trees making a howling noise, and I shivered. This night was trying to swallow us whole.

7

We silently made our way out of the woods. I convinced myself that Abby would be okay. She'd find us back at the party. She'd be fine. She always was.

I walked close enough to Tommy that our shoulders touched. I breathed in his scent and began to believe he could be mine. Things hadn't happened in the best way—but they'd happened and opened up a world of possibility.

The clearing was still full of classmates and the bonfire blazed. I scanned the crowd to see if I could find Abby, but there was no sign of her.

I waited while Tommy walked through the group of people, weaving around classmates downing cans of beer.

"I bet she's already home," he said when he made it back to me, and I nodded.

Tommy and I walked to his truck, and even if someone

noticed us, it wasn't unusual. We were friends. We had been long before my sister staked her claim.

I stared into the woods as we drove home, and worried Abby was still in there, moving through the trees like one of those forest sprites that existed only in fairy tales. I studied the dark edges of the trees at a stop sign and imagined her there, reaching the end of the woods and turning around to be swallowed up again, as if afraid to enter back into our world. A world now full of betrayals and dishonesty.

8

Tommy didn't pull into my driveway. He stopped right before it, so we were half hidden under the canopy of an old oak tree.

The light was on in Abby's room, and I breathed a sigh of relief. She was home.

"Do you want to talk to her?" I asked as his headlights winked off.

"Not tonight."

"What do we tell her?"

"The truth."

Before we could say anything more, the front porch light switched on and I froze, expecting Abby to step outside. Instead, Dad opened the door and waved a hand in the air to us before closing it again.

"I think that's my cue to leave," I said.

"Life's going to suck for a while once everyone finds out

what we did, but this . . . this is us. This has always been us."

Tommy grabbed my hand and squeezed it. A calm settled over me. He was right. It would work out. How could it not after we had finally found our way back to each other?

I got out of the truck and watched him drive away. In the morning I'd have a lot of explaining to do, but for tonight, all I wanted to do was close my eyes and remember what it felt like when Tommy was mine.

Gone

What's done cannot be undone.
—William Shakespeare

1

I fully intended to hide from the morning as long as possible, because whatever faced me outside my door wasn't going to be pretty—even though I deserved it after what I'd done last night. What kind of awful person kissed her sister's boyfriend? Two separate times. I buried my face in my pillow and groaned. Not because I regretted what I'd done, but because I wanted to do it again.

I was surprised Abby hadn't stormed into my room yet. That was unlike her. She was always ready to make it known when she was pissed about something, whereas I was a pro at holding things inside, so it appeared as if everything was fine even if it wasn't. It was eerily quiet, which made the potential of what she was plotting a lot worse. We'd had our fair share of fights before, but I doubted they'd be anything like the one today.

I stayed in bed and tried to make sense of what had happened with Tommy. I hadn't set out to hurt my sister, but I did, and I had no idea how I'd even begin to make things right again. Especially if making it right meant not being with Tommy.

I reached for my phone on my night table, but couldn't find it. The drawer was open and as I searched for it in there, my hand landed on a piece of paper I'd hidden. I pulled out the picture of Tommy and me together in the made-up NYC apartment and thought about what I had wanted and what I did to my sister to get it.

I was granted twenty more minutes to myself until the floorboards creaked outside my room. I waited for the pounding I'd prepared myself for, but instead, the person knocked quickly and then tried to turn the knob.

"Rhylee, are you up? We need to talk." It was my dad, his voice hard and insistent.

Of course this was how it would go. Why would Abby take me on alone when she could pull Dad into it?

I crawled out of bed and had barely unlocked the door before he pushed it open and stepped into the room. He still had on pajamas; a pair of flannel pants that were a little too short and a worn white undershirt. It was rare to see Dad dressed like this, since he was usually getting home from his job when we were waking up. But it was Sunday, and that was the one day where Dad's nights and days weren't backward.

He surveyed my room.

"Is Abby here?"

"No," I said. His words were a glimmer of hope. Maybe I was safe for a little bit longer. Maybe she hadn't told Dad yet.

He certainly wasn't acting like someone who had any idea what I'd done.

"Have you seen her?"

"Not since last night at the bonfire."

"Didn't she come home with Tommy? His truck was outside."

"That was me," I said, afraid my voice would give too much away.

"Why wasn't she with the two of you? Why would he give you a ride home and not your sister?" he asked, and paced back and forth. That's when I knew for sure this wasn't about Tommy.

But I wasn't about to tell Dad the real reason why Abby didn't come home with us; he'd find out soon enough. "She was with her friends. I wanted to leave because I didn't feel good."

Dad stopped pacing, and I could tell what he was going to say even before the words came out. "She hasn't come home."

"I saw her light was on when I got home."

"Your mom thought she left the light on when she dropped off some of Abby's laundry. Her bed is still made with the clothes your mother washed piled up on it. She didn't sleep there and she's shut off her cell phone. We can't get in touch with her." Dad looked around my room one more time, as if he might find Abby. "Dress quickly and come downstairs. This isn't good."

2

I changed in record time and headed downstairs, where I found Collin in the family room watching TV and eating a big bowl of sugary cereal; the kind Mom never let us have but Dad always bought and snuck into the house. I ruffled his hair and went into the living room, where Mom sat on the couch, her shoulders hunched over and the rims of her eyes stained red. Usually on Sundays she was up early, dancing around to the radio that we keep on the kitchen table and making a big breakfast for us. Today she looked like a different person.

She stood when she saw me and I was sure she could see what I had done written all over my face.

"Why did you leave Abby last night?" Mom asked, her voice ragged and hoarse. She was barefoot in a pair of faded jeans and a wrinkled blue blouse that she wore to work. It was as if she'd grabbed whatever was nearby and threw it on.

"I didn't mean to," I told her. It was the truth. I didn't mean for any of this, not at all. "She was supposed to have a ride home. I'm sure she's at one of her friend's houses."

"Abby would've called. She wouldn't make us worry like this."

Mom was right, and it made me sick to think about. This was unlike Abby; she never missed curfew and she always checked in if she was going to be late.

But then again, she'd never had to come home to the person who had betrayed her.

"Calm down. This isn't Rhylee's fault," Dad said. "We need to focus and call as many of Abby's friends as we can think of."

He picked up a pad of paper and passed it to me. I glanced down and saw a list of names.

"What is this?" I asked him.

"We made a list of people to call. Are there any other names you can add? Who was she supposed to go home with?"

"We walked through the field with Mary Grace and Erica. I figured she'd go back with them."

"Okay, I'll call both girls."

I read through the names he'd already written down and saw everyone on the cross-country team Abby ran with, her friends from school, and, at the top of the list, Tommy.

"Have you talked to Tommy?" I asked.

Dad shook his head, and I held up my cell phone.

"I'll call him." I walked into the kitchen before they could object.

Tommy picked up on the first ring. "Hey, you," he said, and I swear I could hear the smile in his voice.

"Hey," I said back and then paused, unsure of what to say next.

"So how are things? You're still alive, huh?"

"Barely. And only because I haven't talked to Abby yet."

"Me either. Her phone is off. I'm surprised she hasn't busted down your door."

"She didn't come home last night," I told him, and saying the words out loud made me uneasy.

"What do you mean she didn't come home?" Tommy asked, and I could hear the same panicked sound in his voice that Dad had.

"She's not here."

"Have you called her friends?"

"My dad is doing that right now. I said I'd check with you and see if you had talked to her."

"I'll come over and help."

"Not right now. Things are too confusing. My parents are trying to track her down. I'll call you as soon as we find something out. Everything will be okay. I'm sure she'll be home any minute now," I said. But a heavy, deep feeling sat in my chest and I was afraid that wasn't the truth.

"Are you sure?" he asked.

"Positive. I'll talk to you later."

I hung up and walked back into the living room. Dad told the person he was talking with to wait.

"What did he say?" he asked.

Mom looked up expectantly, and I wished I had something to say to make everything better.

"He hasn't heard from her since we left," I said.

"I'll keep calling people," Dad said. "She probably overslept at one of her friend's houses."

Mom closed her eyes and took a deep breath. Abby never overslept. She was out running in the morning before any of us even thought about opening our eyes.

Dad and I went through each of the numbers on the list, but each reply was the same: No one had any idea where she was. All of these girls were safe at home with their families and my sister wasn't with them. Mary Grace told Dad that she tried to find Abby before she left and when she couldn't, she figured Abby was with Tommy.

But my sister wasn't with Tommy, and it was impossible to ignore the panic that was welling up inside; it fluttered like a bird that was trapped and couldn't get out.

A phone tree was set up, and in a town our size, that meant pretty much every person in Coffinberry received a message asking if they'd seen my sister.

Each and every reply was the same.

My sister was missing.

Dad moved on to another call. He spoke in a low hushed voice, but I could still tell that he was talking to the police.

Mom's shoulders shook as the tears she'd been holding inside escaped, and I stood helpless, drowning in guilt.

How had this gone so wrong?

3

The police showed up quietly. There were no flashing lights or sirens. Not that I expected cars to speed into our driveway and kick up dust as they screeched to a stop, like in the movies, but there should be something more to make this feel like a big deal. Because this had become a very big deal.

It was rare to need the police in our town. Disturbances were few and usually involved a noise outside that turned out to be a raccoon scavenging for food or a group of kids skinny-dipping at Black Willow Lake.

But this wasn't the first visit from a set of police officers at our house. The last time the police came to our door was a lot different. It was almost a year ago and late at night when the doorbell rang. Hound Dog had started a frenzy of barking that probably woke up everyone within a five-mile radius. I'd stumbled out of bed to the stairs, where I'd sat with Collin, hoping no one would notice and tell us to go back upstairs.

Abby had stood between the cops, dressed in black with smudges of thick dark paint under her eyes, a cross between a ninja and baseball player. She'd grinned at my parents and the cops had looked amused themselves, nothing like the gruff look they had when they walked up the bleachers during a football game and made sure no one was heading down the path of juvenile delinquency.

"Is everything all right?" Dad had asked. He'd stood in front of Mom with the door opened all the way so light snuck out and let anyone who was driving by know that the cops were at our house. "Is my daughter in some kind of trouble?"

The cops had exchanged a glance and then turned back to my parents. Hound Dog gave up his quest to sniff out their intentions and trotted up the steps to me. I'd grabbed his collar in my hand and scratched his ears the way that he loved, to get him to settle down.

"Well, she's not exactly in trouble," the bald cop had said. "We caught your daughter and a couple of other kids dropping off cards and flowers on people's doorsteps."

Mom had raised her eyebrows in confusion. "Cards and flowers? Why would Abby be delivering that?"

"Sympathy cards, Mom. To those on Bolton's team," she'd said, mentioning the cross-country team they'd be competing against at the meet in the morning. Abby had pulled an envelope out of her book bag and passed it to Mom.

"We wrote them out expressing the sadness we felt for the

other team's future loss tomorrow. We gave them flowers to let them know we're thinking of them in this time of great sorrow."

"You've got to be kidding," Dad had said, and tried to look angry for the cops' sake, but I could tell he'd wanted to laugh along with Abby.

"We don't think she was causing harm, but it's after curfew," one of the officers said.

"Yes, thank you, sir," Dad had said, acting serious. "We'll make sure to talk to her about this matter."

The cops had nodded and turned to leave, but the bald one had stopped. He crossed his arms across his chest and stared down Abby. "I think a fair punishment would be to win your race tomorrow."

"I can handle that," Abby had said, and patted the cop on the back as if he were an old friend, something I'd never dare to do.

Dad had waited until the door was closed to start laughing himself silly. "Really, Abby? Sympathy cards?"

Abby had shrugged. "Well, it wasn't as if we were going to congratulate them. We wanted to make the team feel better since we're going to destroy them tomorrow."

She'd grinned, and what could they do? It was the way Abby was.

And true to her word, Abby flew past the other team and reminded us on the car ride home that she had fulfilled her punishment.

Today, there were once again cops standing at our front door, but this time, Abby wasn't with them and no one was smiling.

4

The officers sat at our kitchen table, as if we were about to eat breakfast together. I half expected Mom to pull out one of her famous egg and sausage casseroles from the oven, but instead, she slouched in a chair and cried. I'd only seen Mom cry two times in my life: when Grandma died and on Collin's first day of preschool.

The kettle whistled on the stove as Dad made cups of tea. He moved back and forth across the kitchen, never settling for too long in one place. Collin sat wide-eyed, too enthralled by having real live cops in his kitchen to watch cartoons, and I avoided eye contact, as if they could see my truth just by looking at me.

"Are you here to bring Abby home?" Collin asked, and we fell quiet at the bluntness of his question.

"That's the plan," the older one, who'd introduced himself as Officer Donovan, said. He pulled a stick of gum out of his pocket and gave it to Collin. "You'll be fighting with your big sister again before you know it."

Collin grinned and unwrapped the gum while Officer Donovan focused on me.

"We need to get a statement from you about what happened last night."

"A statement?" I asked. My pulse quickened. That sounded official and important.

"No need to worry," he told me. "It's to help us get the events in order, so we can find your sister faster."

"Okay," I said. I twisted the bottom of my shirt around in my hands.

"When you left the bonfire, your sister was still there?" The second cop, Officer Scarano, asked, ready to note my every word on his pad of paper. He couldn't have been more than a few years older than me.

They sat on either side of me, and it felt as if I were trapped between them. I glanced from one to the other and neither of them relaxed the rigid look on their faces. They weren't messing around, and the seriousness of it scared me.

I hesitated.

If I let them know what really happened, maybe it would help. But I couldn't find the courage to do it, especially in front of the police. I'd told one story to my parents; what would happen if I changed it? They weren't going to care about why I kissed Tommy; all they'd listen to is the fact that I'd done this to my sister.

"Abby told me to leave, that she'd get a ride from her

friends," I said, which was the truth. I wasn't lying, I was simply leaving out the part about her saying it after she had caught me kissing her boyfriend and wanted me as far away from her as possible. My parents would hear all about it when she finally did return home. "Tommy dropped me off, and I went to bed."

"What time was that?" Officer Scarano asked.

"I don't know, around eleven? Dad saw us come home. He flashed the lights."

He nodded. "I thought it was the three of you coming home together."

"Is there additional information you can remember? Any little detail might help us figure out where she is," Officer Donovan added.

I paused, the truth dangling so close.

"Tell him something," Mom insisted, startling us all.

"Rhylee," Officer Scarano said, "time is important in helping us to bring your sister home. Any piece of information might help."

My mind flashed back to the look on Abby's face when she found Tommy and me together. She'd trusted me, and I betrayed her. I'd done this. There was no one to blame but myself.

"Help us find Abby," Mom shouted. She grabbed my upper arm. Her fingers dug into my skin. "Don't you understand? Something might have happened to her. We need to find her."

Mom's voice was close to hysterical. I looked at the floor, ashamed.

"I . . . that night, Tommy and I . . ." I wanted to tell. I really did, but the words wouldn't come out. How do you tell your parents that you kissed your sister's boyfriend? You couldn't. "I don't know. I don't have anything else to say that might help."

"That's not good enough," Mom snapped, and I wished I had the courage to say more.

"Rhylee's trying her best," Dad said to Mom. "Why don't you go see if you can find some pictures of Abby for the police to use?"

It was unnecessary; the entire town knew what Abby looked like. She was our star. They didn't need a photo of her.

"Can I go talk to Tommy?" I asked, and if anyone thought it was unusual, they didn't show it.

Officer Donovan nodded. "Tell him to come over here, if you don't mind. We need to get his statement too, and it'd be easier if we could stay here with your parents."

I agreed and ran toward Tommy's house. I needed him to tell me it was going to be okay.

5

I heard Tommy's music before I saw him.

The sound of notes from a song swelled and floated out the windows of his living room. He was hunched over the keys of his piano, and his fingers moved so fast they blurred. He played with a passion and talent that was unexpected. No one had any idea where it came from. He'd simply sat at their piano one day when he was little and plucked out a tune. His parents enrolled him in lessons, and to his teacher's amazement, he conquered pieces each week that usually took others a month to learn. He began to write his own songs when we were in middle school—silly ones at first that the two of us would make up words for, but now he created pieces that could make your chest swell with emotion. Tommy's music was one of the things I loved about him.

He was barefoot; he always played barefoot. He had on his usual jeans and one of the vintage T-shirts he searched for at the Goodwill a few towns over. The black ink of his tattoo peeked out from under the sleeve, a contradiction on someone who played the piano at the level Tommy did. But that's always been who he was: a contradiction in so many ways, including subverting everyone's expectations of the two of us ending up together when he began to date Abby.

I listened as he played, until his fingers rested on the keys.

I knocked on the window to get his attention and our eyes met. My body vibrated from the adrenaline. Neither one of us moved. It wasn't until a car flew around the corner, its brakes screeching, that I was startled out of his gaze.

"You're here," he said through the screen, and there was such genuine happiness on his face.

Happiness for me.

He still felt it, and my heart hurt for what I had to say next.

"The police are at our house," I told him through the screen. "Abby still isn't home and no one has seen her."

Tommy swung his legs over the side of the piano bench and jumped up. The front door opened and he came outside.

"Where is she?" he asked, his voice fast and frantic.

"I don't know. None of her friends remember seeing her when they left. And now the police are involved and they're asking questions and looking for pictures of her and they want you to come over so they can talk to you. . . ." My words hung in the air, their meaning heavy and serious.

He shook his head, but our denials couldn't erase what had happened. "We shouldn't have left without her."

"I tried get her to come with me," I said. But did I try hard enough? Did I really do everything I could have?

Tommy paced back and forth across his porch, his bare feet slapping against the old boards.

"This is my fault. I did this to my sister and now she's gone." My voice rose until I was yelling hysterically. I thought about the policemen in our living room and my parents and about the truth. Tommy and I had ignited all of this and now the repercussions of our actions were exploding around us. "I did this."

I backed away, but he grabbed me. He wrapped me in his arms and hugged my body against his.

"There's no 'I.' There's us. The two of us. You're not alone."

My knees buckled from the weight of it all, but he held tight. He refused to let me go.

"You're not alone," he repeated.

I gave up fighting and let him hold me.

"I did this," I sobbed, and continued to say the words over and over again into his chest.

6

Tommy and I walked side by side with just enough space between us that we didn't touch. No one knew what we'd done, and now, all of my hopes felt sour in the face of Abby's disappearance. The closer we got to my house, the more anxious I became, but I forced myself to go numb so my guilt wouldn't shine through and reveal everything to everyone.

I filled him in on what I told the cops. "I didn't say anything about the kiss. Or that Abby ran into the woods. They think I got sick and you took me home. I told them Abby was going to leave with Mary Grace." I said all of this in a hushed voice, like I was telling him a secret, and in a way, I was.

"We need to tell the truth," he said.

I shook my head quickly. "No, we can't. Think about how it would look if I change my story. Everything will be fine. Abby will come home, and we'll deal with it then."

I waited for him to argue, but he didn't.

"You're right. She'll be back in no time and everything will come out then," he said. But like me, he didn't sound convinced.

We slipped in through the back door and sat in the living room on the couch. Dad nodded at Tommy, and Mom gave him a sad half smile. I couldn't look at the two cops. I was pretty sure that if I did, they'd see the truth.

"I'm here to help," Tommy told my parents. "If there's anything I can do, let me know."

I put my elbows on my knees and bent forward, as my parents and the police went over and over the same facts about my sister, searching for a clue that would reveal itself in the information that seemed to play on a loop. I acted like things were fine. I pretended I hadn't just come from Tommy's house, where we'd held each other and worried about the role we'd played in all of this. I became a part of the group and focused on finding my sister. That's the way it had to be.

7

When Abby ran, some of her races would be so close that she'd go stride for stride with another runner. We'd hold our breaths as they neared the finish line and wait to see who'd pull forward in the end. Every single second counted and one misstep could cost her everything.

That's how I felt today when we searched for her.

I learned there was a certain protocol when someone goes missing. Things move fast, because the first twenty-four hours are the most crucial in bringing the person home okay. As time ticks away, so does the chance of a happy ending.

When it was clear that Abby wasn't staying at a friend's house, a call went out for volunteers, people who were willing to come over and help search for her. The police questioned everyone at the bonfire and talked with Johnson Franklin, an old Vietnam vet who lived in an army tent back in the woods about two miles from where the bonfire was. He was a fixture of our town and could be found every day pushing his shopping cart along our small main street, a handwritten sign hanging over the side, asking to please "Remember Those Who Served for You." He didn't take handouts, didn't want your money, and the only time he participated in a town event was during the Memorial Day parade, where he made sure to shake the hand of every man who served our nation. If you tried to offer him a place to stay, he'd tell you he "slept in the jungle during the war, and he can sure as hell survive in a forest in Ohio."

"He's been questioned in depth," Officer Scarano told my parents. "We're confident he isn't tied to Abby's disappearance."

"I'm relieved that he isn't a part of this," Dad said. "I only wish we had some answers. A way to bring Abby back to us."

"We all do, Mr. Towers. Believe me, we're looking."

Tommy's parents walked over with steaming carafes of coffee, and Tessa showed up with two giant pizzas from Calloos's, our go-to food when one of us was having a bad day.

"I have pepperoni pizza and cheesy bread with extra dipping sauce," she said as she presented the boxes to me.

"Thanks," I told her, even though I was pretty sure Collin would be the only one to eat the pizza. Food was the last thing on our minds.

"The more important question is, how are you?" she asked.

"I'm fine," I said, but I wasn't, not even close.

"That's bullshit," she said, always one to call me out on a lie.

"Okay, right. Things could be better."

Tessa rolled her eyes. "This is ridiculous. Your sister has

everyone worried. What a screwed-up way of sleeping off a hangover," she said, because years of friendship gave her the power to speak about Abby like that. She pulled a bag of M&M's from her purse and threw a few of them into her mouth. Tessa was always carrying some kind of candy; she devoured it as if her life depended on hourly sugar rushes.

"I'm not so sure it's a hangover," I said, and the words made me feel sick. "Let's go see what everyone is talking about." I pointed toward a large group that had gathered by the barn. Tommy stood at the edge, away from Abby's friends. He was alone, and Tessa headed toward him.

"Hey," he said to both of us. I tried not to look at him too long, afraid Tessa would be able to tell what we'd done just from the electricity that sparked in the air between us.

"This sucks, huh?" Tessa asked. "I told Rhylee it's going to be fine. Abby will come waltzing back home any minute now, and we'll laugh one day about how we overreacted."

"I hope so," Tommy said.

A man in a red polo shirt with a clipboard whistled loudly to get everyone's attention. He directed us to spread out in a line; our heels touched the road, our toes, the grass. We clasped hands and formed a giant chain.

"Okay, everyone," he said, "we need you to move slowly and keep your eyes on the ground. We're looking for clues. Something that might confirm that Abby was here. Don't rule anything out; a piece of paper, crumpled-up wrappers, things that may look like trash. Even if it doesn't seem like anything, it could be."

When we were ready, he gave the signal to move across the field. Tessa shook the rest of her M&M's into her mouth and held my hand tight. Tommy grabbed my other hand, and I flashed back to the day in the park in the tunnel and how badly I had wanted to be with him then. I tried to shake the memory out of my head. It wasn't right to be feeling things for him now, and I needed to focus on what we were doing.

The search reminded me of the game red rover we used to play on the playground with our classmates. We'd stand the same way, our hands clasped tightly as we yelled, "Red rover, red rover," inviting those who looked weak over. We'd tighten our grip, hot and sweaty, squeezing one another so the person from the other side couldn't break through. We stood strong and united, laughing when our human wall held the other side out.

I was part of a chain with thirty-six other searchers and we slowly moved across my family's field, walking the same path I'd walked with Abby and her friends the night before on the way to the bonfire. We took baby steps across the great expanse of our field that Abby could run in eleven minutes flat. Today it took almost an hour to cross. There was no running, no chanting, no laughing. We didn't want to keep anyone out of our wall. We wanted to find something.

Or someone.

We walked across the field slowly and kept our eyes to the ground, desperate for even the smallest clue.

"Hey, can we stop for a minute? This might be important," a man in a plaid shirt said and bent down. A murmur went through the group. People rushed to surround him. He held a gray sweatshirt high in the air as if it were a winning lottery ticket.

I recognized it. Abby had worn it the night before.

I let go of Tessa and Tommy's hands and pushed my way to the center of the circle where everyone was gathered. I stopped at the spot where the man found it. The ground was covered with brittle pieces of grass baked by the sun. Abby had been here. I bent down and pretended to tie my shoe, but instead, I grabbed a handful of grass and stuck it in my pocket, so I could somehow be close to her. I tried to convince myself that she'd dropped it on our walk to the bonfire, but as I stood, Tommy's face was full of fear, and mine reflected the same.

Officer Donovan took the sweatshirt and put it in a plastic bag. He didn't ask me if it was my sister's; he didn't even look at me. It was as if I wasn't even connected to her anymore. As if I wasn't even Abby's sister any longer. I was nobody.

We joined hands and continued our search. When we got to the woods, we walked as close to one another as we could, only breaking to go around trees. Step by step by step. We walked past the bonfire site to where Abby found Tommy and me, and continued to move through the trees. We didn't stop until we reached the edge of the river. No one talked, as if our words would change our worst fears into reality.

Officer Scarano and two other officers I didn't recognize walked a ways down, inspecting something in the dirt. One of them took out a camera and snapped some pictures.

"I'm going over there," I said.

"Maybe you shouldn't," Tessa told me, and Tommy nodded.

"Screw that, this is about my sister."

I let go of their hands and made my way over to the group. Officer Scarano spotted me, opened his mouth to say something, but then closed it. Whatever was out here couldn't be hidden from me. I'd find out. I was family.

But when I saw what they were inspecting, I wish I hadn't.

There were shoe prints in the dirt.

Fresh ones. There was no water gathered in them from the rains earlier this week, nor had the sun baked them dry. I put my shoe next to one of the prints. It was the same size as my own. The same size as Abby's.

I followed them until they stopped. The two officers were already scrutinizing them. They went right to the edge of the river. It looked as if one foot had gotten stuck deep in the mud, while the other foot streaked down and disappeared into the river.

It terrified me to think of Abby here, running along the river our parents had forbidden us to go near when we were younger. We stayed away from it, especially at this time of year when the bank was slippery and the water was high and fast from the heavy summer storms. It was to be avoided.

Except for last night, when Abby ran along the edge to get away from me.

Deep down inside of me, something shifted.

My sister was not okay.

And it was my fault.

8

Mom was waiting when I came back with the group from the fields. The police had told her it would be better to stay at home in case Abby returned, especially since Dad was driving around in his old Buick with some other men from the car factory, hoping to find her.

Mom saw Tessa and me, and she rubbed her hands against the sides of her jeans like she does when she's nervous. As we got closer, most of the group broke away and walked to their cars or the barn.

"Do you want me to stick around for a little bit?" Tessa asked. "Because I will. I'll stay all night if you need me to. Heck, I'll move in if it helps."

I wanted to smile, but it was impossible.

"Thanks," I said, and considered telling her everything.

Tessa was my best friend. She had been since we were six. We didn't keep secrets from each other. Ever. But now, it seemed as if all I did was hide things from people I cared about.

Things that made everything worse.

"Hang in there," Tessa said. "It'll be okay. Abby always lands on her feet."

I nodded, because it was easier to pretend things would work out than talk about how they might not.

"If you need me, all you have to do is text." She waved her phone in the air as she headed to her car.

It wasn't until she was gone that I became strongly aware that my hand was still gripping Tommy's. I took a deep breath and let myself hold on for a moment longer. I wanted to be connected to him, but this wasn't the right time. There might never be a right time again.

"I need to talk with my mom," I told him.

"I'll call you later," he said, but I shook my head.

"I don't think that's a good idea. I'll let you know the minute I hear something about Abby, but maybe it's best if we stayed away from each other."

His forehead creased in that way it does when he's upset. "We need each other."

"My *sister* needs me," I said.

He opened his mouth to say something, but I interrupted him. "I'll let you know if we hear anything, but for now, just give me space."

"Okay, if that's what you want," he said.

"It has to be what I want."

Above us, a helicopter made laps around the woods where Abby was last seen.

9

Abby didn't return for dinner.

She didn't return at all that night.

The police told my parents about her sweatshirt and footprints. Mom hadn't been able to stop crying since.

"Why is Mama so sad?" Collin asked, and it about broke me.

I bent down so we were on the same level.

"She misses Abby," I said. "We all miss Abby."

"Where is she?"

It was the first time I'd heard him ask, and I wondered what my parents had told him.

"She'll be back soon," I said, hoping he'd believe what even I couldn't.

"She's left us," he said firmly. When he fixed his gaze on me, his eyes were a dark blue like midnight. "She's gone."

"Don't be silly. Abby will be home before we know it, and

you'll wish she was gone again because she'll be bugging you so bad!"

My words got caught in my throat. It felt as if I was lying to Collin and that scared the hell out of me.

I threw one of the couch pillows at his head to distract him. He giggled and threw it back. I was about to send it over to him again when he spoke up.

"She visited me last night."

I froze, the pillow in my hands. "What do you mean?"

"When I was sleeping. I woke up and she was scratching on my window screen. She wanted to come in, but I couldn't get it open. Her hair was tangled with sticks and she was covered in mud."

I moved so I was real close to Collin. "Did you tell Mom and Dad that you saw her?"

He shook his head. "She told me not to. She said it was a secret."

"Why would she say that?"

"She didn't want anyone else to know she was out there."

"You were having a dream," I told Collin, but goose bumps covered my arms. "It was a bad dream."

"She was there," he insisted, and I didn't argue. I knew exactly how he felt. I wanted to believe she was out there too, because Abby haunted my every moment, and all I wanted was to see her again.

10

That night the wind blew wildly through my open bedroom window, moving the curtains like tissue paper ghosts.

I pressed my face against the screen and searched for Abby, while another storm rolled in over the field where she ran.

Lightning flashed and illuminated the corners of my room before it plunged into darkness again. But the storm was far off and never reached us.

I waited for her to come, and when sleep finally took hold, I yearned to see her in my dreams. I wanted Abby to appear, so I could tell her I was sorry, that I never meant for this to happen, but my dreams were empty.

There was nothing but black, black space.

11

The alarm went off the next morning, and I slammed my hand on the snooze button.

It went off three more times before I finally yanked the cord out of the wall.

I couldn't get out of bed.

I didn't want to get out of bed.

I didn't deserve to get out of bed.

A new day had come, even though I willed it not to. Abby was still missing. The secret burned hot within me, scorching my insides so it felt as if I might explode.

The sunlight grew brighter through my curtains, but all I wished for was a world of darkness where I could waste away as the blame burrowed deep within me.

The grass I had grabbed from the spot where Abby's sweatshirt was found was scattered across my dresser, a tangible reminder of the nightmare we were now living.

My family moved around the house, doors opened and closed, low voices, except for Collin's good-byes as he got onto the school bus.

At first I thought my parents were going to leave, forget that I still existed, my absence from breakfast not even something they noticed. It would make sense if they did. With Abby gone, I didn't know where I belonged.

But I was wrong. There was a knock on my door.

"Rhylee, are you awake?" Dad asked from the other side.

"I'm here," I told him. "You can come in."

"Hey, kiddo," he said, sitting on the edge of my bed. It felt weird to have him call me that, a term he hadn't used since I was young. "Not a good morning, huh?"

"The worst," I told him.

"I hear you. Do you want me to call you in sick from school?"

I nodded, afraid I'd cry if I spoke. He was being so nice to me, and I didn't deserve any of it. I owed him the truth, but it was the one thing I couldn't bring myself to give him. I was a coward.

When Collin got mad or upset, he'd put his fingers in his ears and sing real loud so he didn't have to listen to us. That's what I wanted to do right now, but I had a feeling that as much as I tried or no matter if I put my fingers in my ears and hummed and hummed and hummed, I wouldn't be able to escape the reality of what was happening.

"I'm going to head out to look for Abby, but your mom is downstairs. Are you okay here?"

"Yeah, I'm good."

"Give me a call if you need me." Dad placed a hand on my shoulder. "We're going to bring Abby home," he said with such certainty that I couldn't help but believe him.

I made myself get up and put my feet on the floor. I went into the bathroom, the door to Abby's room still closed tight. Usually the two of us fought over the tiny space. She'd dry her hair while the I tried to brush my teeth, or I'd want to shower and she'd be washing her face. It was a constant battle. Mom forbade us from locking each other out, but we never listened. It was pretty much inevitable that one of us would wake the rest of the house by pounding on the door for the other to get out.

I'd always wished for my own bathroom.

Just not like this.

Abby's toothbrush sat in its holder, ready for her to come use it. Her pale blue towel hung on the hook by the door and one of her hair ties sat on the sink with some golden hair wrapped around it. Everything waited for her to return.

I brushed my teeth and it felt strange to be doing something so normal when Abby wasn't here. The world moved on and we went through the motions, but none of it felt right. I examined my face in the mirror. I looked the same, but I didn't recognize myself. I was a stranger.

Dad was gone by the time I made it downstairs. I'm sure he was driving the streets in search of Abby. Hoping to find her among the other people in our town, as if it were a regular day and she'd only gone out for a run or to grab a doughnut at Otis's Diner.

I wondered where Tommy was. Did he go to school today? He'd left me alone like I asked, but last night he had gone out with Dad and a few other neighbors. They had searched the dirt roads that were used to access the hunting trails.

I'd picked up my phone a few times to text him, but I never sent them. As much as I missed Tommy and wanted to talk, I couldn't see how that would ever be possible again. Not after what we'd done to Abby.

The only thing I could think about was finding my sister, and as I finished eating a bagel, that's exactly what I set out to do. I didn't bother to leave a note; I figured my parents wouldn't be back until later, and if they did come home, they'd assume I was at school. I slipped out the door and headed into the field.

There wasn't a question about where I was heading. I took the same path Abby, Mary Grace, Erica, and I had walked on our way to the party. The ground was still wet from last night's storms, creating pockets of mud from the ruts where Dad's mower had gone. The grass brushed against the bottom of my legs, and a lazy breeze blew around me until I reached the woods. Once I entered the trees, the outside world was silenced. Except for the snapping of twigs and rustling of the leaves, it was only me.

I followed the trail into the woods and watched everything around me; my eyes scanned left and right as I hoped to catch a glimpse of my sister. It was eerie being here alone. The leaves on the trees created a canopy, so only bits of light escaped through the open spaces and reached the ground.

I caught a flash of movement out of the corner of my eye and froze. I prayed it was Abby, but when I crept forward for a closer look, I saw it was Johnson. He wore a blue thermal shirt that seemed too hot for this weather and clutched a pile of sticks against his chest.

The police had said that he wasn't a suspect, but how could he not be when he lived in the same woods my sister disappeared in? Had he seen her that night? Or heard her? Was he holding something back? I wanted to shout out to him, ask him what he knew, but I was alone in the woods that had swallowed my sister up; I was too scared to do anything more than wait for him to leave.

My hands were in fists. I relaxed them and continued along the path until I arrived at the bonfire site, now just a hole of black soot and charred logs. I kicked at one of the stones that lined the circle and when it didn't budge, a sharp lick of pain surged through my foot. But even that wasn't enough to numb all of my emotions. Abby had been here two days ago, twirling around the flames with her arms held out. How happy and carefree she had been.

I walked over to where the cars had been parked. There were tire tracks in the dirt filled with cloudy rainwater and crumpled-up beer cans. A reminder that people had been here.

Tommy and I had been here.

And Abby had found us.

I sank to the ground as thoughts spun around my head. They made me so dizzy it was hard to think straight.

What had I done to my sister?

Why hadn't I chased after *her*?

Why hadn't I *insisted* she come back with me when I saw her at the river?

Why hadn't I told her I was sorry?

Each *what-if* taunted me. There were so many things I could have done, but I didn't do any of them.

My mind flashed to Max Locke. He was in my class until last year, when his family moved away. He was supposed to stay home and watch his little brother one day, but instead he took his brother with him to the park so he could hang out with friends. When he wasn't watching, his brother wandered into the street, where a car hit him. He survived, but he was never, ever the same. I remember the way people at school treated Max. What they said to him and how they made him into some kind of monster. He never intended for that to happen to his brother. It was an accident, but it didn't matter. People would view me the same way if I told the truth about what happened.

I went in the direction Abby had when she ran away from Tommy and me. I moved through the woods quickly, as if it were that night again, and I was following her. I slapped tree branches out of the way and tripped over roots, but that didn't stop me. I moved faster and faster until I burst out into a clearing.

I was at the river.

The water moved swiftly. It churned and took anything in its way with it. A tree limb the size of a small car passed by me in an instant.

"Abby," I yelled, but the roar of the river was the only response.

I took a few small steps toward the river until my feet were at the edge of the embankment.

"Abby, please, you need to come home," I shouted into the empty spaces around me. "We need you."

I choked on my words.

"I need you."

I shifted my weight to take another step and slipped. My right foot slid down the muddy bank into the water. I grabbed at the roots that lined the edge and tried to pull myself up. I could feel the current tugging on me.

I clawed my way back, moving on all fours like an animal, struggling to get away from the angry water.

My pants got stuck on a rock, and it tore a hole through them, the cold water a shock to my bare skin. A bright red line of blood appeared, and I hurried to pull myself up all the way. I moved a few feet away from the river and fell to the ground.

I lay there, my chest heaving up and down, my heart punching against my skin. I'd almost gone into the water. I could've been swept away.

Panic set in as I imagined my sister too close to the edge so that with one misstep, the water could swallow her up.

The thought took my breath away, and it felt as if I were the one who was drowning.

12

I burst out of the woods and ran through our field as if an invisible demon was chasing me. I moved through the mowed lines my sister ran, and as I got close to our house, my parents and Officer Scarano rushed toward me.

"Rhylee, what's wrong?" Dad asked, alarmed.

I was a mess. My jeans were torn and bloody, my clothes were caked with dried mud, and my hands were scraped.

"Everything," I told him, and I choked back the fear that was threatening to smother me.

"Are you okay?" Mom asked. "Where have you been?"

"I tried to find her. I went back to the woods where the bonfire was. I searched by the river, but she wasn't there."

I broke down. I couldn't be strong any longer. I sank to the ground and brought my knees to my chest. I put my head down and sobbed, too ashamed to look at anyone.

Dad kneeled and pulled me to him. He rocked me like he had when I was young.

"You've been so strong, Rhylee. I know this is hard, but we have to believe she's going to find her way home." The stiff hairs from his beard rubbed against my cheek, and I wanted so badly to believe him.

But it wasn't true. I was by the river. I saw the footprints and how easy it was to be pulled into the water. Abby wasn't okay. She wasn't going to be okay. And if they had any idea what I'd done, no one would want to touch me anymore. No one would want to be near me.

"I need to ask you about that night again," Officer Scarano said when I let go of Dad.

I was suddenly on guard. What else did they want to know?

"I told you everything I know."

"It's about Tommy. You two are close, right?"

"We're friends," I said, and tried to be careful with my word choice because I had no idea where this was heading.

"Do you remember seeing him at the bonfire while you were there?"

"Yeah," I said cautiously.

"Do you remember if there was ever a point when you didn't see him around? Maybe for a little bit?"

"I don't know, maybe. He's my sister's boyfriend, not mine. I don't know what he's doing all the time. Why is that important?"

Mom and Dad exchanged glances. The two of them then

turned toward Officer Scarano. It made me nervous.

"What's going on?" I asked.

Officer Scarano cleared his throat before he spoke. "Tommy's being interviewed by some detectives right now."

"What for?"

"Rhylee, let's go inside. We can talk about this later," Dad said, placing a hand on my shoulder, but I shook it off.

"Tell me what's going on," I demanded.

"Some of your classmates came forward and said that they heard Abby yelling at someone near the bonfire. When one of them went to check on her, they saw Tommy push your sister down and then Abby and Tommy ran into the woods. We're trying to figure out what it was about." Officer Scarano said it as if it were no big deal. As if we were simply having casual conversation.

I sucked in my breath. I remembered how I'd reached out to Tommy to stop him. That wasn't my sister they saw, that was me.

"No," I said, not just to my parents and Officer Scarano but also to myself. "You're making a mistake. Tommy wouldn't hurt Abby."

"We're not saying that he did, but we need to check our leads."

"What leads?" I demanded. "Who's blaming him?"

When the officer wouldn't reply, Mom spoke up. "His shoe prints were found along the riverbank. Near where we found the ones that match Abby's shoe. But he said he never went near the water."

"I have to talk to him," I said, a sense of unease rising within me.

"You need to stay away from him," Mom said, surprising us all. She loved Tommy. She joked that she had four children, since he was over so much.

"You can't possibly believe he did something to Abby, can you, Mom? This is Tommy we're talking about," I said, mostly to convince her but also to silence the sliver of doubt that had edged into my mind.

Mom just stared at me. "Right now, all I know is that my daughter is missing and Tommy is the last person to have seen her," she finally said.

"He's not a suspect, is he?" I asked Officer Scarano, and when he didn't reply, Dad spoke up.

"We're trying to bring your sister home," he said. "That's what we need to focus on."

"Tommy didn't do anything to Abby," I said, but my words didn't sound so confident. And when the three of them said nothing, suddenly it wasn't only my sister I was afraid for, but also Tommy.

13

Tommy is not a suspect.

Tommy is not a suspect.

Tommy is not a suspect.

I sat in my room and wrote the words over and over again on notebook paper. I tried to make myself believe it was true. My pen pressed down so hard that it left an imprint on my desk.

Tommy was a good person. He'd never do anything to Abby.

But the police had planted a small doubt into me, and I wasn't sure I could shake it out of my mind. There were about thirty minutes between when Abby had run away from me and Tommy found me. What was he doing during that time?

I ripped a new sheet of paper out of my notebook and wrote a list of what might have gone on during those lost minutes:

1. *Looking for Abby*
2. *Arguing with Abby*
3. *Trying to talk Abby into returning to the bonfire*
4. *Breaking up with Abby*
5. *Tommy did something to Abby*

My pencil hovered over number five. I was scared to put down what the cops and my parents were thinking.

Tommy couldn't have done anything.

He wouldn't have done anything.

Right?

I crossed off five, then four, then three, then two. I pretended there were no other reasons or answers beyond Tommy searching the woods for my sister.

I grabbed a glue stick and created a new sort of collage. I pasted the scraps that proclaimed *Tommy is not a suspect* over my list. One on top of the other until the list disappeared and there was nothing but Tommy's innocence.

14

Mom might have forbidden me from talking to Tommy, but that was all the more reason I needed to. Forget about leads and what the police thought they'd found. I had to hear it from him that he didn't do anything.

I waited until my parents went to a community meeting to discuss efforts in the search for Abby. Collin was at a friend's house, so it was easy to slip away.

I walked alongside the road, not wanting to cut through the field. It didn't feel right when Abby wasn't here to run it every day.

It was dusk, that time of day when the bottom of the horizon seems to fade beneath the darkening sky. I wondered where Abby was and whether or not she saw the same sky.

Tommy's light was on in his room. His curtains were drawn, but a shadow moved in front of them. I pulled out my phone and dialed his number.

"I need to talk to you," I said when he answered. "I'm outside your window."

The curtains parted and Tommy appeared. The light behind him illuminated his face, and I felt the familiar pull toward him.

He held his index finger up, indicating that he needed a minute, the curtain dropped, and he disappeared again.

I waited for what felt like forever and almost thought he'd changed his mind when he walked out from the back of the house.

"Is something wrong?" he asked.

"The police questioned you," I said. "They said someone saw you running into the woods after Abby."

The light from his eyes faded.

"They're calling you a suspect," I continued.

"I'd never hurt Abby. You can't believe that," Tommy said.

I shook my head. "I don't know what to think, this is all so crazy."

Tommy sat on his front step and put his head in his hands. I reached out and my hand hovered over his back. In the life before Abby went missing, I never would've hesitated to offer support, but here, in our current reality, I pulled my hand back, unsure of what was right or wrong anymore.

Tommy finally raised his head. "I tried to find her. I looked for her everywhere. I went back to the woods after you had called and told me she hadn't come home. I searched through the trees, by the river. I wanted to bring her home, but I couldn't find her."

"You went to the river?" I asked.

"It was a dumb idea, all of it was. She'd run away the night before, but I had this strange feeling that something wasn't right. I didn't know what else to do."

"The police found your footprints there," I said, and it made sense. He'd gone back to find my sister.

"I told them I didn't hurt her. I was there because I tried to find her. I swear, I didn't hurt Abby."

"I believe you," I said with a certainty even I didn't understand. And this time I did rest my hand on his back.

"I told the police everything I could. About what happened at the bonfire. I told them Abby and I got in a fight because I planned to break up with her. I admitted to chasing after her, but told them I couldn't get her to come back with me. I didn't tell them you were there. They don't know you were involved. You're safe, Rhylee, and I'll make sure it stays that way."

Safe. I was safe. He couldn't know how much his words twisted inside of me. How could I ever be safe again after what I had done? Until Abby came home, I'd never feel safe again.

15

I stayed home from school again the next day and returned to the woods to look for Abby, but once I made it to the river, I couldn't move on.

I stood at the edge, because where did I go from here?

The water swirled and churned as if it waited for one wrong move to swallow me whole and claim me too. I stayed rooted to the edge, and my mind spun with reminders of how I'd betrayed my sister and the fear that no amount of searching would fix what I'd done.

16

My parents were waiting for me when I got home.

"We were hoping to meet with some of the neighboring cities' police officers to talk about ways to expand the search. Do you mind staying here until we get back?"

Translation, "We want someone here in case Abby returns," as if we needed to catch her and hold on to her so she doesn't run again.

"Sure," I told them, even though the idea of sitting in an empty house was the last thing I wanted to do.

"We're going to find her," Dad said, and I felt that familiar clutch in my stomach, the deep knot of fear, the whisper of doubt.

I turned on the TV after they left, because silence was impossible.

Mom had plastic bins full of pictures sitting on the dining room table. She'd been sorting through them and pulling out images of Abby to scan and upload onto a tribute page she created to help bring her home.

I grabbed a stack and laid each picture out, one after the other, until the whole table was covered. I moved each around and placed the images in chronological order the best that I could. My sister's life scene by scene.

I sorted through one of the stacks and found a picture of Tommy and me that I'd never seen before. We were on my front steps with Popsicles in our hands. There was purple juice from Tommy's Popsicle running down his hand and my lips were stained bright red. It was the summer before sixth grade, because I had Band-Aids on both my knees, my elbow, and my forehead. Tommy had dared me to climb the tree in his backyard after his dad had been picking apples and left a ladder under it. The limbs were too high to get to from the ground, but the ladder made it the perfect climbing tree. At least it was until the branch I was on snapped and I slipped. The two of us had gotten in big trouble for going up in the tree, and for a week we weren't allowed to see each other. Abby and I had spent the days together, and I remember how upset she was when our parents got sick of Tommy and me whining and we were finally allowed to see each other again.

I'd chosen him over her, always. Nothing had changed. And now Abby was gone because of it.

I swiped my hand across the table and knocked the pictures on the floor. This was useless. It was all useless.

My thoughts were interrupted by a loud knock on the front door. For a second, a brief second, I thought it was Abby and she'd returned home, but that was silly. If it was her, she'd open the door and let herself in.

I tried to hide my disappointment when I saw it was Tessa.

"We missed you at school today," she said, and dropped the bag she carried so she could give me a hug. Her hair tickled my cheek as she wrapped her arms around me. I wanted so badly to be folded into her comfort. To take what she was offering. But how could I after what I'd done? I deserved none of it.

She let go and pulled a pile of mail from her bag. "Here, this was falling out of your mailbox."

"Checking the mail hasn't been our top priority these days," I said and took the stack. I noticed a bunch of college brochures on top. Texas A&M, Pepperdine, Boston University. I'd been so excited a few weeks ago about Boston University when I found out that they had a program where you could study art for an entire year in Europe. I'd imagined days filled with museums and evenings sitting at cafés and outdoor bars where I'd savor the memories of seeing the great works of art in person. I'd pictured myself there so easily, but now that felt like a lifetime ago.

Tessa followed me through the front hallway into the kitchen. I dumped the brochures in the trash. It was pointless. Who was I kidding? I wasn't getting out of this town. I wasn't going anywhere as long as Abby was missing.

We went into the family room, and even though the pictures were strewn all over the room, Tessa didn't say a word. Instead, we sat on opposite sides of the couch, our feet touching in the middle. The TV played in the background, some commercial about a sale at a furniture store.

"Have you heard anything else?" she asked.

"The cops think Tommy is a suspect," I said and hated the words on my tongue.

"Everyone at school is talking about it."

"He didn't do anything to Abby," I said, and wished I had the courage to tell her the real story about what happened.

"I never for a second thought he did," she said with a certainty that reminded me of how much I loved Tessa.

"Thank you," I told her.

When she spoke next, her voice was almost too soft to be heard over the television. "I'm worried about Abby."

"So am I."

"Where do you think she is?"

"I have to believe she's somewhere safe."

"We all do," she agreed. The mood in the room had shifted. The two of us focused on the television because what more could you say after that?

The afternoon news came back from commercials and Abby's face filled the screen. It was her school photo from last year. She wore a mint green shirt that made the blues of her eyes even more brilliant. Her hair was down and I remembered her braiding it the night before so the curls would be perfect. My sister smiled back at me from the television as a news anchor talked.

"Efforts are being made to help find a missing teen who disappeared this weekend. Abby Towers, a high school junior at Coffinberry High School, was last seen at a bonfire with classmates. A community-wide search is in effect, as everyone helps to locate her."

The woman went on to give a phone number for the police if anyone had tips or information, but I wasn't paying attention. Instead, I focused on the images that were on the screen.

It was Black Willow Lake, which was where the river flowed. The lake that was usually full of Coffinberry kids trying to find a place to cool off in the summer heat. Only in the images on the news, it wasn't full of my classmates but divers in black suits, sleek as seals.

I hit the mute button. I didn't want to hear what the newswoman had to say. I'd seen enough crime shows and movies to understand why someone would be diving in a lake.

They were searching for my sister.

Or more specifically, her *body*.

I jumped up from the couch, ran into the bathroom, and threw up. My hands gripped the sides of the toilet, unable to find absolution for what I'd done.

17

Officer Donovan showed up that evening as we sat around the dinner table. My parents had picked up a pizza on their way home, but Collin was the only one eating any of it. The poor kid pretty much subsisted on pizza or peanut butter and jelly these days. Next to him sat a stack of my collages that I'd made him.

"Can you make me another?" he asked me.

"I don't know, Collin . . . ," I said and trailed off, not quite sure how to tell him that wasn't going to happen anytime soon.

"Please? Something with Abby in it too. It's okay if she wants to share one of my pictures. The two of us could be doing something together. Like when she was here."

"I'll see what I can do," I told him, and the hope in his eyes made me feel even worse. It was as if someone had closed their fist around my heart.

Our doorbell rang, and Collin ran to the door.

"It's the police," he called to us. The police meant Abby, and we needed to be there for whatever it was they came here to tell us.

"Good evening, Mr. Towers," Officer Donovan said to Dad after he opened the door.

"Please, call me Will. Do you want me to make some coffee for you?" he asked. Never mind the fact that Dad didn't even drink coffee. He said even the smell of it made him sick.

"No, I think it's best that we go into the living room to talk." He gestured at Collin.

"Hey, buddy," Dad said to my brother. "I'm going to turn on some cartoons and you can stay in the kitchen. Does that sound okay?"

Collin nodded and I wished I could be like him, so easily swayed and made happy by having his favorite show turned on.

Mom, on the other hand, was the opposite. She shook her head like she was the one having a tantrum.

"I can't," she whispered. "I can't hear what you have to say."

Dad placed his hand on her shoulder, but she shook it off.

"What wrong, Mom?" Collin asked, now concerned with the conversation a second ago he couldn't care less about.

"Everything is okay," Dad said, and looked pointedly at Mom. "Rhylee, why don't you stay here with your brother?"

He gestured at me to take him upstairs.

"I'm coming with you," I said. "Abby is my sister; I need to hear what they have to say."

Dad looked from me to Collin, back and forth. I crossed my hands over my chest. I wasn't going to be left out of this conversation. He ran his fingers through his hair and sighed. "Fine. Collin, stay in the kitchen and watch your show."

Collin nodded, so we took the opportunity to move into the living room. Once we were all there, Officer Donovan spoke again.

"As you're aware, we had divers searching the lake today," he said, and I fought back a swell of bile that rose up from my stomach at the mention of the water. "We looked as much as we could, but the current was rough from the storms and visibility was near zero. The recent rains stirred everything up and debris and logs made it dangerous to search. However, the team found an item that belongs to your daughter."

"What is it?" Mom said in a voice louder than I'd heard her use in days.

Officer Donovan closed his eyes for a moment, as if what he had to say next was hard to get out.

"They found one of Abby's tennis shoes at the bottom of the lake. It was tangled in a bunch of weeds about halfway from shore."

"Are you sure it belongs to her?" Dad asked.

Officer Donovan eyes remained fixed on a spot beyond Dad's shoulder when he talked to us next. "It had her road ID on it."

I could picture the tag he was talking about in my mind.

It was metal and had Velcro so you could put it around the bottom of your laces. Her name and phone number were stamped on it in case something happened to her when she was out running. I'd made fun of her for wearing a tag like Hound Dog did. Now, it seemed, the tag had done exactly what it was supposed to do. Identify my sister.

"The footprints we found on the shore match the tennis shoe in the lake. It places Abby at the edge of the river," he continued. "Does she swim? Is there any reason she would've been in the lake?"

"No," Dad said. "Abby isn't the strongest swimmer. She stays away from the river. We've told her to since she was young."

Dad was right. Abby may have been the best runner our school had ever seen, but her athletic ability only existed on land. She was a terrible swimmer, usually opting to sit in the grass and tan while everyone else swam.

"She could have lost a shoe when she was in the woods," Mom said, her voice flat and hollow.

But that wasn't true.

People fool themselves into believing what they want to be real. They had found the proof. No amount of lies we told ourselves could undo the evidence the police had.

I had to get away. I couldn't hear Officer Donovan tell Mom she was wrong. That a person doesn't lose their shoe and then it ends up tangled at the bottom of a lake.

I slipped out of the room and went outside before he destroyed Mom's hopes.

I ran, even though I hated to run. I moved down the same stretch of earth that my sister's feet had followed so many times. I pushed myself even when my lungs ached for air. I went farther and farther and crossed the field into the entrance of the woods. The sun was nearly gone. The trees cast shadows everywhere, but still I raced forward until I was once again at the river's edge.

"I did this," I cried into the water, my words getting lost in the rush of the current. I yelled my guilt over and over again and prayed that wherever Abby was, she could hear me. I yelled until my voice became hoarse and raw, and it hurt to swallow.

I collapsed on the grass and crossed my hands over my chest. I tried to catch my breath, but it was thick and labored. My mind was tangled up with sins, about Tommy and me and how destructive love is.

This was it.

The end.

It had to be.

I could never, ever be with him again.

I made a promise to the universe.

"Tommy and I are nothing, just bring Abby home! Please!" I begged, my voice choked with sobs.

The river continued to rage. It taunted me for my foolishness, thinking that one could wish everything okay.

I closed my eyes and created a different ending to the story Officer Donovan just told us. In my version, when Abby fell into the water, she kicked off her shoes and striped off the clothes that were heavy and pulling her down. She swam to the surface and climbed out, running barefoot all the way back home to us, and I was there waiting. And Tommy never came between us again. There was only my sister and me, and everything was the way it used to be.

18

The police assumed the worst. They concentrated their efforts on the river, and even though nothing was said, there was a heavy feeling in the air that my sister's disappearance was now a recovery effort. Cadaver dogs were brought in to scour the woods, their noses kept low to the ground as they tried to catch a scent of Abby. The police would deny it if you asked them, and wanted to keep what they'd found in the water a secret, but I knew they were no longer looking for a missing person, but for a body.

The town wouldn't accept that my sister was gone from our lives forever. How does one come to terms with something like that? It was asking the impossible. So as day faded into night and night faded into day, we clung to the idea that she was still out there and would walk through our door at any moment.

A news conference was set up in front of our house, and my parents pled with everyone watching to come forward if they had any information to share. It interrupted the morning talk shows broadcast on every channel. I watched from the little TV in the kitchen, because there was no way I could hold it together enough to stand beside them on live TV. The news crew had put makeup on Mom, but it wasn't enough to hide the black circles under her eyes and the hollowness that sank deep into her cheeks. Everyone could see how broken she'd become as she and Dad spoke straight to the camera and begged Abby to come home.

I didn't go back to school that week. I stayed home and looked for my sister. How could I not? Abby was missing, and I needed to find her. No one said I couldn't, even on those mornings my parents were still in the house when I woke up. It was as if there was an unspoken rule that our lives would stay suspended until Abby returned.

I ignored Tommy's text messages. It was awful of me, but I was afraid if I read them, I'd answer them, and that could never, ever happen again. Tommy and I could never, ever happen again.

The thing about guilt is that it bites its teeth deep within you and doesn't let go. And why should it? Instead of getting easier, the days got heavier and heavier, weighing on my shoulders until I thought I'd explode. The moments when Mom would stare off into space and her eyes would gloss over, the lines on Dad's face that I don't remember existing a week ago, and Collin, who slept with the light on in his bedroom now and often woke up crying from nightmares he refused to tell us about.

I wanted to tell the truth, but at what cost? I practiced what I'd say to my parents, testing out words, but there was no right way.

I covered one wall in my room with Abby's missing person flyers. The picture had been taken at a picnic last summer. Abby was laughing at the camera, holding up a pinwheel. She and Collin had held them out of the car window on the way home, letting the breeze turn them around and around.

I hung each so it was perfectly aligned with the one next to it; her face smiled back at me over and over again. I hung up picture after picture of Abby, but no matter how many I added, they couldn't fill the space that she had left behind.

19

Dad opened my bedroom door Sunday morning and sat on the end of my bed. I was awake, but not ready to start another week without my sister.

"How are you doing, honey?" His voice was gentle, and it made me feel worse, because I didn't deserve it. Dad was doing his best to hold us together, to be the strong one, but it couldn't be easy not to fall apart in front of everyone.

"About as well as the rest of you are."

"Not good, then," Dad said, and I nodded.

"Not at all."

"This is hard for everyone." He nodded at the flyers I'd hung on the wall, but didn't say anything about them.

"It's pretty much impossible," I told him.

Dad took a deep breath and let it out. He looked exhausted. He never stopped moving. If he wasn't home trying to coordinate search efforts with others on the phone, then he was out himself with the groups trying to find Abby. I didn't know when he slept, but then again, maybe he didn't want to sleep. Nightmares clouded my dreams, and I wasn't sure what was better: what haunted me in my sleep or my reality.

He picked up a picture that was face-down on my desk, one of Tommy and me, and examined it. I'd gotten rid of everything else that reminded me of him, but I couldn't bring myself to throw away this image.

The picture was the two of us at the carnival that came to the nearby city every summer. We were standing in front of one of those rides that spins you around and around until you get sick. The two of us had huge grins on our faces, proud that we'd gone on it three times in a row.

"You know Tommy wouldn't hurt Abby, don't you?" I asked. "Mom thinks he did something to her."

He lowered the picture and walked over to my bed. "Your mom is trying to make sense of this."

"But how can she blame Tommy? Where's the sense in that?"

"No one is blaming Tommy. We're just trying to find answers so we can bring your sister home."

"Tommy isn't a part of this," I told Dad, and I needed him to believe me. "He'd never hurt her."

"I know that, honey." He pulled open my window shade and let the morning light flow in. "What do you think about going back to school tomorrow? You've already missed a week."

"I need to look for Abby."

"The FBI are bringing in a search team from out of state.

They'll look during the day, and we need to let them do their job. You can help when you get home, but I think it would be a good idea if you went back," he said in a way that told me this was an idea I couldn't turn down.

"I'm not sure I can handle being at school when she isn't."

"We need to keep moving," Dad said. "Try it for one day, and if it doesn't work, we'll talk again."

I nodded, but returning to school was the last thing I wanted to do. It didn't seem fair. It made me feel as if I were giving up on Abby; like I was going back to my normal life when she couldn't.

Dad placed his hand on my shoulder and squeezed. "Thanks for being so strong," he said, and I flinched.

I was anything but strong. I was weak and afraid I'd fall apart at any moment.

20

The next morning I got ready as if it were a regular school day. I showered, dried my hair, picked out an outfit, and even put a little lip gloss on. I had the radio on to the station I always listened to and had my usual breakfast of a piece of toast and a banana. I grabbed my bag and waited for the bus, and when it came, I climbed on and took a seat just like I always did. I forced myself to follow my usual routine, but it felt so very wrong. I shouldn't be allowed to do any of this, not after what I'd done.

I kept my eye on Tommy's house and wondered what he was doing. If it had been any other morning, Tommy would pull up, beep twice, and Abby would run out. He'd point to the middle seat if I was around and let me know I could squeeze in, but I never did. Life hurt a lot less when I didn't have to watch the two of them together.

Today, I stared at the screen on my phone to avoid the

stares of everyone around me. I searched "missing teens" on the Internet and read reports about others who had disappeared like Abby. There seemed to be hundreds of accounts about people who had vanished. I clicked on the image button at the top of the search engine and face after face appeared. I scrolled through and wondered what their stories were. Where did they go and had they returned?

The bus pulled up in front of the school and stopped with a giant lurch. I expected school to look different. I expected everything to be different now, because I was different. But everything was the way it always was, which made it even harder for me.

The chain-link fence that ringed the stadium had become a tribute to my sister. Styrofoam cups were stuck in between the links and spelled out ABBY COME HOME. My classmates used the fence to cheer on our sports teams or convince one another of who should be class president, but now it was a plea for my sister to come home to the place I'd once so desperately wanted to get away from.

I hid out in the bathroom before the first bell because there was no way I could talk to anyone and still hold it together. As I moved from class to class, it seemed as if my shame burned so bright that people must be blinded by it, but that wasn't the case. It was the opposite. People I never met before gave me sad half smiles and teachers spoke in low voices and asked if I needed anything. They told me not to worry about the lessons I had missed, that we'd figure out a way for me to catch up. The whole school treated me as if I was fragile and would break at any moment, which I might, but not for the reasons they believed.

I found myself searching for Abby in the halls. I prayed I'd spot her laughing with her friends or racing to get to class, her blond hair flashing as she dodged anyone in her way.

Friends of my sister walked around in a daze, a shocked look on their faces, as if someone had turned the light on in a dark room too fast. Her locker had become a shrine, notes were stuck through the slats, a pair of running shoes left below it, and a sheet of paper with the words WE MISS YOU taped to the front. She'd only been missing for a week, but Abby already haunted the halls, like she haunted my every second.

I hovered at the doorway to my art class. It had always been my favorite time of the day. I certainly wasn't talented enough at it in the way that Abby was with running, but art was one of those things I was really into. I loved that it was a time when I could forget about everything else and get lost in my work. However, the roar of silence in my mind that was usually so welcomed was the last thing I wanted today.

The bell rang, and the rush of students forced me to go through the door. I went to my cubby and pulled out the picture I'd been working on. My teacher had us doing a piece using contrast art, where the main image was blank and the background was full of colors or words. We took the negative space and used it to create a picture. I'd been working on a silhouette of me. In the middle of the page, my face was outlined. I'd begun to write words to fill the space around it.

Travel, Explore, Wanderlust, words that were so silly and insignificant now.

I erased them all, so I was left with nothing but blank space again. I pressed the pencil tip into the paper and wrote a new word.

Gone.

And then, *Lost.*

Where.

Are.

You.

I repeated the words until they filled the entire background of my picture. The words stretched and curved around the outline I'd made of my face. But when I stepped back to look at it from farther away, the silhouette created in the blank space of the picture didn't resemble me. It looked exactly like Abby.

21

The school day continued, even though it felt as if time should stand still. How do we keep moving forward when Abby isn't here? How do you exist when there's such a hole in your life? It didn't feel right. Why was I allowed to do such normal everyday things when my whole world was kicked off its axis and spun out of control?

Tessa found me in the lunch line. I'd grabbed a bunch of food to simply fill my tray, even though I had no appetite.

"Why haven't you answered my texts?" she asked. "I've been trying to talk to you for days."

"I haven't felt much like talking."

"I didn't know you were coming to school today."

I wished she'd stop talking. People around us were listening. I moved to the front of the line and gave the woman at the register my money.

"I didn't either," I said. "But right now I don't know what

the hell I'm supposed to be doing anymore."

My eyes filled with tears and Tessa wrapped her arms around me. My lunch tray jiggled in my hands. I pushed against her to get free and lost my grip. Everything fell to the floor, the silverware clanging as it hit.

I waited for the people around us to clap, like they always did when someone dropped something in the cafeteria, but instead the room got quiet. Abnormally silent for a cafeteria full of teenagers.

I hated it.

I hated that they didn't do anything because it was me. That even dropping my tray in the cafeteria wasn't normal anymore.

Tessa bent down to help pick up my things.

"I'm so sorry, Rhylee, I didn't mean to make that happen. . . ." She babbled on. It was so quiet; the whole room could hear her apologize. My cheeks burned with embarrassment, and I couldn't focus on anything but how much it hurt. A hand grabbed mine and jerked me forward.

"Follow me," Tommy whispered.

He pulled me out of the cafeteria. Some kids jumped out of the way, as if touching him might burn them, and a bunch of others looked at him with disgust.

Kyle Tanner, a boy on the cross-country team, shoved his shoulder into Tommy as we walked past. Tommy stumbled forward as he lost his balance. He grabbed on to a locker to steady himself.

"Watch it," Kyle called over his shoulder as we moved down the hallway.

"Asshole," Tommy said under his breath.

"This isn't right," I told him. "The way people are treating you. You don't deserve this."

"Just keep moving," Tommy muttered and elbowed his way forward. He walked in front of me and blocked everyone. We didn't stop until we reached the indoor pool, a contradiction to the rest of our run-down school. Some rich alum had donated the funds to build it over a decade ago and a swim team was created, those students arriving at class after early morning practices with wet clumps of hair, the smell of chlorine perpetually bouncing off them. He pushed opened the door and we slipped through. His hand still gripped mine as he led me up the steps to the observation deck.

"Hey, it's okay. You're okay," Tommy said, and I realized I was shaking. The water in the pool was still and blue, and I focused on that. The sun came through the windows above and created shadows in some sections and sparkles of light in others.

"It's not okay," I said. "I'm not okay, and *this* certainly isn't okay."

Tommy nodded, but didn't make a move to get up.

The bell rang, signaling the end of lunch period, and I could hear students outside in the hallway. Their voices rose and fell in conversation as they passed the entrance to the pool. The bell rang for the next period, and still, the two of us stayed. I thought about all the times I had wanted to be with Tommy. The daydreams I'd had of the two of us doing something exactly like this, slipping away during the school day, and it turned my stomach.

"What if something really has happened to her?" I finally asked.

"We can't think like that," Tommy said.

"But she was down by the water."

"Please," Tommy interrupted. "Stop."

"We can't be together," I said, and kept my voice monotone.

"Rhylee . . . ," Tommy said, but I wouldn't let him finish.

"I'm sorry. But this is the only way it can be. I owe it to my sister. We don't *deserve* to be with each other."

"We didn't mean to hurt her," Tommy said.

"But we did."

"We did," he agreed.

"I wasn't even sorry that I was taking you from her." My voice broke. Watching Abby and Tommy together had been impossible, but this was a hundred times worse. "We can't be together."

"Then what are we supposed to do?" Tommy asked.

"Survive," I told him, because really, that's all we had left.

22

Four more days passed without Abby.

Dad decided to go back to work on Monday. I heard him talking with Mom when they thought no one was around. His boss wanted him to take more time off, but he told Mom that we needed the money and he'd still be able to spend his days helping with the search. I thought about my own job at Webster's and how I never went back after Abby disappeared. I never even called to tell them, and they never called to see where I was. It was as if my family was given a pass to pause our lives, but for how long? And what were the consequences when everyone around us kept moving?

Life became an endless stream of hours, minutes, and seconds without my sister. We were essentially living, without really living. Our lives suspended, our breaths held, until she returned.

I began to create collages again, but not the ones Collin wanted and I didn't put myself into them. Instead, I invented new lives for Abby, reasons for why we hadn't heard from her. I placed her in islands with water so blue it hurt your eyes. I put her among crowds of thousands at rock concerts and alone on mountain peaks. She hiked through national forests and crossed sidewalks in cities congested with cars, people, and smog. She was everywhere, even though we couldn't find her anywhere.

We all wished for a miracle.

Even when each day ended and a miracle didn't come.

The time rushed by and still we hoped, because everyone seemed to know Abby, and even if they didn't, they pretended that they did because her disappearance was the biggest thing to happen in our town. Our own personal tragedy, and everyone loved to be connected to a tragedy, especially when it wasn't your family involved.

So it shouldn't have come as a surprise that the night the circles came, we didn't notice.

It was easy not to notice things these days, because we were so busy being consumed by just one thing.

Mom was the first to see them in the early hours of dawn when she opened the door to let Hound Dog out for his morning pee. She ran into Abby's room to get a better look.

"Will, come in here," she yelled, her voice high and insistent, also pulling Collin and me from our beds. We jostled into each other trying to get down the hall, tired, disoriented, and confused as to why Mom would be in Abby's room.

She stood in front of the window that faced the field. Dad hadn't mowed it since Abby went missing and the paths she had run through were thick with grass and weeds.

Except for the circles that were now cut into our field.

Crop circles in the middle of Coffinberry, Ohio.

They stretched about the size of a football field, and I counted four large circles and three small ones. *Seven circles. Abby's cross-country number.* But I told myself I was being silly.

The circles were attached, forming a pattern that seemed deliberate. The grass around the shapes pushed down. There were no paths outside of them. It was like someone had dropped something and pulled it back up to create the design, their feet never touching the ground. Like in one of those movies where aliens invaded. I half expected a little green creature to jump out of the weeds.

"What are those?" Collin asked as he rubbed sleep from his eyes. He clutched the teddy bear that Abby always slept with.

"Some kids' idea of a joke," Dad said, but Mom didn't think it was a joke. She squinted her eyes and studied them as if the reason for their appearance would suddenly show itself. I thought about my classmates, specifically the farm boys who drove their trucks to school, the backs full of feed and dirt. They sat in our parking lot before school blasting their country music, revving their engines. They were the type of kids who would do something like this; make a joke out of our family's tragedy for a laugh. I could picture the boys creeping into our yard last night, laughing and telling one another to stay quiet in hushed whispers. They'd be drunk, burping out breaths of stale beer and pissing in our grass.

I gazed out at the field my sister once ran and wondered how we didn't realize how lucky we were only weeks ago.

23

An hour later, Dad honked the horn of his car to get us to move.

While the circles were important, we had other things to do. Today was the first cross-country meet of the season, and they'd dedicated it to Abby. I had no idea how I was supposed to sit through the whole thing without breaking into tears. But there wasn't any way to get out of it, even if it would feel next to impossible to be there.

As hard as it was for me to go, it was even harder for Mom. Her bad days seemed to be outnumbering the good, and this morning even Dad couldn't convince her to come with us.

"I want to go," she had said when Dad tried to reason with her. "But I can't. I just can't do it."

I'd watched the two of them from the hallway. Dad had taken Mom into his arms and stroked her hair as if she were a little kid, rocking her back and forth.

Everyone says that the pain of grief lessens, but it was the opposite for us. The grief was elastic and continued to stretch further and further into everything around me, especially moments like that, when my family was so different than what we once had been.

Mom stood at the screen door as we backed out of the driveway. I willed the car to get a flat tire or break down, but no such luck.

I pressed my face against the window and watched the circles disappear from sight as we drove away.

It was a gorgeous day, the sky a blue so vivid it was as if you were living within a picture. It was the type of day where you wanted to stay outside and soak in all the sun you could.

Collin sat in the backseat and flipped through the pages of a comic book; something full of bangs, pows, and kabams with superheroes who saved the world in a single bound. They seemed the opposite from our reality where we had learned that a world where good prevailed and the bad guys perished seemed impossible.

"What planet do you think the circles came from?" Collin asked. "Mars? People say there's life on Mars."

Dad slowed for two kids walking across the street and glanced at Collin. "I don't know, buddy. Let's let the police figure that out."

"So you *do* think they came from outer space?"

Dad sighed. "They came from Earth. We'll find out exactly how, so you don't have to worry about it."

"It's weird," Collin continued. "Why didn't we hear anything? Hound Dog goes nuts when there's an animal in our backyard."

"It probably happened when we were sleeping," Dad said, and turned up the radio to try to stop the conversation, but Collin continued to push the topic.

"No, I bet it was because a human didn't make the circles."

"Collin," Dad said, "we're not talking about this anymore. We need to focus on what's happening today rather than the circles."

But today was the last thing in the world I wanted to focus on. It was Mary Grace who had suggested that the school dedicate the race to Abby. As a way to keep her in the town's mind. But it's not like she needed to; everything these days was about Abby. The school even named it the Abby Towers Hope Run.

A race named after my sister. She would've thought the whole town had gone nuts.

And maybe we had.

Dad, Collin, and I headed into the stadium so everyone could turn their gaze on us and give sad, pitying looks. I tried not to make eye contact, afraid they could see it all on my face. Mom was the one had stayed home, but I should have been the one who didn't go. After all, none of this would be happening if it wasn't for me and what I'd done.

You did this, I reminded myself. *And you weren't even sorry.*

My classmates stood on either side of the entrance with plastic bags in their hands. These were the same people who'd come to our house for pre-meet dinners where Mom would make pot after pot of spaghetti while they carbo-loaded for their races the next day. They all had the tall muscular look. Their legs long and arms lanky. The group ran together as a team, and I always thought they looked like one another after the first few weeks of the season. The girls with their hair held back in elastic bands and everyone in red track jackets with warm-up pants. Tessa and I called them the Cult of Coffinberry. I swear they'd run off a cliff like lemmings if the person in the front led them there.

"Hi, Mr. Towers," Amy, a senior who always wore her hair in a thick braid, said when we made our way to the girls. "It's good to see you." She dipped her hand into the bag. "Thanks for coming."

She pushed a purple bracelet into my hand with the words HOMEWARD BOUND printed on it. I twirled the bracelet around in my fingers. I didn't need to ask what it meant; they were the must-have accessory since Abby had disappeared. Purple was her favorite color, and the slogan was from one of the songs she'd played over and over. She loved old folk music: Crosby, Stills, & Nash; Bob Dylan; Neil Young—anyone who would go on and on about the world needing a' changing. We'd groan when she had control of the radio during a car trip. There was only so much rambling and sappy singing one could take. Dad would joke that it reminded him of his days in college lying in the grass and smoking a joint, and Mom would then elbow him or give him a look that made him apologize and quickly turn the joint into an ice-cream cone.

"We're glad you're doing this for Abby," Dad said.

I put my bracelet on even though it felt more like a shackle. They were supposed to show our solidarity, but it didn't mean anything. It wasn't going to bring back my sister. When they had first passed out the bracelets at school, I couldn't even look them, another constant reminder that Abby was gone and I was still here. I'd thrown mine into my locker, where it probably still sat.

Collin took his and slipped it over his wrist next to the four he was already wearing.

"Do you think Abby will be here?" he asked.

"I sure wish she was," I said. "Everyone is here because they really want her to come home." I wrapped my arms around him in a tight hug and tickled him to get him to smile.

"She's been gone long enough. She better come home soon," he said, and I wished I could promise him that.

My French teacher, Mademoiselle Lang, was the first to come up to us after we made our way into the stadium. She was short and dressed like she was going to some fancy cocktail event. She always wore pearls and pantyhose and heels, even when it was early in the school year and the days still blazed heat. Or at a cross-country meet on a Saturday morning when the rest of the world was looking like lazy bums in jeans and T-shirts.

Abby had urged me to sign up for French when I had to pick a foreign language.

"We'll both know a secret language that Mom and Dad can't understand," she'd said.

I chose it because Abby wanted me to, and while she

had picked up the language quickly and would walk around the house pointing at objects using the French word, it was obvious that I stunk. The words wouldn't come out right, no matter how much I rolled my tongue to make that stupid "r" sound that the rest of the class seemed masters at creating. Mademoiselle Lang would pucker up her face like she'd sucked a lemon when I tripped over my words. Once, when Mademoiselle Lang was particularly frustrated, she said, "I can't imagine how you can be so different from your sister. *Abby est magnifique avec le français.*"

Of course she was. Abby was always the better one. And now she was gone. How could I have ever thought to take her place—even just with Tommy? Would I have measured up to her in his eyes? And how would it be if things were reversed? If I was the one missing? Would people be as upset? Would the town hold out the same hope for me?

Mademoiselle Lang took Dad's hand, holding it between her own. "I'm so sorry to have to meet up with you under these circumstances, but it's good to see you here."

"The same to you," Dad said. He cleared his throat and spoke louder. "Thank you for coming to support my daughter."

"Abby was a wonderful girl," she said.

"Is," I corrected her.

"Pardon?" she asked, confused.

"You said Abby *was* a wonderful girl. She *is* a wonderful girl. There's no past tense to Abby." I said the words slow and steady, my voice firm.

Dad stepped in front of me, creating a blockade between

126

the two of us. "I'm sorry about that. This is hard for everyone."

Typical Dad, always trying to make things better. He was a master at pretending and apologizing for us. It was like he'd become some politically correct robot who only focused on facts and tried to please everyone. It was as if he followed the police's script, only repeating what we knew and not daring to talk about the things we feared.

I let him continue to make excuses and walked up the bleachers. Tessa was at the very top with her back against the press box.

She stood when she saw me and waved her hands in big sweeping motions. She looked like a bird about to take flight.

"Rhylee. Hey, Rhylee, over here."

I hurried up the rest of the steps to get to Tessa and silence her. There were enough people staring at me already. I didn't need her to create even more of a spectacle.

She had on a red Coffinberry High sweatshirt over black leggings and cowboy boots. Her hair was braided into two long pigtails and she had the bracelets for Abby all the way up both arms. She must have been sporting at least fifteen of them. I imagined Mary Grace's pursed lips when she saw how many Tessa had swiped.

Tessa threw herself at me when I finally reached her, wrapped me in a tight hug, and tried to pick me up off the ground.

"Okay, that's enough love from you," I said and swatted at her to get her to let me go.

"I want you to know that I'm sacrificing for you here."

"You are?"

She nodded and pointed to her red sweatshirt. "I wore my school pride even though my school pride clashes with my hair."

"I'm honored that you undertook such a great hardship for me."

"You should be."

She sat down and patted the spot next to her for me to do the same. I joined her and she pulled a bag of Swedish Fish out of her purse and offered them to me. I shook my head.

"I can't believe these people showed up today for Abby."

"Yeah, I know." I looked around the stadium. The place was packed, and most people had on the purple bracelets. A man a few rows down looked at me, nudged his wife, and pointed me out to her. "We're here on display so everyone can watch Abby's poor, sad family."

Tessa took a fish out of her bag and bit it in half. "They're here to *support* you."

I knew that. Logically. But still, I hated to be the center of attention and pretend everything was okay.

I scanned the crowd of my so-called supporters and found Dad and Collin on the sidelines of the field. Dad talked to the cross-country coach, Mr. Hoch, and Collin warmed up with some of the team as if he were going to run with them. My eyes continued to search the bleachers. There were kids who sat next to me in classes and never said a word to me and upperclassmen who didn't give a shit about cross-country. They wore a sea of purple, dressed to show their solidarity for

Abby's return. A stadium full of people who wouldn't be here if it wasn't for what I'd done.

It was in the very right hand corner near the top that I spotted Tommy. His feet were on the bleachers in front of him and he rested his elbows on his knees, his face in his hands and earphones around his shoulders. His foot bounced like he does when he's nervous. He was sitting alone, the seats around him empty, as if he were in his own personal VIP section. But there wasn't anything special about his seat. Tommy stared straight ahead and ignored everyone; his jaw muscle clenching and unclenching the only indication that the stares of those around him were affecting him. I thought back to how he pulled me out of the cafeteria when everyone was looking at me. And here I was, leaving him alone. It wasn't right.

"I should go sit by Tommy," I said. He'd do the same thing for me in an instant without even debating it. I couldn't leave him alone like that. Could I?

"You what?" Tessa asked.

"Nothing," I told her, because I couldn't go over there. Not after my promise to the universe. I could never sit near him again. "It's just that Tommy is over there alone and everyone is avoiding him like he's got some kind of deadly disease. He doesn't deserve that."

"They're looking for someone to blame. It's easier than not having an answer."

"It's bullshit," I said, my voice rising as I got madder and madder. I was the one they should be blaming for Abby missing from our lives. "Tommy didn't do anything, but everyone is acting like he did. Even my mom thinks he has something to do with Abby's disappearance."

"I know he didn't do it, and you do too. That's got to count for something," she said, and I was so happy she was my friend at the moment.

"I wish it did," I said. "The whole town believes he's the reason Abby is gone. It's like they're on some witch hunt to destroy him. Everyone's gone mad."

"Except you. Tommy has you," Tessa said, but that wasn't true. We hadn't talked since the day at the pool. He'd stayed away from me like I asked, but I couldn't help thinking I was abandoning him, when he was the one who was protecting me and letting everyone believe he was the reason Abby was gone.

But before I could do anything, Mary Grace stepped up to the microphone. The rest of the runners entered the field and stood in a line behind her, their hands linked. The crowd became quiet without her having to say anything.

"Thank you for joining us today. It's so important that we come together. Two weeks ago we lost someone very special to us," Mary Grace said.

"Lost?" I asked Tessa, my voice rising. "Why the hell is she talking as if Abby is dead? She can't really believe that, can she?"

In front of me, a woman turned and shushed me. Her face turned from a look of annoyance to one of recognition when she saw me.

"Sorry," she mouthed, and faced forward again.

Mary Grace went on. "Today we're here with Abby's family to send out prayers for her safe return."

The team let go of one another's hands and walked around Mary Grace, forming a semicircle.

"What the hell did they do? Choreograph this?" I asked, loud enough this time that a bunch of people turned around to look at me.

Tessa placed a hand on my knee. "Relax, it's going to be okay."

I pulled my leg back and tapped my foot against the bleachers. This was not going to bring Abby back, none of this would. As each day passed and Abby remained missing, the longing inside of me to see my sister again would destroy me.

Mary Grace turned to my family. "Mr. Towers, why don't you and Collin come stand with us?"

To give Dad some credit, he seemed a bit bewildered. His face froze in a look not much different than the one on animals who find themselves in the street with a car suddenly right in front of them. But Dad's expression quickly changed and he smiled at Mary Grace, ever the gracious community member, and stood, offering Collin his hand.

If Mary Grace was surprised that Mom or I were missing from the group, she didn't show it.

"Mr. Towers and Collin, I want you to know that every single person here is praying for Abby's safe return," Mary Grace said. "We miss her so much, and we need her to come home."

She wiped away tears and some of the girls on the team

131

stepped out of their formation to wrap their hands around her. I glanced at Tommy and locked eyes with him. Even across a crowd of people, he could still unnerve me.

I turned away, my attention on Dad instead as he stepped forward and took the microphone. Collin stood by his side, fidgeting with the pockets on his shorts. He looked confused and unsure of what to do, and I wished I could go swoop him up and take him away from everyone's prying eyes.

Dad searched the stands for a moment before he spoke. I slouched down and tried to hide from him. He finally gave up and talked to our community. "Thank you, everyone. I can't express how much your support means to us. My family owes you so much for your efforts and never-ending hope."

A few people in the crowd clapped. It got picked up by more and more people until the entire audience was applauding, and I swear it was so loud, Mom must have heard it all the way at our house.

But it didn't matter. It didn't help. Everyone was here for my family, but I never felt more alone. I couldn't tell the truth, and I couldn't be with Tommy. There was no end to any of this in sight, and I was afraid that if I stayed any longer, I'd break down in front of everyone.

I stood up. "I need to get out of here," I said.

"It's almost over," Tessa replied, but it wasn't. This wasn't close to being over.

"I *have* to get out of here."

I rushed down the steps of the bleachers, and almost lost

my balance and fell. My sandals made loud echoing slaps against the metal. I didn't look back at Tommy, Dad, or the crowd, all of whom were probably staring at the poor upset sister of Abby. I'd seen enough. My hand played with the bracelet Amy had given me when I entered.

I pulled it off and dropped it into the wastebasket outside the stadium.

24

I wasn't sure if Dad saw me leave the stadium, but it didn't matter. I needed to get away and calm down before anyone came to check on me.

The high school wasn't far from my house, but it also wasn't close enough that I'd ever willingly make the choice to walk home. I'd missed the bus last year and when my parents didn't answer their phones, I'd been forced to start the journey by foot. It was nasty and sweaty and everything nightmares were made of. My book bag had dug into my shoulder as cars whizzed past me, junior and senior boys leaning out with jeers and beeping the horn. When I'd finally made it home almost an hour and a half after leaving the school, I'd told myself that was never, ever going to happen again. I'd hitchhike if I had to, even if the guy who picked me up was in a big white van with no windows and had a creepy mustache.

But today was different. Heading home on foot didn't feel

like torture, but a necessity. My body hummed with adrenaline. I needed to get out of here before someone tried to find me, and I was pretty sure that I'd left a pair of tennis shoes in the car, which would make the walk home a lot easier.

I got to the car in the parking lot and opened the door. Just like the houses in Coffinberry, no one bothered to lock their cars. Besides, if anyone did break into my family's old Buick, all they'd find was empty bags from McDonald's, mountains of flyers with Abby's face on them, and wadded-up gas station receipts. Dad would probably thank them for stealing the stuff and cleaning out the mess.

I found the old pair of shoes that stank like gym class and put them on. My jeans weren't exactly workout-worthy clothes, but they'd do. I sent Dad a text that I was heading home on my own and not to worry.

My body vibrated. It was as if my thoughts were moving at a million miles per minute and I couldn't seem to get myself to calm down. Like the time Tessa and I each drank three energy drinks to stay up and study. We ended up staring at the clock as the hours passed, unable to focus on anything. That's what was happening to me now. It was too much, and I needed to leave it behind.

I picked up my pace to a jog. The road remained empty, even though I half expected Tessa to drive by and laugh at me. I didn't do jogging. Ever.

But today I was. And it wasn't hard.

In fact, before long, I was running. I kept waiting for my breath to catch in my throat or a cramp to start in my side, but it was easy. It was as if I'd been running my whole life.

I fell into a steady pace, chanting a word with each footfall.

"I . . . did . . . this," I said, the words beating a rhythm into my head.

I recalled a conversation I'd had with Abby last summer. I ran with her one afternoon, a brief flirtation with getting myself into shape, but after we got about six minutes away from the house, I stopped. My body yelled, fought, and revolted.

"That's what running is, Rhylee," Abby had said to me when I voiced my protests. She ran in place and spoke to me. "You run for that feeling."

"You run for the pain? Why would anyone want that?"

"You run because you can control the pain. You cause it and you can take it away. Running makes your body feel something. It makes you feel alive."

And she was right. Running was freeing. Today, it was as if Abby and I had switched roles, and I held on to that thought. I ran the rest of the way to my house as if I were my sister. As if I could fill the hole I'd created, and give back what I'd taken away.

25

Mom was in the kitchen when I walked through the door, sweaty and out of breath.

"What are you doing back so early?" she asked. She had a sandwich in front of her, but it was untouched. She'd always been thin, but now she looked especially frail. People had been dropping off casseroles and pasta dishes, but she rarely ate more than a few bites. Just the other day, Tommy's parents had brought one over. Dad had accepted it politely, but then made up an excuse about waiting for a phone call and quickly closed the door. Mom had watched them walk back down the road, and then promptly picked up the meal and dumped it into the wastebasket.

We'd lost so much more than my sister. My parents were shells of their former selves, and I don't remember the last time I'd seen either of them smile. They never went out, Mom stopped cooking, and Dad no longer joked with us. Instead, our house was a collection of hushed voices and quiet apologies as everyone tried to get through each day.

My parents used to be good friends with Tommy's too. The four of them would get together a few times a week, meeting for drinks after dinner or to play games, but now Mom wouldn't even acknowledge them. If I had to make a list of things that I'd ruined, I feared it would stretch on until infinity.

"I couldn't handle it," I explained. "It was too hard, so I left Dad and Collin there."

Mom didn't argue with that, because how could she? She'd used the same excuse earlier today.

"I'm going to take Hound Dog outside for a walk." I left her at the table, the circles in our field visible out the window behind her.

I called for Hound Dog, and he ran down from upstairs. He hung out in Abby's room more than the rest of the house; he'd been her pet, a present for her tenth birthday. A gift that surpassed anything I'd ever received. I'd asked for a pony when I was ten, but all I got was a new winter jacket. Abby had named him after Elvis. We'd protested the name, considering the fact that he was actually a big black poodle, but Abby insisted on calling him that.

Hound Dog endlessly searched for Abby. I'd find him whining in her room or sniffing around her shoes that sat waiting for her in the mud room. I was pretty sure I detected a bit of disappointment when I came home and he saw it was me and not Abby who walked inside.

But right now he was tail wags and wiggles, jumping up

and licking my face. I tried to push him off me and get him to sit, but he wouldn't stay.

"What's gotten into that dog?" Mom asked.

"I have no idea. Usually he couldn't care less about me."

"He's acting like he does when Abby comes home."

Mom was right. Hound Dog had now pressed himself against the side of my leg and stared up at me adoringly.

The two of us headed outside. He strained against his leash and pulled us toward the circles that spread throughout the fields. Dad wasn't here to stop me, so I followed Hound Dog's lead until we were standing right in the middle of one of the huge crop circles.

He ran with his nose pressed to the ground and whined, as if he picked up on a familiar scent. He darted back and forth between the sides of the path cut in the circle, and I pulled the leash tight, anxious from his pacing.

The grass crunched under my feet and the weeds were overtaking everything. In some places brambles, leaves, and vines twisted together, and thorns reached out, threatening to cut your legs if you tried to cross the field.

It hadn't rained since Abby went missing, and the weatherman didn't believe we'd have relief anytime soon.

I followed Hound Dog through the circles and felt a strange sort of unease. This was my house, my backyard, but it didn't seem right. A breeze lifted the tips of my hair and whistled past my ear as if it were trying to let me in on a secret.

Hound Dog froze and faced the woods. He barked three times, and then made a high-pitched whining sound. I expected to see something, but it remained dark and empty. The trees at the edge of the woods were still, but around me, the tall stalks of grass bent from some invisible wind that only seemed to be around us. He tugged to go farther, but I was done. This place was giving me the creeps.

"Let's go," I said, and pulled him in the other direction.

At first he balked. He sat back on his heels and refused to move, and for a minute I panicked. It was as if something was about to sneak up behind me and I wanted to get inside.

"Now," I said loudly and yanked him again. He gave up and followed me. I walked out of the circles quickly and then broke into a run as if I were being chased, and sprinted to my house.

26

I sat down with my lunch on Monday, and Tessa immediately turned to me with a serious expression on her face.

"We need to talk," she said, and I had a feeling this talk wasn't about last night's homework or what I wanted to do this weekend.

"I need you to explain the secret you've been hiding from me."

She pulled a newspaper out of her bag and shoved it at me.

"Why didn't you tell me about this?" she asked, and I detected a bit of hurt in her voice.

"Oh Jesus, you have to be kidding me," I said as I caught sight of the article.

"I could've come over and helped or something," Tessa said.

I put down my peanut butter and jelly sandwich and grabbed the paper. I took a deep breath before looking at it, a habit I'd developed to prepare myself for whatever I'd see. It seemed like every morning I'd look at the paper lying on our kitchen table and see a picture, a story, a sentence about Abby. It had been almost three weeks since she'd disappeared and her face still smiled back from the front page of the paper pretty much every day.

I scanned the article and saw that it did in fact mention our name. But for the first time in what seemed like forever, it wasn't about Abby. There were no words on her cross-country accomplishments or disappearance. Today's article was about the circles.

"What's going on?" Tessa asked. She tapped her fluorescent yellow nails against the table. "You're not going to tell me aliens landed in your backyard, are you?"

I pushed the paper away from me. "The circles aren't from outer space; they just showed up Saturday. Dad went to the police, but no one made a fuss about them."

"Well, it seems as if they're a big deal now. My mom said every news station in the area is reporting on them. She drove by to try to see the circles and your yard is full of people."

I groaned. "Great, just what we need, another circus outside our front door."

"I'm coming home with you," she said, not bothering to ask me if it was okay. "You shouldn't have to deal with this alone."

I glanced over to where Tommy sat alone at a table in the corner of the cafeteria and wished that none of us had to deal with this alone.

27

Tessa was right. The circles had exploded into something huge. Cars were parked along my street and tall gray antennas jutted out of news vans and stood at attention against the blue sky. It was like the first days of Abby's disappearance all over again.

I spotted Collin with a group of his friends and Dad in the middle of a circle, arguing with a bunch of men. I wasn't surprised. Ever since the circles showed up, he'd been adamant about them not meaning anything. He wanted nothing more than to remove them, but the police had asked that he keep them until they determined who made them. What I couldn't believe was that Mom was also outside. Unless she was going with Dad to look for Abby, she hadn't stepped outside in the last couple weeks.

She stood off to the side, next to the big oak tree with the tire swing hanging from one of the branches.

Mom had come out for the circles.

Cameras swung toward Tessa and me as we walked up the driveway. I held my arm in front of my face and tried to conceal my pain, while Tessa put her head down and refused to look at anyone.

I dropped my book bag on the front porch and walked over to Mom.

"Rhylee," she said, with this strange half smile on her face.

"What's going on?" I asked.

There were news anchors positioned at different spots on the circles. I told myself they must be hard up for news to focus on some lame circles made as a prank in our yard.

Before Mom could answer, a heavily makeup reporter in a short dress began to talk. "We're standing outside the Towers residence, home of missing seventeen-year-old Coffinberry High School student Abby, where crop circles have mysteriously appeared in their field."

"This is ridiculous," Tessa said, and I was so glad to have someone who agreed with me, but deep down there was a twinge of fear. Everything was getting so big now; not only were the police involved, but so was the news. My destruction was taking over more and more lives, and I could only imagine what would happen when everyone found out that I was the cause of this.

People were interviewed and everyone speculated about where the circles came from. I tried to catch Dad's eye to get him to put an end to this craziness, but he was still with the same group of men and seemed as frustrated with them as I was with the group around me.

"Maybe it's a brain-slurping monster from space," Richie Fagan, one of Collin's friends, shouted. He was standing with a group of kids who nodded in agreement. They were actually speculating about it and from the sounds of things, it seemed as if they were trying to one up one another to see how absurd their guesses about the circles could get.

Another boy from the group spoke up and said, "I bet our town has been picked for some kind of extraterrestrial experiment where we'll be taken up to a spaceship."

A little girl with pigtails sticking straight out of both sides of her head shrieked and her mother wrapped an arm around her.

"Relax, there's some reasonable explanation for this," Officer Scarano said.

"It's some hillbilly's idea of fun," Jeff Vichaikul, our mailman, declared.

I wanted everyone to stop talking, to stop trying to figure out a reason for this madness, because the truth was, there were no answers. There was no way anyone could make sense out of what I'd done to Abby, and I hated that those around me thought they could.

"It's some high school kids' idea of a joke," Heather Tuck, the town's hairstylist, shouted at the camera. "How much grief can one family go through? Do you really think they deserve to be the punch line of some late-night trouble a group of kids decided to get into?"

"It's a sign of the Armageddon," a boy with a face full of freckles shouted. "I read it on the Internet. When things like this happen, it means the world is going to end. This is it.

145

Next thing you know, the whole state will be infested with zombies coming to track each of us down."

The little girl with the pigtails cried harder, and her mother shot the boy a dirty look.

Collin looked at me with panic in his eyes, and I shook my head no. "It's nothing. The police will figure out who did this, and then everything will go back to normal." He seemed to accept my words, but I knew better than to believe something as simple as that. Things wouldn't go back to normal. Life would never be normal until Abby came back. We were fools to believe otherwise.

"What if they have something to do with Abby?" One of our neighbors, Karin, spoke up.

I stared at her, incredulous. This had nothing to do with Abby, but before I could object, she elbowed her way to the front of the camera and continued to speak straight to the lens as if she were asking this question to everyone who might possibly be watching. "What if it's some kind of sign from Abby?"

"How is Abby a part of this? That's rubbish," Jeff said, and kicked the heel of his boot into the dirt. A cloud of dust wafted up between us. A few of the adults nodded in agreement.

"These are the fields she used to run," Karin insisted. "If she was going to return anywhere, it would be here. She disappeared in the woods, so she'd have to cross this field to get back home. She's trying to tell us something."

Was she for real? She didn't know us, and there was no reason she should act as if she did now.

"What is she thinking?" I asked Tessa.

"One of the things I liked about Abby," Karin continued, "is that she was always outside running her heart out. That girl loved to run, and it's true, it was this field that she always seemed to soar over."

"It would make sense that she'd return to it," Heather said, somehow won over easily by this awful reasoning. She wasn't the only one either. Other people's heads moved up and down as their thoughts filled with false optimism and imaginary ideas.

"No," I shouted, probably louder than I should have. The group turned toward me and a cameraman moved in closer, but I didn't care. "This isn't about Abby."

"But what if it is?" a voice asked. It was Mom. And for the first time in what felt like forever, her face turned into something that wasn't the expressionless wilt of her thin, chapped lips. Something moved behind her eyes that had long since been at a loss for expression.

The news reporters took the idea and ran with it. They connected our fields to Abby, and I could hear my sister's name now addressed to the camera. This would be the lead story on the news tonight, and I hated how they could talk about Abby so easily. They were using us, finding a way to put words to the nightmare of what was happening to our family.

But apparently, I was the only one who felt this way. All other discussions were stopped. The people in our yard had come to a conclusion: The circles had something to do with Abby.

28

I was on edge until the news trucks and reporters packed their gear and drove away when the sun went down.

Dad waited until the field was empty of people and then left for work. Collin sat in front of the living room windows with Abby's comforter wrapped around his shoulders to watch the circles. He'd pulled it off her bed, and when Mom didn't say anything he began to drag it around the house like a giant baby blanket. Collin was officially obsessed with the circles. After it was suggested that they might have something to do with Abby, he couldn't take his eyes off them.

Mom sat in front of the computer in our family room and signed into the missing person's page she had created for Abby. News about Abby had spread through word of mouth and there were now thousands of people who had liked the page and followed along to see how my sister's story would end.

Mom continued to upload pictures of Abby, driven by the

possibility that someone may have some kind of clue as to where she might be. She posted throughout the day, writing detailed posts full of updates and pleas for people to share any information that might help. And people were sharing. There were hundreds of messages from all over the United States, and it seemed as if everyone thought they had a clue to help.

Mom managed the page like it was her new full-time job. She pored over these messages as if they could bring Abby home. She had a notebook where she tracked each message. A column for the name of the person who posted, another for their location, and then a meticulous written record of any information they'd offered. She filled page after page with the so-called evidence she found here and studied it late into the night. She highlighted information, wrote her own notes on Post-its, and passed whatever she thought was important on to the police.

Mom was obsessed with this page and if she wasn't at the computer, she was on her phone, checking for new posts. I'd sneaked a look in her notebook to see if anyone had any ideas about Abby, but it all seemed so far-fetched. People said they saw Abby at the Brookline Hills subway stop near Boston or at Jensen Beach in Florida. Locations I'd never even heard of and couldn't believe Abby would be at. But Mom followed up on each clue, passing the information on to the police, poring over Google Maps and zooming in on the places, and sticking a pushpin in the location on the giant United States map she'd hung on the wall. Most people bought maps to mark off the places they've been; Mom used hers to mark the invisible world Abby was inhabiting. Cities, highways, and towns full of her, as if these people were haunted by her every moment.

Tonight she stuck a pin in a town about two hours away from us called Perry. It bordered Lake Erie, and I imagined Abby sitting on the shore watching the sun go down. Could she really be there? Maybe she was living the new life I so desperately wanted.

I ran my hand from one pin to another and created an imaginary path that Abby had run as she zigzagged across the whole United States. Even missing, she did the things I wanted to; these phantom sightings got her out of this damn town.

I moved to the window that overlooked the field.

"Dad should mow over the circles tomorrow," I told her. "It would keep everyone away from our house."

"Your father won't do that," she replied, her eyes going back and forth from the computer screen to her notebook.

"Of course he would."

"Those circles are important. They need to stay there."

"You're joking, right?" I half expected Mom to burst out laughing. She didn't.

"We don't know where they came from and what they mean. So until we figure it out, the circles stay."

"Isn't it obvious? Someone made them as a joke."

Mom finally looked up at me. "They stay, Rhylee."

There was no getting through to her. Dad would say to let her be. This was her way of coping. But I didn't understand how denial and forgetting about the rest of your family was the way a person coped. Although, what did I know? I wasn't dealing with this any better than Mom was, so I couldn't pretend to have the answers.

Outside, the fog rolled in over the field. Thick wisps like ghosts touched down for a brief moment and then swirled back up again. They'd do this dance over and over, rising and falling until they blew out of sight into the parts of the field where the light wouldn't touch.

I pictured the way Abby used to run across those fields; smooth and fast so if you squinted in the sun, you could almost pretend she was flying.

Where was she? Had she run so fast that she let the wind push her faster and faster, until she too was picked up and blown forever into the dark parts of the world that you weren't allowed to see?

29

In the deep hours of night, someone whispered my name.

I sat up in my bed. My eyes worked to adjust to the pitch black around me.

"Hello?" I asked, but there was no answer.

I stayed there, unmoving, for a few minutes and waited to see if I heard the voice again. Across the hallway, I could see a light glowing under Abby's bedroom door.

I squinted at the narrow strip and tried to remember if anyone had gone in there. Mom avoided it like the plague, but Collin went in from time to time. He took little items of Abby's. Her bear was first, then her comforter, and now it was stuffed animals. I noticed his bed was filled with Abby's old toys.

But it was too late for him to be in there right now. My clock said it was 3:41.

The air was hot and sticky, and my damp hair clung to the back of my neck.

I stared at the light in my sister's room and remembered all the times I'd listen to her move around in there as she got ready to go out with friends or when she came home from being out with Tommy. I took it for granted that she'd always be on the other side of the door.

A shadow flashed across the doorway and for a moment the hallway went dark before the light was back.

Someone was in her room.

I threw the covers off and walked to Abby's door, even though I was scared out of my mind. I put my hand on the doorknob and turned it.

It was locked.

Whoever was inside didn't want anyone else to get in.

I softly knocked. "Hello, Mom? Collin?"

When no one answered, I went to Collin's room. He was curled up in his bed, Abby's stuffed animals around him and his legs tucked against his chest. I peeked in the crack of the door to Mom's room, and she, too, was fast asleep.

The hairs on the back of my neck prickled. I told myself I was being silly. There was nothing to be afraid of.

I knocked again on Abby's door, but it was silent on the other side.

I grasped the doorknob and twisted it.

"Open up," I said. I didn't care who I woke. When nothing changed, I pounded on the door.

"Who's in there?" I yelled. I continued to beat on the wood, terrified about what was beyond, but I needed to know. I had to find out. I hit the door over and over again, until my hands throbbed and my voice was hoarse.

"What's wrong?" Mom rushed down the hallway, in nothing but a giant T-shirt.

"There's someone in here," I told Mom and pointed at Abby's room. But now the light was off. And when Mom tried the knob, the door swung open as if it had never been locked.

My sister's room was completely empty.

I told myself it had been a dream. It had to be a bad dream to add to the nightmare that was already our lives.

30

Mary Grace and Erica slid into the empty seats across from me at lunch the next day. I was flipping through biology note cards and cramming for a test I had that afternoon. Tessa was taking her time in the food line, probably trying to decide what would do the least amount of damage, a Salisbury steak or foot-long hot dog. I could've told her she was fighting a losing battle; both looked and tasted nasty.

"How are you holding up?" Mary Grace asked. She had a bag of mini carrots and took tiny bites out of each, unlike normal people who tossed the whole thing in their mouths. She probably also ate baby corn as if it were on the cob, one row after the other.

I shrugged, uncomfortable, and opened my bag of barbe-que chips so I could shove a handful into my mouth to avoid answering. What was I supposed to say? *I kissed your best friend's boyfriend, and she caught us and ran into the woods. Where I left her. But I'm fine.*

"Can you believe Tommy is a suspect?" Erica asked.

"Tommy isn't a suspect," I told her.

"The police questioned him," Erica answered, as if she were an expert on the case of my sister's disappearance. Anger swirled inside of me.

"They didn't connect him to anything." I waited for Mary Grace to speak up and defend Tommy; she had hung out with him and Abby a lot, but she didn't say a word.

"Yeah, well, you never know," Erica told me. She acted like she was talking about some detective show on TV and not my sister. It made my food spoil in my stomach.

"Actually, I do," I snapped and wished she'd stop talking, but she seemed oblivious to the fact that I couldn't stand her right now.

"Have you found out any more about the circles?"

"No," I said, and it was the truth. It had been three days since the circles appeared, and I tried to ignore them, which wasn't easy considering that this morning the news stations had arrived again and continued their report in front of our house. More and more cars drove slowly down the stretch of road that usually had no more than five cars a day on it. Our house was now a tourist stop, a celebrity's home on a Hollywood bus tour.

"Everyone thinks they have something to do with Abby," said Erica.

"They don't have anything to do with Abby," I said, my voice a bit harsh. All of these people interested in the circles were nuts, and I wasn't about to feed into it.

"It's okay, Rhylee," Mary Grace spoke up. "I understand why you're angry. You're allowed to be mad. My mom says that sometimes people do that when they're hurting."

I swear she was about to reach out for my hand and stroke it. I pictured her pulling out some ginger ale and crackers from her lunch bag and offering them like Mom did when I was sick.

"It doesn't matter," Erica sighed. "We're not trying to fight with you." She pulled a purple bracelet out of her bag and put it in front of me. "You aren't wearing one. You can have mine."

"Why? It's not like it's going to bring her back," I snapped again.

Mary Grace spoke up. "We miss your sister. We don't want to forget her. A bracelet might help you feel like you're doing something."

Was she implying that I wasn't?

Maybe she was right. I felt so helpless about everything that was going on.

And what would she think if she knew the truth? She sure as heck wouldn't be sitting here, handing me a bracelet if she did. She and Erica would hate me, they'd shoot me dirty looks, trip me in the halls, and make it their mission to destroy me. Like everyone had with Max Locke. Like they were doing to Tommy.

I grabbed my lunch bag and stood. "Stop pretending that these things you're doing are going to help. Cross-country meets, prayers, and bracelets aren't going to bring my sister home."

"It's like you don't even want her to return," Mary Grace said, and her words sliced through me.

"How can you say I don't care?" I said.

"How can we not?" Erica replied.

"She's my sister. She's *my* sister, and she's gone." I squashed my lunch bag into a ball and made a fist around it, I was so upset. "I want her to return more than any of you. I *need* her to return."

"It doesn't seem like it," Erica said. "All you do is get mad at us when we try to help."

"Don't you get it? I can't act like I care. If I get caught up in all of this, it means she's gone. And she's not gone. She can't be," I yelled, and I didn't care that my classmates turned around in their seats to watch me. "I need to act like this because what's the alternative?"

And no one could reply because to admit any other alternative would be impossible.

31

I couldn't get away from Mary Grace and Erica fast enough. I blamed all the thoughts that clouded my head for why I wasn't thinking about where I was going. I'd been so careful about the corners I took at school, the hallways I walked down, and stairways I moved up, all so I could avoid Tommy.

Except today, I rushed away from Mary Grace and Erica and ran right into him.

"Sorry," I mumbled, and tried to calm myself so Tommy wouldn't see how upset I was. I focused on the floor where my biology index cards now lay. If I hadn't blown off studying last night, I'd leave them on the floor, spread out like confetti after ringing in the New Year. I bent to pick them up at the same time Tommy did.

"Let me help." He handed a few cards to me, and his arm brushed against mine. I paused, remembering what it felt like.

I shook my head to clear it and went back to collecting the cards.

Tommy handed a few to me. "Can you really not even stand to be near me?"

I held on to the stack of index cards so hard they cut into my palm. I reminded myself of the things that could never exist between us. Not now. Not ever. Not after what we'd done.

"I told you. I can't. We can't."

"We can still talk to each other," Tommy said, loud enough that people stopped to look.

"Quiet down," I told him. Most of my classmates walked right past on their way to class, but there were a few who had slowed and seemed to be waiting to see what exactly was happening between the two of us.

"You okay?" Kyle, the same boy who had shoved Tommy that day in the cafeteria, asked. "Is he giving you trouble?"

"We're fine," Tommy said.

"I wasn't talking to you," Kyle replied. He looked straight at me. "Everything good?"

"Everything is good," I said, my tone every bit as unfriendly as Tommy's was. It was obvious what Kyle was getting at, and I wasn't going to allow it.

Kyle nodded and headed back down the hallway, but shot one more look at Tommy over his shoulder.

"Asshole," Tommy said when Kyle was gone.

"It's my fault."

"Nothing is your fault."

"But it is. The way Kyle just treated you. It's because he thinks you had something to do with Abby."

"Don't worry about it," Tommy said.

"Are you kidding me? Don't *worry* about it?"

"I can handle it. Just ignore them."

I squeezed my eyes shut as if it would erase the awful feelings I had about myself and what Tommy was going through, but all it did was make things worse. "All I *do* is worry about it. You shouldn't have to be used to it."

"Rhylee, I'll be okay," Tommy said, but how could that be true? There was nothing okay about any of this.

32

Collin tackled me when I arrived home after school. His hair was messed up and he had smears of chocolate on his face. He must have had one of the pudding cups he was obsessed with. He dipped a spoon in peanut butter and then ate it with the pudding. It was absolutely brilliant; I'd be lying if I said I hadn't tried it myself. But Mom never let him do it. I wished I could believe she let him have it as a treat, but it was more likely she wasn't paying attention so he helped himself. Mom tuning out from the world seemed like the norm these days.

Our field was still full of people, but it looked as if the news trucks had backed off. It was mostly adults from our town. Officer Scarano stood off to the side. Dad had insisted that if we were going to keep these circles, the police needed to provide someone to keep a watch over things. But Scarano sure wasn't doing that great a job; he was on his phone more than he was keeping order.

Collin tugged at the bottom of my T-shirt. "What took you so long? I've been waiting for hours."

"More like half an hour. I know when your bus drops you off," I said and messed up his hair more. He pushed my hand away and made a face.

He dug around in his book bag and then shoved a pile of books at me. A few fell to the floor, but he left them there, too excited to show me the one still in his hand. He opened it to a page and shoved it in my face. "Look, Rhylee, look."

"What are these?" I grabbed the book out of his hands. The cover read *Urban Legends: Fact or Fiction*.

"The librarian helped me pick them out. They're research."

"Research?" I asked, giving him a look to let him know he wasn't fooling me.

"Hello—the crop circles. There's tons of information in these books." He pointed at a specific picture and jumped up and down, excited for me to look at it. "And this one looks like the ones we have. In 1976 Clayton Thorp discovered them in his cornfields."

"Clayton who?" This was getting a bit ridiculous.

"Thorp," Collin said and pointed at the grainy pictures of a field similar to my family's. A man with a long white beard stood in front of one of the circles, his lips set in a grim line like this was all very serious. "The circles showed up in his yard too. They came out of nowhere and then strange things began to happen."

"Like what?" I took the book out of his hand and glanced at the page, not wanting to encourage him, but they were interesting.

"Unusual stuff. His horses appeared in the road near his house even though he locked them in the stable at night, the leaves on his trees turned red and orange in the summer, and he'd find windows in his house wide open. It's like when Abby visited me. The circles are connected to her, I know it."

I thought about the other night with the light in Abby's room. *Stop it,* I told myself. *This is nuts.* I shook my head to clear it from any creepy ideas Collin's books were giving me. I refused to believe any of it. I closed his book and gave it back to him.

"The only strange thing about the ones in our yard is that a bunch of idiots find them important enough to stand around and stare at them for hours. Everyone needs to get a life."

I counted fourteen people in our field. They stood in the circles and faced the woods as if waiting for something. Something they had lost because of me. I yearned to tell them that the circles were useless, just like all the other things the town had tried to do to bring Abby back.

33

Later that night, while I was in the bathroom brushing my teeth, Mom called my name. I nearly choked on a mouthful of toothpaste when I realized she was in Abby's room. She hadn't been able to even walk by her room without crying.

"Are you okay?" I asked.

"Look outside." She sat on the desk chair, which she had pulled to the window. Her hand was draped over the back, lying against a purple sweater of my sister's that waited for her to return and put it on. "Tell me what you see."

I hesitated, afraid of what was out there, but when I looked, it wasn't any different from earlier that afternoon.

"A bunch of people," I told her.

"What do you think they're doing?"

"I have no idea." I pressed my face against the glass and tried to get a better look at the group that was outside in our field. I counted nine of them, six women and three men. They were older, maybe my parents' age, and wore thick-soled shoes better suited for being outside than the heels and shiny dress shoes the news crew had worn. I recognized a librarian from the children's room who always saved new books for me and a teacher from my elementary school. It was strange to see people from town hanging out in our yard. They walked in a line through the paths that cut into the circles.

I opened the window, half expecting one of them to notice me, but nobody did.

"Did you tell Dad?"

"He left for work before I saw them."

"They're saying something." I put my ear against the screen. I very faintly heard bits and pieces of their words. I turned back to Mom, puzzled. "It sounds as if they're praying."

We both fell silent, our heads tilted toward the outside. Mom's eyes grew dark and serious.

"They're praying for Abby," she said, and I listened again. When meaning was connected to the words, they became clear, and she was right; they were out there for Abby. I thought about all the prayers I had sent out to bring my sister home and how useless it seemed. I'd begged and pleaded with fate, willing to trade the world to have her back. I wondered how many more prayers would be sent up to Abby. And if anyone was listening.

34

I woke that evening to a light shining into my window.

Someone was in the woods behind our house.

The person stood there, unmoving, and held a flashlight with the bright beam pointed directly at my window.

It hit the wall where I hung Abby's missing person flyers, her face illuminated and then fading into the dark edges where the light didn't touch.

I placed my palms against the window screen and stared at the light. It was steady, held at the person's middle, and only wavered slightly every few seconds.

I ducked down onto my bed, as if whoever it was could see me, and counted to one hundred. When I came back up, they were still there. The light in the same position, the inky darkness swallowing up the edges.

It wasn't Abby.

It couldn't be Abby.

But a nervous thrill went through me.

What if it was Abby?

When my sister and I were younger, we used to play a game we called I Haunt You. We'd stand somewhere in the dark, usually a bedroom, the hallway, or the backyard, unmoving. Sometimes one of us was brave enough to walk up to the other person to see if that person was really there or if it was only shadows in the dark. Usually the game ended with the person jumping out and scaring the other or the light being flicked on. Tonight, as I watched the person with a flashlight, my mind went back to that game. What if Abby was waiting there for me? Maybe she was testing my courage to see if I'd come out and discover her.

I considered telling my parents, but they'd want to investigate, and I couldn't scare away whoever was there.

I needed to find out what was going on.

I threw on a sweatshirt over my pajamas and slipped out the door.

I tried not to be terrified, but I was.

The light pulled me toward it, as if I were connected to a string. I moved through the field; the dew-soaked grass clung to the bottom of my pants. With each step, I expected the person to leave or move, but they remained, and so each step brought me closer to whoever was out there.

The dark shadows of the woods played tricks on my eyes. They warped and changed so it looked as if people were hiding everywhere, a line of bodies at the edge of the forest.

This had to be a prank. Some kid from school messing with us like when the circles were created.

But what if it wasn't, a voice in my head kept saying.

"Abby?" I asked.

I took baby steps. One foot in front of each other. A wind stirred the leaves in the trees. It lifted the ends of my hair.

I continued to move forward, even though all I wanted to do was turn and run back to my room, lock the door, and hide under the covers until the morning light erased the night. But I couldn't run. I couldn't do that now, not if it really was Abby.

I was about ten feet away, but it was so dark, and the flashlight blinded me.

I stopped when I was close enough to reach out and touch the person. But I didn't touch them. Instead, I held my hands palm up, as if offering everything, even though I had nothing left to give. I'd lost it all.

I could hear their breathing. Deep and heavy and labored. As if it were impossible to take in air.

I took the final step toward the light and reached straight out. But as I touched skin, the flashlight went off.

I was plunged into darkness as whoever it was turned and ran away. I was left reaching out into the emptiness with the memory of brief contact with skin so cold it took my breath away.

35

A fight erupted between my parents the next morning at breakfast when Dad saw that a few people had spent the night in our field. I wondered if one of them had been the person who had stood at the edge of the woods. It had to be. There were no other explanations that didn't make me sound certifiably crazy.

"This has to stop," Dad argued with Mom. "I've put up with way too much this last week. I let the news crew come here and report for some ungodly reason, I allowed practically the entire town to converge here and hash out some insane conspiracy about how the circles had to do with our daughter, and said nothing when it was obvious some of the people here just had a sick curiosity to check out our tragedy. But this, this is where I draw the line. I'm not okay with a bunch of random people spending the night in our yard."

"They're not random," Mom said, the surprise advocate for

this strange group who had nothing better to do than hang out in our field. "We know every one of them. Jen, Gavin, a few parents from the kids' schools were there. No one is a threat."

Dad shook his head in frustration. "I didn't say they posed any threat. But our field does not have to be the gathering place in town."

"They're staying," Mom said with more force than I'd heard her use since Abby disappeared. "They're trying to help."

"Sitting in a field is not going to help anything," Dad shot back.

"No one knows what to do, and this is something. They're here for Abby. How could you be against that?"

Dad sighed and scratched his beard. "I'm not against it. I just don't like the idea of this."

"Nobody is hurting anyone," Mom said. "Let it be."

"I don't think that's a good idea . . . ," Dad said, the struggle apparent. Mom hadn't shown this much passion for anything since Abby left. But this. These people. It was all so strange.

"Please," Mom begged. "I'll talk with Officer Scarano. Check to see if he can patrol the house a few times a night. These people are doing good; they're praying for our daughter. How can we fault them in that?"

"We can't," Dad said and the decision was made. He'd allow these people to continue to search for some kind of meaning in a bunch of circles that were more than likely mowed into our fields by some of my asshole classmates with nothing better to do on a Friday night.

171

36

My parents weren't the only ones caught up in the circles. My classmates were fascinated too. The whole school talked about them. Not directly to me—that would be too awkward—but I'm sure they wanted to say something.

Two girls in my history class were whispering about them a little bit too loud when a student aide came in with a note. It was during the last class of the day, ten minutes before the bell rang, and all I wanted to do was get out of there.

"Rhylee, you need to go to the office," Mr. Scott said after he had read the piece of paper in his hand. "You can take your stuff, since class will probably be over before you get back."

I stood slowly. I was afraid. The office never called for me, and I hadn't done anything to earn a trip to see our principal. What if they had news about Abby?

What if it was bad news? Confirming what we were all afraid to say out loud.

My head spun with worries and fears as I made my way to the office. I wanted to walk past the door that led inside. I could keep going, right out of the building. I could go somewhere else, stay away from my house and live in perfect oblivion for a few more hours. But I couldn't do that. I had to face things no matter what the cost.

I relaxed a little when the secretary, Mrs. Hastings, smiled at me. I figured you couldn't tell someone bad news if you looked happy. At least I hoped that was the case.

Our principal, Mr. Ralston, walked out of the meeting room.

"Everything is okay, right?" I blurted out.

"Yes, yes, sorry about that, I didn't mean to make you nervous. Thanks for coming down." He shifted from the front of his feet to the back and looked uncomfortable.

"No problem," I mumbled, and prepared myself for a lecture. If this didn't have to do with Abby, I had a feeling it was about my grades and how bad they were. I wasn't a fool. I understood that I had to do well in school if I wanted any chance of going to college, especially since I wouldn't be able to pull it off without some sort of financial aid. But sitting down and studying wasn't exactly at the top of my list of things to do right now.

"Listen, I talked to your mother and we have some . . ." He paused for a moment and then spoke the last words quickly, ". . . possessions of your sister's. We gathered the stuff the police didn't take out of her locker, and when I talked to your mother, she said you could bring it home." He walked into a small room, and I stood there stunned. This was not what I'd expected when I got called down here. Was I supposed to follow him? I didn't want to. And I didn't want him to come out. I didn't want a bunch of Abby's stuff. Was Mom so clueless as to think I wouldn't mind bringing it home?

I couldn't believe they'd cleared out her locker as if to make way for someone else. It had only been three weeks. Something bitter bubbled up, and when I tried to push it back down, a sound that was half laugh and half cough popped out my mouth.

Mr. Ralston came back with a cardboard box. It had been used to ship something; the address blackened out with a thick marker. Pieces of masking tape stretched across the top to keep it closed, but you could still see inside if you wanted to look. I didn't.

I took the box as if it held a dead animal. It was surprisingly light, but too big to hide.

"Thanks," I muttered, and turned to leave.

"Of course. It's the least I can do to help." Mr. Ralston put his hand on my shoulder. "I heard about the circles. I was thinking of stopping by one of these nights."

I wanted to jam the box back into his hands and tell him that he could take the damn thing to my house then, but I simply nodded.

I left without saying a thing, the weight of Abby's items in my hands growing heavier with each step.

37

I stuffed the box into my book bag. The corners cut into my back and just knowing it was there made it feel as if it weighed a million pounds.

Instead of getting on the bus and having to give its contents to my parents, I went to the grocery store, since no one in my family remembered to buy food anymore. We grazed on the scraps around the kitchen: odds and ends, peanut butter and jelly or tomato soup for dinner, dry cereal for breakfast. We never seemed to run out of food, but we also never had the right food for a complete meal. Poor Collin had dined on a gourmet dinner of instant mashed potatoes and breakfast sausages last night.

I grabbed a basket and filled it with milk, fresh veggies, fruit, bread, some lunch meat, and two chocolate bars I planned to share with Collin.

On my way out, the bulletin board near the automatic

doors caught my eye. It had one of my sister's missing person flyers stuck on it.

Men in business suits rushed out with small bags of food and mothers walked in with sleepy babies in one hand and lists in the other. They moved past me without looking at the flyer, but I couldn't tear my eyes away from it.

I touched Abby's face. There were tabs at the bottom of the flyer with the police department's number to call if you had anything to report. Three of the tabs were ripped off. It reminded me of my collages, the images torn apart and pieced back together to create the reality I wanted. What if these tabs could do the same?

There was a slight twinge of excitement in my stomach. Usually when I saw these, they were intact, whole, but someone had touched this one. The numbers at the bottom were in someone's fist, pocket, purse, or sitting on top of a dresser. My mind spun. Did someone have knowledge about Abby? Could we be wrong about the river? The thought made me giddy with hope.

I pulled the flyer with the missing tabs off the board and stuffed it in my purse. This sheet of paper represented something to me. Maybe Abby was still out there and I needed to find her. If I could make sense of anything I'd done, it was that I shouldn't give up. I had to make things right.

38

Mom was at the living room table in front of the computer clicking away on Abby's tribute page when I got home. I waved the carton of milk at her as I tried to rush past, hoping she wasn't thinking about the box in my book bag. "Have no fear; we won't die of calcium depletion this week."

She looked up, "I didn't know we were out."

Of course not, I wanted to say. *You don't notice anything these days.*

I could create a whole list of things Mom didn't see these days, starting with the pile of unopened mail in our front hallway, the dust and dirt that collected on our floors, which hadn't been swept or mopped in weeks, and the fact that Collin got away with not taking a bath for almost a week before I noticed. My grades were falling so fast that I wasn't even sure if I could salvage them and Collin was practically a walking zombie from exhaustion, since Mom didn't enforce his bedtime anymore.

When I glanced back, she was already bent over her stupid notebook full of Abby sightings again, and frustration built inside of me. Her obsession with the messages on Abby's tribute page, Collin's obsession with aliens, the town's obsession with the circles—they were nothing. Nothing that would help.

But the flyer, I told myself, *that was something. That could mean something.* And the idea calmed me.

I put the groceries away and headed upstairs with the candy bars. I planned to unload the box of Abby's stuff and see if I could find some kind of connection to her. The box promised new ways to remember my sister.

I hesitated for only a second and considered handing it over to Mom or Dad. It would be the right thing to do, but this might be my only chance to see what was inside. If there was something in the box I could hold on to, I wanted to pull it out before one of my parents found it. Mom would probably set it on Abby's desk, another shrine to gather dust.

I locked the door to my room and dug my nails under the packing tape, not even bothering with scissors. The tape cut into my hands and twisted into tight ropes, so I broke it with my teeth. I yanked open the flaps at the top of the box and stuck my hand in.

The first thing I pulled out was a pair of her running shoes, held together with knots joining the bright purple shoelaces she loved to use. All of her shoes had purple laces; it was her trademark. I pictured her running ovals on the high school track during the school day. If you played a sport, you didn't have to take gym, so the period when Abby would've chased a volleyball around or done enough jumping jacks to keep your heart rate up, she instead went out and ran. I could see her from the upstairs bathroom window of the school. Abby had a hypnotic effect on people. There were times when I'd let ten or fifteen minutes go by as I watched my sister, and then the bell would ring and break me out of my trance.

I tried her shoes on and they were the perfect fit. I stretched my legs in front of me, and it was as if Abby was sitting there. I pulled them off, because it didn't feel right. I stretched my own feet in front of me. The pink polish she had painted on my nails was chipped and almost all gone.

I dug back into the box and pulled out a half-empty bottle of the lemon-scented body spray she always doused herself with. I pumped the top of the bottle and caught the scent in the air, letting it settle around me.

There was a bunch of papers stacked on top of one another. I shifted through them and wished for a note, something personal, but they were all school papers, her slanted handwriting crowded together on each line, one word almost running into the next.

I found a pair of sunglasses that was missing one of its lenses and a hair tie, which I used to gather my hair into a ponytail. I pulled out her school-issued agenda that everyone was given the first day of school. I paged through it, but it was empty. I grabbed a pen from my desk and put a number one on the date she went missing. I numbered each day after it until I got to today. Day fourteen. I paged through the rest of the book and wondered how many other days would be empty of my sister. I couldn't think about it; she had to come home. I pushed the agenda aside and went back to the box.

There was a worn-out T-shirt folded neatly on the bottom. I recognized it immediately. I knew about the hole in the left corner and the blue stain on the backside without even looking. It was the shirt Abby had worn when she ran her first marathon on her sixteenth birthday. Most normal people would go for their driver's license, but not Abby. She'd wanted something more, so she'd set out to train months before, ignoring Dad's pestering that she should be practicing her driving skills. He'd made it more than obvious that he was counting the days until Abby got her license and could take over the job of chauffeuring Collin and me around.

"Why would I need wheels when I can run everywhere?" she'd asked, and it was true. Abby did run everywhere: to the store, friends' houses, and even school, which I didn't understand. I'd be a big sweaty mess if that was my means of transportation, but somehow Abby always managed to look as if she had taken a leisurely stroll.

"It's a goal, something to work toward," she'd told us when we teased her about the race.

"Nothing says celebration like a twenty-six-mile race," I'd joked, because even the idea of running that far made my legs ache.

"Twenty-six point two," she'd corrected me with a grin.

My family got up on the morning of her birthday not to watch her eat cake and open presents, but to watch her cross the finish line before coffee and cold air had fully woken us up. She'd ended the race with her hands held high in the air, and

180

we'd wrapped our arms around her sweaty body, her T-shirt covered in messages we'd scrawled before the race.

I read the words on her shirt now and remembered when Abby had proclaimed, after running twenty-six point two miles, that she could now take on the world.

The last item in the box was a notebook with math problems written on the first few pages. I turned to the next page and a photograph fell out. It was of the two of us, hands slung around each other's shoulders with our heads tilted back as we were caught in mid-laugh. I couldn't remember when it was taken, but the happiness on both our faces was impossible to look at.

"I'm so sorry, Abby." I traced the outline of her face. "Please come home."

I flipped through the rest of the notebook and stopped when I found a page of her writing. It looked like the draft of a note, the words scratched out and written again.

A note written to Tommy.

I closed the notebook. It was private, not meant for me.

But what if I held a clue? I found the page again and read the words.

> Tommy,
> I don't know what I'd do without you. You saved me.
> You have no idea.

The note stopped there, and I imagined her writing it in class and having to turn the page when her teacher walked by or the bell rang.

You saved me. Saved her from what? What did he have no idea about? And if Tommy had saved my sister, what had *I* done to her?

"Destroyed her," I said out loud. "That's what you did."

I picked up the picture of the two of us and ripped it in half. I removed myself from the image because I didn't deserve to be with her. Not after what I'd done.

I hid the picture in my desk drawer. I couldn't bring myself to throw it away. I placed everything else back in the box.

I carried it to my parents' room and left it on their dresser. The scent of her perfume clung to my clothes, and if I closed my eyes, I could pretend that I wasn't standing here all alone.

39

I added the flyer I'd taken from the grocery store to the wall in my room.

Three missing tags.

Three chances to bring home Abby.

The paper was jagged where the tags had been ripped off, and I had to believe that they meant something.

If people were pulling off our number, then I was going to continue to plaster it all over town. I wouldn't be like Mom; I'd do something—something useful. I'd make sure the flyers were everywhere so no one could miss them.

"We need to hang more posters of Abby," I told Dad the next morning at breakfast.

"I think everyone did a pretty good job putting them around town, but I can talk with the police and see what they can do," Dad said, always the practical one, even when practicality was useless.

"No, that's not enough," I argued. "I want to go out and distribute them myself so we can make sure we have them everywhere."

It was probably pointless. I'm sure Dad was right about the town being blanketed in flyers, but what if more tabs were taken from some of them? What if all the tabs were taken from one and someone needed to take one? And I needed to get a new flyer up at the grocery store to replace the one I took. If I helped pass out the flyers, I'd know exactly where they were going, and I could keep track of them. If there was a chance Abby was still out there, I had to help.

"Please. We need to make sure the town is flooded with these posters," I insisted.

Dad must have realized how important this was to me, because he didn't even hesitate. "Sure, we can go this afternoon. I'll pick you up at school," he said.

"You can come too," I told Mom.

"I'd like that," she said, and I hoped she'd still be willing to go when the time came. It seemed as if her mornings were better than her afternoons. She got up, made us breakfast, and watched Collin leave for school. It was in the hours after that she seemed to forget about us. Something happened during the hours in between the morning and afternoon, so the Mom I said good-bye to in the morning was often different than the one I saw when I got home. She'd be sitting in front of the computer screen filling her notebook with name after name. The pins on the wall continued to multiply until it seemed as if Abby was everywhere.

"We need to keep her in everyone's mind," I said, as if anyone could think of anything but Abby. Her disappearance was a heavy weight, draped over us, dragging us down.

"What about me? I want to do something," Collin said.

"You can take care of Hound Dog for Abby. He misses her," I told him.

"Okay, the two of us will watch the circles," he said, and tried to coax the dog to the window.

Collin's obsession with the circles was getting worse.

Despite all of our conversations with him that there was nothing out of this world happening in our backyard, he wouldn't stop talking about it. If my parents were smart, they'd put blackout curtains on the windows so he couldn't stake out the field.

"The circles don't need anyone to watch over them," Dad said firmly.

"They mean something. These things don't appear without a reason," Collin insisted. He pulled sheets of paper out of his pockets. He laid images of circles all over our table. "The signs are here. The circles are from somewhere far away."

He talked fast, in an excited voice, as if someone might stop him. His finger traced one of the circles, moving around and around the intricate pattern. "This one was found in Michigan. That's not too far from here. And this field has a whole bunch just like our house. Maybe they're connected."

Dad shook his head and gathered the plates. "Collin, believe me, it's an awful joke. Nothing more. Don't get yourself worked up about something that doesn't mean a thing."

I nodded my agreement, but when I turned to Mom for her affirmation, she was bent over one of the pictures, studying it intently.

Collin saw the same thing and turned to her, speaking as if she were his singular audience. "This field had circles found it in it three times. They kept showing up." He continued to talk about the different pictures and Mom listened. She stared at the sheets that were spread out in front of her as if she was lost and was studying some map that would lead her back home.

40

"Where are we heading?" Dad asked when he picked me up after school with a backseat full of flyers for my sister. It was only the two of us. Dad apologized for Mom not "feeling up to joining us."

"The town square. I figure we can hit the stores on both sides of the street, and after, we can grab dinner."

"Now you're talking," Dad said. "I've been craving Deagan's."

"Maybe we could try something new?"

"Somewhere new? But you love eating at Deagan's."

"I used to love it. When we'd go together."

It was true. Deagan's was a family favorite. I craved their burgers, and Dad liked how they served breakfast whenever you wanted it. He was a firm believer that a person should eat a good breakfast at the start of their day, even if his day started in the evening because he worked the late shift. More often than not, he'd come home from work when we'd be eating cereal or toast before school and he'd have a plate of spaghetti or leftover meat loaf. It frustrated Mom to no end, since she battled with Collin, who hated any type of breakfast food that wasn't a sugary cereal. Collin still didn't think it was fair that Dad got to eat the dinner leftovers while he was stuck gagging down Cheerios. We usually went to Deagan's once or twice a month, but since Abby disappeared, we hadn't been back. It didn't seem quite right. It was just another reminder of what I was able to do and Abby wasn't.

Dad placed his hand on my shoulder. "I hear you. We can go somewhere else."

I relaxed, relieved. "Thanks."

Dad and I went along the strip of stores that was Coffinberry's downtown. It wasn't a huge area, but the sidewalks were always crowded. People came here to get odds and ends, to listen to the weekly outdoor concert, or socialize. Our flyers would be seen.

I told Dad about the flyer at the grocery store.

"There were three phone numbers ripped off." I tried to hide the excitement in my voice. I'd been thinking of them and imagining scenarios that all ended with Abby coming home.

"That's three more numbers than we've seen in a long time," Dad said, which was true. "But I haven't heard anything new."

"Do you think someone knows something?"

"It was probably more likely a person interested in what was going on in our yard right now."

"I hope that's not the case," I said.

Dad was right about the flyers. There were piles of them in each store we stopped in, but I reminded myself of the three tabs. People were noticing, and I'd make sure there were enough flyers to do just that.

After we left the fifth shop, Dad suggested splitting up.

"How about you drop off flyers over there, and I'll get this side. Then we can meet for dinner at Otis's Diner when we're done."

"Sounds like a plan," I said.

He crossed the street, and I entered the first store, a little bakery that every bride in town ordered her wedding cake from. I refilled the stack of flyers. I hung another one on the bulletin board near the entrance of the coffee shop before I moved on to my next stop. I waved to Tessa's mom, who worked at the post office, and dropped a bunch off on the table they had set up near the stamp machine. I moved from store to store, making sure Abby's flyers were everywhere, so even if people wanted to keep her out of their minds, they couldn't.

I dropped off the rest of them at the little antique shop with a bell that rang when the door opened. The gray-haired woman who owned the place was working with some customers, so I put the papers near the register and felt a tiny bit better that at least I'd done something.

I was about to text Dad that I was done when Johnson appeared about a block in front of me. I studied him with a strange fascination.

He attempted to push his cart up a curb, the wheels not cooperating and the entire cart leaning to the left dangerously. People walked past without helping. A mom grabbed her daughter's hand and dragged her across the street, so the two of them wouldn't have pass him. It didn't take a genius to see that even though the police had cleared Johnson, the town wasn't letting him off that easily.

"Just like Tommy," I said to myself.

I joined the group of people who stopped and stared as Johnson tried to pick up the front of the cart and put it on the curb. There was this little voice in the back of my head that made me wonder if maybe, just maybe, he knew what happened to Abby.

A man in a Coffinberry High School football shirt walked up to Johnson and put a hand on his shoulder.

Johnson shook it off. "Hey, listen, no problems," he said and held his hands up in defense. "I want no trouble."

"How about you get out of here then," the man said in a way that made it clear it wasn't a question, but a statement.

"That's what I was trying to do," Johnson said.

I wanted to turn away, to leave all of this, but instead, like those around me, I stood glued to the spot, unable to move, and hated myself for the small bit of doubt about his innocence that had crept into my mind.

"Do it a little faster, asshole," the man said, and spat at Johnson. It hit him on the cheek, the wet blob dripping down.

Johnson made a fist and pulled his arm back as if he were

going to hit the guy. I tensed up, scared to see what would happen.

"Go ahead and hit me," the man said, and laughed. "It'll just prove to us that you had something to do with Abby's disappearance."

Johnson dropped his arm and pushed his cart forward, not even wiping the spit off his cheek. He moved down the street and the crowd dispersed, everyone going their separate ways as if nothing had happened.

I walked in the opposite direction, shocked. This must be how people viewed Tommy, too. It didn't matter that they were both officially cleared. When there wasn't an answer, the town needed to find one, and Johnson and Tommy were their targets. I was ashamed that I'd stopped like everyone else to watch what would happen with Johnson. How was that any different from the way people treated Tommy?

Things weren't going to change. I could scream the truth about Tommy, and people would not only go after him but me, too. Because we needed to find a reason that my sister wasn't here. And until Abby came home, the town wouldn't stop blaming people for taking her away.

My phone buzzed with a text from Dad. **Grabbed table at Otis's. Meet me when done.**

I headed to the restaurant and found Dad sitting near the back in a booth. I slid in across from him and he smiled.

"That was a good idea you had, putting up more flyers," he said.

"I feel like we need to keep doing things," I said, Johnson

still on my mind. "We need to bring Abby home, so we can end this nightmare."

A waitress came and took our orders, and Dad and I fell into an easy conversation with each other about school, the weather, and Hound Dog. Insignificant things.

I was halfway through my burger, dragging a French fry through some ketchup, when an older woman approached our table. She stopped in front of us.

"You don't know me, but I've been watching your family on the news," she said, as if it was perfectly okay to come up to people during dinner and interrupt them. "Every time I see a picture of your beautiful daughter, my heart breaks. And to think, that boy who she trusted might have hurt—"

I dropped my fork and it clattered against my dish. "He didn't do anything," I said.

She opened and closed her mouth as if she was trying to say something but didn't know quite what.

"Tommy," I clarified, just in case she didn't understand exactly what I was saying. "He isn't a suspect, so stop trying to make him one."

"Excuse me?" she said, confused, as if I were the one who crossed some kind of line at the moment.

"Rhylee, calm down," Dad said so loud that people at other tables turned to look. He apologized to the woman. "What she's trying to say is thank you."

"I was only trying to help," she said, pulling back.

"Of course, we appreciate your kind words," Dad said, and it took every ounce of control inside of me to stay quiet.

Dad pushed his plate away and leaned toward me. "Do you want to tell me what the hell that was about?"

"What? How she thought it was okay to interrupt us while we're eating to chat it up about Abby? How she accused Tommy, just like everyone else in this damn town?" I asked.

"You might not agree with her, but you need to respect her," Dad said.

It was the word "respect" that pushed me over the edge. I thought about the way everyone had treated Johnson, the way I had treated Johnson. How Tommy was now a target and about all the people in our yard, the endless news reports, the way my classmates stared at me with pity and Tommy with disgust. What was happening to our town had nothing to do with respect. It was about me and what I'd done and what I'd ruined. This, all of this, was my fault.

"How can I *respect* them when they treat Tommy like a criminal? Like he's the one who hurt my sister."

"The town is hurting," Dad said "Something like this makes people afraid—that this could happen to them, too."

"Then let them hurt," I shouted, not caring that I was causing people to look over at us. "But Tommy isn't the one they should blame."

"You're right, honey. It isn't fair, but we're trying to get through this. Everyone is searching for an answer in the nightmare that we're living now."

"I just want her home," I said, a truce to Dad. A signal that I was done fighting with him.

"We all do," he said. "There's nothing more that I want in the world than for your sister to come back to us."

It suddenly felt very important to tell him the full truth. If Dad was noticing a change in me, everyone else must be too. Abby was slipping further and further away from me; I couldn't do the same.

"What if I did something really bad; would you still love me?" I asked, terrified of his response. "Something that would be hard to forgive me for. Something awful."

"I'll always love you, no matter what," he said, and I wanted to believe that was true.

"I need to tell you something," I told him, and my heart sped up.

Dad leaned in, as if he could sense that this was important, but before I could confess, our waitress came over to our table.

"How are you two doing?" she asked.

"Great, we're great," Dad said.

"Are you thinking you want any dessert?"

I shook my head. I didn't have an appetite anymore. Not even for one of Otis's Diner's famous salted caramel sundaes.

"I think the bill is fine," he said.

She fished around in her pocket for a moment before pulling out a slip of paper. "Thanks so much. Have a great night."

Dad counted out a bunch of money and I waited in silence. My heart slowed and now that I had a few minutes to think, I realized how stupid I was to have tried to say something. I pictured Mom's face that first morning when Abby went missing. How she'd looked at me as if she hadn't recognized me.

194

How even though she tried to hide it, she blamed me for not coming home with my sister. Would admitting my role in all of this make things better or worse? Would it show that there was even more information Tommy was withholding or could it help him? I wasn't sure, but what I did know was that I didn't want to do anything that might possibly hurt Tommy even more. It had been selfish of me to want to shove the weight of my secret off my shoulders. What good would that do? Just so I could hear that my dad still loved me?

"What was it you wanted to tell me before I paid the bill?" Dad asked as he put his wallet back into his pocket.

"Nothing. It was nothing," I told him, even though it was really everything.

"You sure?" he asked, and I nodded.

"All right, ready to go?" Dad asked, standing up.

I slid out of the booth and followed him. He put his arm on my shoulder, and I wanted it to feel okay, but it didn't, not at all, because there was no way he could love me if he found out that my selfishness was what had made Abby run away.

41

Instead of going to lunch at school the next day, I walked over to the gym and stepped outside. There was a pay phone attached to a metal stand on the wall. Probably the only one left in America. It was covered in graffiti so thick with different colors that it looked like an abstract painting.

I grabbed the receiver and fished around for some change in the bottom of my purse. Pay phones were safe. Unlike cell phones, no one could identify the person on the other end.

I pulled out the magnet we'd gotten during homeroom when Abby first went missing. It had a list of phone numbers that "might be important during a time like this," said one of the crisis counselors they'd brought in to talk to us. Most of my classmates had rolled their eyes and stuck the magnets on the back of our metal seats or in the trash when they left the room. It did sound kind of crazy that anyone would actually call one of these numbers, but today I needed to talk to someone about what I had done. Anonymously, maybe, I could find some relief. I found the number I was looking for and punched it onto the keypad on the pay phone.

"National suicide prevention hotline," a female voice said. "Do you need an ambulance?"

I paused, taken aback. Nothing like expecting the worst right from the start.

I counted each breath to remind myself that I was still living. A boy wandered out of the gym, his eyes blinking in the sunlight. He walked toward me and I gripped the phone tightly against my ear. Not a lot of people used this phone anymore. It was once important to secure rides after practice or games, but now everyone had cell phones. The only people who still used it were probably kids who planned to call in bomb threats or make shady drug deals.

Regardless of what this kid wanted, he wasn't going to use the phone. I stared him down with a scowl on my face until he left.

"Do you need immediate medical attention?" the woman asked again, her voice firmer.

"No," I whispered at a level so quiet that I didn't think she could hear me. But she did.

"I'm glad you're okay, and I'm happy you called. My name is Kara." She sounded all soft, like butter left on the table, and I imagined her living this perfect life. I pictured her going home from her job, pulling on faded jeans, and ordering takeout with her boyfriend. They'd eat on the couch, and while they might fight over the remote, he always let her win.

"What's your name?" she asked.

"Abby," I said. That surprised me. I'm not sure why I gave her my sister's name.

"Abby, that's a nice name," she answered back, as if making a decision. As if she were picking out a dress to wear or deciding on a meal off a menu. "What has your day been like, Abby?"

"Awful," I said. I figured the direct route seemed to be the best way to go.

"Why is that? Sometimes it helps to talk."

"It's not fair," I told her.

"What isn't?"

"The fact that some people are here and some people aren't."

"What do you mean by 'here?'" She spoke in that same calm voice, and it made me want to talk more.

"Here. Earth. Living."

"Do you not want to be here?"

"No, the opposite. I'm missing someone really bad right now. So bad that it hurts to breathe when I think about it."

"Did someone you know pass away recently?"

"I don't know."

"You don't know?" Kara repeated after me, and I could tell that I was confusing her. I was confusing myself.

"That's why I'm calling," I said. "Someone disappeared, and I'm afraid she isn't coming back."

"Can you look for her?" Kara asked.

"We already have," I told her.

"Maybe you're not looking in the right spot," she said. "Maybe she's waiting to be found."

A door opened a ways down and a group of girls piled out with shorts and tennis rackets.

"I have to go," I told Kara.

"You don't," she said. "You can talk to me for as long as you like. I'm here for you."

"I know." I was impatient to finish the call before the girls made it to me. "I'm not going to hurt myself if that's what you think. I'm okay."

I hung up the phone before she could say anything more, and repeated the word "okay" over and over again until it didn't even sound like a word I was familiar with anymore.

42

On the second week of the circles, the police had to intervene because traffic had grown so heavy it blocked the intersection a quarter of a mile from our house. The light would change from green to yellow to red and no one would move because so many cars were trying to turn down our street. Officer Scarano directed those making the pilgrimage to our house to turn in to an empty field across the street from Tommy's front yard. The slam of car doors and engines turning on became part of the normal noise of the spectacle that had formed outside our house.

The school bus had begun dropping me off at the top of the street because it took forever just to get down my street. Today, I counted seven cars that passed me before I even made it to Tommy's house, and I was willing to bet that most of them were headed toward our field.

A beat-up Subaru pulled up alongside me, and a man

leaned out the window. He had a toothpick in his mouth that he chewed on.

"Excuse me, maybe you can help," he said. "Is this where the girl went missing?"

I didn't bother to answer. I continued to walk down the road. He followed me in his car.

"Did you hear me? I'm looking for the fields where the circles appeared. For the house where that family lives."

I turned toward him. "Why?"

"Why what?" he asked, confused.

"Why the hell do you care? What would seeing the house and the field do?"

He pulled the toothpick out and flicked it out the window. "Shit, I don't know. I thought it would be interesting. Something to do. You know what I mean?"

"No, I don't," I snapped.

"Aww, come on. It's all anyone is talking about. Most of these people are here for the same reason. You can't tell me you aren't curious."

It might have been the way he assumed I thought my family was a freak show. It might have been the way he joked with me as if what he was doing was perfectly normal. It might just have been that I was sick and tired of being on display. Whatever it was, I snapped. I was done being someone else's entertainment.

"Of course I'm curious. And do you want to know why? Because that's my house. That's my family and that's my sister missing. So how about you stop and think for a minute how *interesting* I find it that assholes like you drive all the way out here because they want to stare at someone else's tragedy."

"Well, I'll be . . . ," he said and instead of being apologetic for getting called out, he seized the opportunity to get a first-hand look at exactly what he had come here to find. His gaze felt unsettling and gross. "You're that girl's sister."

"And you're a pathetic human being," I said. I stepped in front of his car. Then I turned and continued down the middle of the street so that if he wanted to follow me, he'd have to run me over. It was nearly impossible not show how shaken up I was. But I did it. I walked all the way back to my house and never moved out of the road. He followed behind me at a slow speed. When I got there, I turned and stared him down. I placed my hands on my hips and made it clear I was not budging.

"Screw this," he finally said. "It isn't worth it."

He reversed his car into the grass along the side of the road, turned, and peeled out. There was a squeal of tires.

"Good riddance," I said. It might have only been one person I stopped, but it was one less person who made it to our house to use our family's heartbreak for their personal fun.

43

I wasn't the only one against the circles. Dad was fed up with them, and it had become a constant battle with him and Mom.

"This is ridiculous," he argued with her. "Our yard has become a circus."

But she wouldn't budge. She refused to destroy them.

"Why don't you go out there and mow them down?" I asked. "You can't tell me the police want you to keep them still. They've become nothing but a giant pain in the ass to everyone."

"I can't," he said. "I don't have the heart. Not when your mother finds some kind of solace in them."

And so the circles stayed and our family's misfortune continued to be Coffinberry's daily entertainment. We were our own morbid sideshow of loss, and people loved to gawk to see how we were holding up.

People brought food; picnic baskets with salads, cakes, and cold cuts to the field. They passed their plates around as they spoke about Abby and our field and faith. Everyone was praying for Abby. They wanted Abby home. I couldn't fault them too much because I wanted the same thing.

I slipped into the house after school one day without Mom or Collin stopping me to talk. Collin had parked himself in front of the window to watch the circles, and Mom sat at the dining room table uploading more pictures of Abby on the tribute site.

I should've been trying to catch up in my classes, since I seemed to be falling more and more behind, but it was impossible to concentrate on school. I had too much energy. The worry, the fear, the shame, everything was bottled up inside me, and it needed to get out. The urge to run surged through me, and I didn't think I could fight it.

I changed into shorts and an old T-shirt, but couldn't find my running shoes. I searched all over the house and they weren't in any of the usual places: near the door, outside in the garage, or hidden under the piles of clothes in my room. They were missing and I needed to run. It was as if my body craved the rush.

I remembered the pair that had been in the box from Abby's locker and ran upstairs to grab them. I laced up her shoes and slipped out of the house.

The sun began its slow crawl down, but people sat in the yard as if they'd never leave. There were twenty-three people out there now. They held hands and gazed at me as if I could give them some kind of answer to a question I didn't even understand.

I started with a slow jog, but then picked up my pace so I could leave them behind.

I ran the side roads of the neighborhoods, up streets that connected to the main road, and snaked my way through my city. I pushed myself so I breathed hard enough that there was no way I could think about anything else in my head.

Maybe that's why I ended up at Tommy's house. At least, I told myself it wasn't intentional.

The first thing I saw was his black pickup truck. He'd bought it himself, after saving up from his job stocking shelves at the grocery store. The day he got it, he'd picked me up and we drove around Coffinberry, savoring the feeling of being free. After Tommy and Abby began to date, she'd joke that he loved it more than her, and it wasn't unusual to see him outside cleaning it or doing god knows what under the hood. Tonight, though, he had a bucket of water and was scrubbing at the side of it. He rubbed the same area repeatedly.

"I think you got that spot clean," I yelled to him.

He spun around and stood with his back against the truck. "Yeah, it was dirty," he said. He played with the sponge in his hand, twisted it around.

I walked up the driveway toward him. He threw the sponge into the bucket of soapy water but didn't move.

I pointed to an invisible spot on the truck. "I think you missed a spot over here."

He moved to my side quickly. "Where?" He inspected the metal as if it were about to fall apart at any moment.

"Calm down. I was kidding. I don't get why guys are so into their trucks." I crossed back behind the truck and he hurried in front of me, blocking my path.

"What's going on?" I asked. "Why are you acting so strange?"

"I'm fine," he said, but he clearly wasn't.

He jumped into the truck bed and motioned for me to do the same. He reached out his hand and I climbed up. There were bags of grass clippings toward the back, and I sat against one. It made a soft hissing noise as the air escaped from it. I stretched my feet out in front of me. My calves burned from running, but it was that pain that I yearned for, just like Abby had told me.

Tommy pulled on one of my laces. He wrapped it around his finger and let it go. I'm sure he recognized Abby's purple laces.

"Why are you doing this?" he asked, and I couldn't tell if he was talking about the shoes or us.

"I have to," I said, and wasn't sure what I was talking about either.

We sat in silence and watched the clouds roll past overhead. I was too aware of how close he was and how just weeks ago I was willing to give it all to him. How I would've traded everything to be with him and how still, when it's the deep dark of night and I can't sleep, I think about those moments when I thought I finally had it all.

I jumped up. This was a bad idea. I shouldn't even be here.

"I'd better go. I'm not even sure why I ran past your house." I climbed down from the truck and walked around the side of it.

"Wait," Tommy said and tried to follow me, but it was too late. I found the reason why he was scrubbing his truck and why he didn't want me to walk around it. Written on the whole driver's side with red spray paint was the word "KILLER."

"Who did this?" I asked, sickened at the thought of Tommy walking to his car and finding this.

"It doesn't matter," he said. "It could've been anyone in Coffinberry."

"This isn't right. We need to do something about it."

"It's okay, Rhylee. I can handle this."

"You shouldn't have to. It's my fault. I can't let you carry this alone."

"I'm not alone," Tommy said, and I understood.

I stuck my hand in the bucket of soapy water and found the sponge. I brought it up to the letters and worked to scrub away the words that spelled out the sins of both of us. We rubbed the surface of his truck so much that little bits of paint chipped off. We scrubbed and scrubbed, but no matter how hard we rubbed, we couldn't get rid of that word.

44

It was late when I left Tommy's house. I ignored the people in my yard, their flashlights and candle flames waving back and forth. I opened the front door as silently as I could, easing it against the frame so it made no noise except for a small click.

Mom stepped out of the dark living room. "Where have you been?" she demanded. "Do you know how worried I've been?"

"I told you I was out running. I left a note."

"That was over two hours ago. It's dark outside; you could've been anywhere. Anything could've happened to you. Like your sister . . ." Mom's voice cracked and she swiped the back of her hand across her eyes. "You have to be careful."

She was right. It was stupid of me. Even though I'd left a note in the kitchen, I could only imagine Mom's fear.

"I'm sorry. I didn't realize I'd run as far as I did. By the time I turned around to come back, I was far from home."

I followed Mom into the living room. She took a seat on the couch, and I sat on the floor near her, my feet stretched out in front of me, my back against the chair Dad sat in.

She hummed an old lullaby she sang to us when we were young. A song she still sang to Collin on nights when storms rattled our windows and he was scared to go to sleep.

"I thought she'd come home," Mom said.

"Abby?" I asked, confused.

"I feel like she's everywhere. With the lights off, anyone could have mistaken you for her. You even smell like her," she said.

I thought about the perfume I'd found in Abby's box and wondered if the scent had found a way to creep onto me.

"Since when do you run?" she asked.

I shrugged, even though it was too dark for her to see me. What was I supposed to say? Now that Abby was gone I felt as if I had to do the things she couldn't do. That my penance was to live the life that I'd stolen from her. I couldn't very well tell her that one day I decided to run and found I could easily go for mile after mile. She'd never believe it. I couldn't believe it.

"I miss her so bad," Mom said.

Her words surprised me. She didn't speak like this, ever, and it was the first time she'd said anything like that since Abby disappeared. I moved closer and took her hand.

I figured she'd fight to let go, but instead, she let me hold on.

"I do too," I said. "And I miss you."

"I'm right here."

I gripped her hand tight. "It doesn't feel like it."

The words hung between the two of us.

She made a noise, and I couldn't tell if she was laughing or crying. "We're all still here, honey."

"Sometimes it feels as if I've lost you, too."

"You didn't lose me, honey," she said, but there was no comfort in her words because it was so hard to believe that was true.

45

When I untangled myself from my sheets and stepped out of bed the next morning, no one was awake. Yet the house already felt claustrophobic. I might not have been able to see the people in the field, but they were there and that made it even worse.

I was never a morning person before Abby disappeared. In fact, I despised the sound of the alarm and its insistence that it was time to get up.

But for running, I'd make an exception.

It was a few minutes before five a.m. Abby used to wake at this time every morning before any of us even hit the snooze alarm five million times. Her cross-country team appeared outside our house at precisely 5:11 a.m. every day. They were never late; keeping a close mark on their running time was essential to training. Even after Abby disappeared, they took the same route, moving as a group past our house. Maybe they hoped Abby would appear out of our front door and run with them.

Today, I wanted to be a part of their group. I had no clue how they'd react, but I planned to find out.

I didn't bother searching for my shoes. The team would run past at any minute, and I had to hurry. I grabbed Abby's pair and stepped outside. I imagined them moving in a pack, feet rising and falling together, ponytails bouncing in unison.

I waited on the porch, Abby's shoes tied tight on my feet. The team came into view and I jogged toward the sidewalk. I kept my eyes forward, so I wouldn't have to acknowledge those gathered in our field.

A few people on the team nodded or smiled, but most simply accepted me. They folded around me like sheep, so I was no longer a single person but part of the group. I moved in unison with them and pushed myself harder and harder until my heart thrummed against my chest.

My breath burst out in strong spurts and back in through thick gulps.

I realized why running was so important to me now. This was the pain Abby had been talking about. A feeling so real and sharp. I carried it like I carried my guilt, deep within me, so I felt it everywhere I went.

I ran to feel a pain so intense that it reminded me I was still here. I was still alive, and I hated myself for it.

46

Mom must have gotten something out of my words the night before, because she did start living, little by little. At least, her version of living, because after I got back from running, I found her dressed and ready to walk Collin outside to catch the bus.

"What are you doing?" I asked her.

"I wanted to talk to the people in the circles."

"No fair," Collin yelled and threw his book bag on the ground in protest.

"Collin, cool it," I said because Mom wouldn't.

"You won't let me go out there. Why are you allowed?" he shouted at her, which was true. He begged to go out almost every day but Dad refused. "What if you find something? What if the aliens come back?"

"There are no aliens," I told him firmly. I waited for him to explode, but instead, he gave up his fight with one final

213

rumble of frustration. Good, at least he was quiet. I turned to Mom, "You're going to hang out with the Miracle Seekers?"

"The what?" she asked, confused. I realized my mistake as soon as I called the group by their nickname.

Tessa and I had dubbed the group outside the Miracle Seekers because of their belief that standing in our yard praying could bring my sister back. It seemed like a contradiction because my family was never religious.

That's why I was surprised when Mom not only accepted the Miracle Seekers, but decided to go outside with them. Couldn't she see that she was substituting one obsession for another and neither would bring Abby home?

47

I crossed more days off in Abby's agenda. More days that we were lost without her.

Mom became friends with the people in our yard, Dad continued to alternate his time between work and search efforts, and Collin built forts inside our living room. Big elaborate ones with blankets and sheets. He covered the couch, table, and chairs and then lined them with pillows. It was a labyrinth of rooms with different sections, some narrowing so you had to crawl through them and others so wide and open that you could sit up.

He worked on them for hours, constructing his new hideout, and when completed, refused to sleep in his bed. Not that Mom even noticed, especially when I was the one changing our sheets since she had given up any type of household chores.

Dad hated the fort, and it would've been simple to pull the sheets down, but no one had the heart to do that.

"I need to be near the fields in case they come again," he told Dad.

"Oh for heaven's sake, there is no 'they,'" Dad said, no longer trying to soften the words.

"Something made those circles, and I'm not going to miss it when they touch down on Earth again," Collin insisted and crawled deeper into his fort. He made his way to the section against the large window facing our backyard. The sheet rustled and he was a bulge in the center. He wouldn't budge and no one wanted to crawl through those tunnels to try to get him to come out.

So Collin hung out under the blankets constantly and sure enough, that's where I found him when I came home from school. Today had been quiet; no one talked about the circles or my sister, but I'm sure that wouldn't last. I wasn't naive enough to think gossip just disappeared. It rose and fell like waves, some days crashing down on you so hard it was almost impossible to stay on your feet and other times a gentle lull that tricked you into believing everyone had moved on to something new. Tomorrow I'm sure my sister and those circles would again invade the lips of everyone in the school, much like they had invaded our backyard.

"Rhylee, come over here," Collin said from inside his fort, and I got on my hands and knees so I could see him.

"Where are you?"

"You need to come in all the way."

"Collin, I don't really . . ."

"Just do it," he said, and something in his voice made me

216

want to crawl toward him and wrap my hands around him. I moved carefully, so I wouldn't upset the city he'd created under the sheets. I found him on a pile of old blankets, the sheet above him dipped slightly in the center, so it brushed the top of his head.

"Welcome. I'm so glad you could make it," he said in the formal way that Mom had taught him to use when we had company. He nodded at my feet. "Please take off your shoes."

Collin pushed a plastic bowl toward me. "Would you like an appetizer?"

I smiled and took a handful of peanuts he must have swiped from the container that Dad kept next to his easy chair.

"I love what you've done to the place," I told him.

"Not everyone is allowed in here."

"I feel honored."

Collin turned so that he was low to the ground. He crawled toward a tunnel on his right and I followed, not knowing what else to do. He headed to the windows that faced out on the field. The space was now big enough to sit up in and was lit by the sunlight that streamed in from outside.

"This is where I keep watch," Collin said.

People milled around the field, and I thought for the millionth time how weird it was that strangers would want to hang in our yard. I couldn't stand being in my house anymore; how could these people make the choice to willingly be here?

"You watch everyone outside?" I asked him.

"No, I keep an eye out for the aliens."

"Collin, there's no such thing as aliens."

"There are too," he argued. "They made the circles and they took Abby."

"Aliens didn't take her," I told him, but it would have been as plausible as her simply vanishing.

"They did, Rhylee," Collin said, his voice calm and even. There was no convincing him otherwise; he spoke with the authority of one who might have seen it with his own eyes. "They took her from us, because everyone loves Abby. It was only a matter of time."

"She'll be back," I told Collin, but my words didn't sound as believable as I wanted them to.

48

I woke in the middle of the night to ice cold air. The scent of mud and earth filled the room.

Someone was here.

I couldn't see them, but I could feel their presence.

I remained still, and told myself I was disoriented. I counted to one hundred and when nothing happened, I convinced myself I must have been dreaming.

I burrowed under my sheets and had almost drifted off again, when my bed moved. Just a slight shift, but it was as if someone had sat on the edge.

"Collin?" I asked, but no one answered.

The curtains in my window stirred as if a wind was blowing.

Except, the windows were closed.

I didn't move. I couldn't move. I was terrified.

I pulled the sheets tight around me and told myself I only thought I felt something. I was in the room alone.

I don't know how long I stayed frozen, but I refused to budge or turn on the light, because I didn't want to see what the dark hid.

The bed shifted again.

I pulled the covers over my eyes and stayed buried underneath them until Dad's car pulled up when his work shift was over and the door slammed shut. I crawled out from under the sheets and glanced around my room. The morning light had fought its way through my window, and landed on Abby's running shoes that I wore when I ran.

The bottoms were covered in fresh mud, the purple laces wet and dirty.

And the missing person flyers and pictures of Abby lay on the ground. Every one of them ripped off of the wall and crumpled in a heap on the floor.

49

It was impossible to focus that day in school. Instead of listening to my teachers talk, my mind was stuck on what had happened the night before. It didn't make sense. None of this did. It was as if Abby was trying to get in touch with me, and the idea both excited and terrified me.

The thought that she was out there hiding from us seemed crazy; that wasn't who Abby was. And if she wasn't hiding, then what did it mean?

Tessa offered me a ride home from school. It was one of those rare days when she was able to use the car. Even though she'd had her license for a few months now, her mom usually drove the family's second car and Tessa and I were still doomed to take the bus forever.

"How'd you get permission to drive today?" I asked.

Tessa rolled her eyes. "My mom's having a bunch of friends from the neighborhood over this afternoon and she needed to clean the house. They call it a book club, but they don't really talk about books. It's more like their monthly gossip session and excuse to drink way too much wine.

"Maybe we need to drive around so you're not subjected to that torture."

"I like the way you think," she said. "Let's stay away for a while."

And so we did. For the next hour, Tessa drove the stretch of road that bordered Coffinberry. She rolled the windows down and the air twisted through our hair as we passed farms and fields full of hay bales. She turned the radio up and sang along with the songs. When she opened the can of soda she had and it sprayed all over her, I busted out laughing. I quickly put my hand over my mouth. I hadn't laughed since Abby disappeared. It felt strange and unfamiliar.

"You're allowed to have fun," Tessa said, reading my mind.

"It sure doesn't feel like I should," I said.

"We're still here," Tessa said.

"And Abby isn't," I countered. The mood shifted in the car. I didn't want to live in a world where I existed and Abby didn't. I wanted us both to be able to laugh. At the dumb stupid things we used to joke about together. It shouldn't be about what I was allowed to do and not do.

"Abby wouldn't want you living this way," Tessa said, and I wanted to ask her what way that was, because ever since my sister had disappeared, I had no idea who I was. Who I was supposed to be.

Tessa turned down a side road, and I realized we were headed toward the part of the woods where Johnson Franklin lived.

"Slow down," I told her. She gave me a funny look, but did what I asked.

What if Johnson really did know something? The idea had been poking at the edge of my mind for some time now. Abby had run into the woods that night, and he had been there and could have some kind of clue.

I was fully aware that this was wishful thinking. If he knew something, he would've told the police. But I didn't have any other ideas, and I needed to bring my sister home.

A thin strip of smoke rose in the air from the woods. He was there.

"Can you stop for a minute?" I asked when she was parallel to the smoke.

"In the middle of the road? There's nothing here."

"There kind of is." I pointed toward the woods. "Johnson's tent is out there."

Tessa turned to look at me. "You're kidding, right?" But she pulled over anyway.

There was a small opening into the woods. When we were young, we'd dare one another to go in there and touch his tent when he walked the main road in town. I could find it again easily.

Before I could think it through, I opened the car door and jumped out. My feet raced across the field. Most of the town now avoided the woods like the plague. It had become a place full of monsters, goblins, and evil waiting to swallow you up. Parents forbade children to go inside and hunters carried their rifles a little closer to their bodies, but I couldn't let those fears rule me right now. I needed to take action. I needed to find Abby and set this right.

Tessa stood in the middle of the field and gestured at me to come back to her. I put my finger to my lips and moved to the opening to take a step in. I paused, waiting for something to happen; perhaps giant fingers would scoop me up and carry me away into the dark creepy places. But nothing stopped me. I stepped in farther.

Johnson didn't live too far from the entrance, and I imagined at night he could hear the same sounds Abby and I used to listen to. The cars and trains in the distance. We'd sit on the porch in the summer, when the heat was so hot it was almost suffocating in our house, and listen to the sounds of the night. Abby once told me that a train carried Abraham Lincoln across the U.S. and every time you heard a whistle late at night, it was the same ghost train carrying his spirit across the Earth, the whistle wailing the tears of the mourners. A few years back she even tried to run alongside a train, racing it as it sped through our town.

She was fearless. And now I had to be the same.

I smelled Johnson's fire before I saw it. The orange shimmered through the trees, the smoke twisted around the leaves. I crept closer but stayed hidden behind a bunch of trees. My clothes, a pair of jeans and navy blue shirt, weren't exactly camouflage, but at least they were dark.

I took a few more steps and there he was. He sat on a

bucket turned upside down, twirling a branch in his fingers. He mumbled something, but I was too far away to hear. His beard hung to his chest, and he wore a red wool hat that looked as if it had seen better days. Mom knitted hats for our city's food pantry to give out each Christmas and I wondered if he'd ever ended up with one.

His fire spat and snapped once in a while, but otherwise, it was silent. So silent that it seemed possible if Abby had come this way that night, Johnson would've heard her. I took a step forward. Things like being careful didn't matter now that Abby was gone. What mattered was finding her.

I held my breath as I moved. I didn't know what I'd do when I reached Johnson, but it seemed important to reach him. He kept poking at the fire until Tessa's voice rang out, spooking both of us.

"Rhylee, get out of there. I'm leaving," she yelled.

Johnson's head snapped up. He looked right at me and there was no turning back. I lifted my hand in a half wave and put it down.

He threw his stick into the fire and stood.

"What are you doing?" he yelled, and it wasn't in the welcoming way. "You have no business bothering me. Get the hell out of here."

I walked backward a few feet. I wasn't entirely afraid of him; I just didn't know how to act. He stood his ground and so did I.

"I wanted to talk to you. About my sister."

Tessa must have walked back to her car, because a horn

225

blasted through the air and a flock of birds flew from the trees, screeching at the sky.

"Get out." He took a few steps toward me; his patience had run thin. Tessa honked the horn in short bursts, and if I didn't get out of there soon, I'd have to walk home. I turned my back on Johnson and ran toward her car. This wasn't the last time I'd see him. I wouldn't let it be.

50

I woke the next morning to yelling in our back-yard. Collin ran into my bedroom.

"Something is going on in the circles," he said. "We need to get outside."

"Calm down. Let's wait and see what Mom says." I wasn't sure what had happened, and I didn't want to bring Collin out there if it was something bad.

"Please," he said. "We have to go."

"It's not a good idea," I said, but he wasn't listening. He ran down the stairs, so I rushed after him.

Light had begun to soften the dark edges of the woods into daylight and the dew had settled on the grass. Collin made his way to Mom, and she wrapped her arms around him. I kept my distance, not quite sure of what I was walking into.

"What's going on?" I asked.

"It's Abby. She was back near the woods."

"What?" I asked. A small flicker of hope ignited in me. "What do you mean?"

Mary Grace's mom stepped forward and spoke. "I saw her while everyone else was sleeping. I was reading my bible. Something moved over by the edge of the woods. I thought it was a large animal, a deer perhaps, but when it got closer, I realized it was Abby."

The group gathered together, and Mom stood in front of them, as Mary Grace's mom tried to recreate the image she claimed she'd never forget. "Abby was in her cross-country uniform, but it looked old, faded almost. It was foggy around her, so it was hard for me to see."

I thought about the mornings I ran with the team and the fog was sometimes so thick it was as if we were in the middle of the sky. The sound of our shoes slapping against the street would be the only way to tell there was someone else beside you. I knew exactly what Mary Grace's mom meant; that when the weather was like that, it was impossible to distinguish between what was real and what might not be.

Some of the Miracle Seekers stared at her, their heavy-lidded eyes fixed and unmoving, but others were more hysterical. A few went back to the edge of the woods where Abby was spotted and moved through the trees, trying to spot her again. A man near me held a rosary in his hands and prayed loudly, and a woman sat and rocked back and forth. Tears fell from her eyes.

My old piano teacher, Jodi Hunter, said, "She's telling the truth. I saw Abby too. I told myself it was a dream, so I went back to sleep. Abby was different. It was as if the fog followed her. Everything around me was clear as day, but she seemed transparent. She was there, but she wasn't."

Collin broke away from me and paced back and forth.

"I told you she was still here," he yelled to me. "She was out in our field, but no one would listen. Why did Mary Grace's mom let Abby leave? Why didn't she stop her?"

Collin buried his face into my arms and cried. I was jealous of him. He was still young enough to cry and yell and hurt openly, when that's all I wanted to do too. Honestly, I think it was all a lot of us wanted to do.

"You let her slip away," Mom said, and she wrapped her arms around herself. It was as if the cold had settled into everyone and no one could escape it.

"I wasn't thinking," Mary Grace's mom said. "All I could see was Abby. I couldn't take my eyes off of her."

But she wasn't really there, I wanted to shout. *This is all ridiculous. You're all ridiculous. How can you blame someone for something that didn't happen?*

Collin continued to sob. His heart was breaking, and I couldn't fix it.

"What does this mean?" Mary Grace's mom asked, standing beside me.

Everyone turned to one another searching for an answer, but like everything else in this mess, no one had a clue about what any of it meant.

51

I promised Collin I'd take him to the library to get some new books about the circles, which is how I found myself walking to our town's measly excuse for a library after school. It was one big room with the sections divided in each corner. I swear I read every picture book there at least five times each when I was younger.

I picked him up at his elementary school, and he practically dragged me the entire way. His eyes focused on every person we passed. He was looking for Abby. And how could I fault him? As ridiculous as it was, I did the same thing.

"We don't need to move as if we're being chased by a rabid dog," I told him. I carried both my bag and his on my shoulder, and the straps cut into my skin, making it impossible to keep up.

"What if there are no books left? What if someone else came and took them out?"

He had such panic in his eyes that I quickened my pace a bit to calm him down.

"I'm sure there'll be plenty of books for you to check out. I doubt there was a stampede to the library for books about aliens."

"You don't know that," Collin said, and I didn't argue. Who knew, he might be right. Everything I expected to be normal had flipped itself upside down these last few weeks; I wasn't sure what normal was anymore.

We were about to head inside the library when I saw Johnson.

Of course Johnson was here. I didn't need to creep into the woods to find him; he pushed his rusted-out shopping cart here every day.

He moved with his head down, but he didn't need to worry about making eye contact. Everyone around him still avoided him.

"Let's go, Rhylee." Collin drew out the last letters of my name into a high-pitched whine and tugged on my sleeve.

"Go ahead, I'll be right there," I said. He didn't have to be told twice. He raced into the library and I took a few steps forward so that I could have a clear view of Johnson. It was stupid and irresponsible of me to let Collin go into the library alone, but I was too focused on Johnson and what he might know about Abby. Besides, what could happen in the library? A stack of falling books crushing him?

I followed Johnson. I lagged behind, so I could keep my eye on where he was going and think about what I should do.

I doubted that he'd let me come up to him and ask a bunch of questions about my sister, but I didn't really know any other way to approach him.

I asked myself what Abby would do. She'd probably stop right in the middle of his path with a big smile on her face and introduce herself. So maybe that's what I should try. I ducked inside the small coffee shop that sat right next to the library. A few people glanced up from their newspapers for a second and one old woman gave me a sad smile, probably recognizing me, but no one tried to talk to me or offer me pitying words, thankfully.

"What can I get you?" a girl in a polka-dotted dress asked.

"Two coffees to go."

She took my order, and soon the hot cups were in my hands. I added cream and sugar to one and left the other black. I wasn't sure how Johnson took his coffee, and I didn't want to mess this up.

I couldn't find him when I stepped back out, but there was no way he could have gone too far. His cart kind of hindered a quick getaway. I headed in the direction I'd last seen him, and it wasn't long before I spotted him on a bench, his cart parked close to his side.

I closed my eyes, took a deep breath, and summoned every bit of Abby's courage I could find in myself. This was nuts, but it felt as if this was my only option. I owed it to Abby to talk to him. I sat at the other end of the bench and he shifted closer to his stuff as if I was going to steal his pile of junk. He kept his back turned to me, toward his cart, and didn't acknowledge that there was another person sitting next to him.

Great, this was a bit anticlimactic.

I scooted closer and caught a whiff of someone who definitely lived in the woods.

I moved even closer until we were almost touching. The coffee cups were warm against my hands, the heat radiating from them almost unbearable.

"I don't have anything for you to steal," he grumbled.

"I'm not planning to rob you," I said and thrust the coffee at him. "I brought you coffee."

"Coffee messes with my mind," he said.

"Good thing it's still early," I said and pushed both of the cups toward him. "Which do you want, black or cream and sugar?"

He turned to investigate me, a flicker of recognition on his face.

"Why are you bothering me, girl?"

"I want to . . ." I stopped and thought about how I'd phrase this. How could I get him to honestly listen to me? Because it seemed as if he was about to get up and leave. I decided to dive right in. "My sister was Abby. The girl who disappeared."

"Aww, shit. I had nothing to do with that." He stood and pushed his cart forward. "You have no right to—"

I jumped in front of him, banging my shin against his cart. "Wait, I don't think you did anything."

"Get out of my way," he said and tried to push his cart around me. I'm not sure exactly what happened next; his cart might have caught on a rock or something, but suddenly it tipped over on its side. He tried to right it, but the cart was too heavy and it crashed to the ground. "Son of a bitch. Look at what you did."

"I'm sorry." I bent to help him pick up his stuff. The coffee cups had flipped over on their sides and the liquid was making a slow descent toward the items in his cart that were strewn about the sidewalk. I handed him a flannel shirt and a garbage bag full of something soft and tried to stuff them back in the cart after he righted it.

"You don't know how to leave well enough alone. All of you. Messing in my business. Asking questions, looking at me like I'm some sort of criminal."

"I don't think you did anything. I'm just trying to find out if anyone saw anything. My sister . . . there's nothing . . . I was hoping maybe . . ." I spoke in disjointed sentences, but it wasn't making a difference. He wasn't listening to me.

"I told them what I knew. I've got nothing else."

"Rhylee," a voice yelled. Collin. I had forgotten about him. For a brief second it was as if two people had taken hold of each of my hands and were fighting over me, each person yanking me from side to side. I didn't know which way to go at first, but then turned toward my brother. How could I have forgotten him? I must have left him alone at the library for at least half an hour.

I stuffed the items in my hands in Johnson's cart. I didn't want Collin to see what I was doing, because he'd tell our parents.

"I gotta go. My brother is over there. I was only trying to find my sister. I didn't mean to bother you; I don't know what else to do."

Johnson continued to pick his things off the ground and acted as if I didn't exist.

"Collin!" I yelled and jogged over to him. I expected to see tears, but instead, he grabbed my hand and tugged me back toward the library.

"Come on. They're holding my books. They said you needed to check them out for me."

"Sounds like a plan," I told him and followed him up the steps of the library. "What kind of books did you find?"

"All different types. One of the ladies helped me. She got me a big huge stack. I'm going to be reading all night long, and Mom can't do anything to stop me."

"Of course she can't." I listened as he chattered on about his adventures at the library. I was glad he didn't think there was anything odd about finding me outside on the street talking to a homeless man with a shopping cart.

I followed him into the library shaken up about the whole conversation with Johnson. I repeated his words over and over again in my head, making sure I'd heard them right. He said he told the police everything he knew, but the police hadn't mentioned anything to my family. At least, nothing I heard about. That might mean there was something I didn't know, and I was determined to find out what that was. I owed it to Abby to find out.

52

The next day, I ran up and down roads looking for my sister. The real version, not the so-called ghost girl who haunted the town. I searched everywhere; through the center of town, past Webster's, the church we'd go to at Christmas and Easter, and the park where Tommy and I kissed. I moved faster and faster until I was afraid I was going to trip over my feet. Even then, I couldn't go fast enough.

I looped around the high school and into the stadium where they'd had the memorial for Abby. The cross-country team was doing timed runs on the track. I headed up the steps of the bleachers until I reached the top, and lay on my back so I could watch the sky. It was one of those days that warned you fall was creeping in. The kind where the clouds held on to the edge of the horizon and made everything look all doom and gloom, and if you squinted, you could picture the leaves on trees changing colors.

Someone yelled "10:13," calling out the time of a runner.

"That's pathetic!" a voice shouted back, and from the high-pitched whine, I recognized it as Erica's. "I bet Mr. Taylor could beat me in a race at that speed."

I laughed despite myself. Mr. Taylor was the seventy-six-year-old English teacher who seemed intent on teaching until he dropped dead.

Voices shouted back and forth below me, and I closed my eyes. I thought about how the world should be right now. Abby would be running on that track, and I'd still be aching for Tommy in secret. Collin would be annoying me by stealing stuff from my room, and my parents would be their normal boring selves, making small talk at dinner and writing our daily activities on the big calendar in the kitchen.

A whistle blew from the track and jarred me from my memories.

Someone walked up the bleachers, the clang of heels against metal. I peeked out through the slit of one eye. It was Tessa, looking ridiculous in jeans, cowboy boots, a plaid shirt, and a bandanna around her neck. Her hair was in two pigtails.

She nudged me with her foot.

"Last time I checked, cowboys don't live in Ohio," I said.

"Today was show choir practice," she told me, as if it were the most obvious thing in the world. "We're doing a medley of *Oklahoma* songs."

"Right, got it." I tried not to laugh at her outrageous outfit, but I couldn't hold it in.

"What's so funny? You're dressed in a costume too," she shot back.

I glanced at my shorts and tank top and then back at her. "What are you talking about? I went for a run."

"A run? And what's with your hair?" Tessa kept going.

I touched the French braid I'd put in earlier today. Abby always wore one when she ran, and I thought I'd give it a shot.

"Since when did you become an athlete?"

"Why does everyone find it so hard to believe that I could actually do something that involves physical activity?" I asked and then gestured toward the field. "I was thinking of joining the team."

"Sure you were," Tessa said, not buying a word of what I was saying. I had a hunch that even if she saw me running with the girls in the morning, she'd still think I was joking.

"What are *you* doing here?" I asked.

"I was leaving play practice when I spotted you here." She fished a box of Hot Tamales out of her bag and pushed it at me. I took a handful and jammed them into my mouth.

"Remember how Abby hated it when we watched her run?" I asked. "She never wanted to see us in the crowd before a race. She said it messed up her thinking."

Tessa laughed. "And you used to come up with the craziest costumes so she wouldn't know it was you."

"It always worked. We'd spend days inventing who we would be."

It became a joke in our family, what we could wear to throw off Abby. We tried to see how outrageous we could get with our costumes and still not have her notice us. Dad and I would go to the thrift store or garage sales and pick through racks of other people's discarded clothes. The two of us brought home hats, wigs, and oversize pieces of clothing to drape around ourselves. We stood next to families we knew at the away meets, and laughed because they didn't recognize us either. Abby acted as if she hated it when we crowded around her in running suits and sweatbands or wigs of long dark hair and sunglasses, but Mom would always pull something out of her purse for Abby to put on to become a part of our group instead of wearing her cross-country uniform, and she'd happily comply.

I realized Tessa was right about my outfit. I was in costume now, a costume that looked a lot like my sister. But was that so bad? Abby had always been the better one. Would it be so horrible if I disappeared and tried to bring her back in small ways? Especially when she's the one who should be here right now after what I did.

"Maybe Abby's hiding somewhere out there now, in her own costume, and we don't recognize her," Tessa said.

"I wish she was." The weight of my words hung between us.

"Listen." Tessa changed the subject for me. "If I ask you something, will you promise to think about it before you say no?"

"If you have to ask me that, I have a feeling I'm not going to like what you're about to say." I knew Tessa, and more often than not, her plans were a bit nuts.

She ignored me and launched into her idea, talking really fast so I wouldn't have time to interrupt.

239

"Jarrett and I are going to homecoming, and I think it would be good if you came along. We'll make it low key."

"How do you make a dance 'low key'?" I asked. It got crazy at school during homecoming and prom time. The girls talked about nothing but dresses and hair and nails and all that other stuff I didn't get involved in because I'd never been asked to a dance before. It was enough to make you want to crawl into a cave and hibernate until it was over.

"We won't make a big deal out of it. It'll be fun. We haven't done anything in forever, and you know how lame Jarrett is about dancing."

"I'm not sure this is such a good idea," I told Tessa, watching the team set up hurdles along the track. "It doesn't feel right to go to the dance with Abby gone."

"Your sister would want you to live your life," Tessa said. "Will you at least think about it?"

I sighed, a big heaving sigh mainly for her benefit. "Okay, I'll consider it for a minute or two, but that might be all the attention I give it."

"Perfect!" Tessa reached out her hand to me, and I grabbed it. She yanked me to my feet, and then draped her arm around me. "Let's get out of here."

I followed her as she clanked down in her cowboy boots. I watched the girls on the track and thought again about how Abby should be practicing with them. How she should be the one here.

53

I pushed the dance from my mind, but it was clear Tessa wasn't going to let it slide. I about jumped out of my skin two days later when she came up behind me and put her hands over my eyes as I was pulling books from my locker.

"God, freak out much?" She unwrapped one of the scarves from around her neck. She had at least four, and looked like a gypsy who'd escaped from the loony bin. "I've been looking for you everywhere."

"You have my schedule memorized; you couldn't have been looking too hard."

"But doesn't it sound more dramatic to think that I've been scouring the school from top to bottom for you?"

I pushed away the scarf that she now waved in my face. "You're nuts."

"Well, I have some news for you." Tessa got that look on her face I knew too well; the one where she gets a funny half smile, so you know she's up to no good. She does it when she's trying to figure out how to convince me to do things that'll probably end badly. Like the time she asked me to help dye her hair black and we ruined her parents' fancy towels after we used them to clean the countertops, or when we were in fourth grade and she thought it would be an adventure to hitchhike home. Our elementary school principal picked us up, and we had to listen to her lecture us about the dangers of taking rides from strangers the entire drive. Tessa was up to no good, there was no doubt about that. "We're set for Saturday, so you can't back out now."

"Saturday?" I said, playing dumb.

Tessa pulled an envelope out of her purse and passed it over to me. She shook her head back and forth as if I was a little child forgetting something. "The dance. I got us tickets, but you don't need to pay me back; it's no big deal. We just need to make sure you have a dress. Do you have a dress?"

"I didn't say I'd go. I told you I'd think about it."

"Come on, don't back out on me. You never do anything anymore, and Jarrett is excited that you're coming too."

"I find that hard to believe. No one likes a third wheel. What am I supposed to do during the slow songs, dance in between you two?"

"You won't be the third wheel; you know Jarrett hates to dance. That's why you have to come, and then I don't need to spend the entire night begging him to go out on the dance floor."

"There's no way I'm going to dance either," I tried to argue, but it was obvious Tessa wasn't going to let me out of this. We hadn't gone to last year's homecoming; most freshmen weren't brave enough to show up without a date, so instead, Tessa, Abby, and I had binge watched a new TV series while stuffing our faces full of ice cream and cookie dough. Tommy hadn't gone either. He'd told me we should go together as a joke to laugh at everyone dressed up in uncomfortable clothes. I pretended that would be funny, but I should've told him the truth. That I wanted to go with him and be one of those people dressed up.

I rubbed my temples. "I don't know, Tessa."

"What do you have to lose? Please, live a little," she said, and I could tell that she really did want me to go.

"Okay, but I don't think it's a good idea."

"It's a great idea," she said and hugged me.

The bell rang and our classmates scattered. As Tessa ran off down the hallway, I hoped she was right.

54

I lay awake that night staring at the ceiling. The air was still without a breeze. It hadn't rained since the day after Abby disappeared, and the weather stations had declared us officially in a draught. It had been weeks without more than a quick sprinkle, and people whispered their worries about the dangers of days with all sun and no relief in sight. September was almost over.

I had the curtains open to try to let some air in, and the faint strains of the Miracle Seekers' songs drifted above the whirl of the little fan I had on my night table.

There was a noise downstairs where Collin was sleeping in his blanket tent. He insisted on staying there since Mom refused to let him be out in the fields all night.

"Abby!" he yelled.

I lay still and waited for something to happen, almost as if my sister would answer.

"Abby!" he yelled again and began to cry. I jumped out of my bed and raced toward him.

He was curled in a ball, and his body shook.

"Hey, it's okay, Collin." I sat next to him and put my hand on his back. He had on his Spider-Man pajamas, the bottoms too short for his long legs. He climbed into my lap, even though he was too big to do that, and I let him because I needed it as much as he did.

The shaking stopped, but he continued to cry. "I missed you, Abby," he repeatedly said.

I hesitated. Did Collin really think I was Abby? *He's half asleep*, I told myself. *He doesn't know what he's saying. He probably won't even remember any of this.*

So I didn't correct him. Instead, I let him believe what we all wanted to believe.

"I miss you too," I told him and rubbed his back to calm him down.

He clung to me in the darkness and his body relaxed.

"I didn't think you were coming back," he said.

"I've always been here. I'm not going to leave you," I told him, because in the dark, you could pretend to be anyone you wanted to be.

55

I slept downstairs with Collin and didn't leave until I heard Dad pull up outside. I untangled from Collin carefully and headed upstairs to take a shower. It felt more important for me to stick around this morning than to go running.

Dad was frying bacon when I came back down, and Collin read the back of the cereal box. His hair stuck up in blond clumps and he swung his legs under the table as he hummed a song.

I slid into my usual seat at the table and nudged Collin with my elbow. He nudged me back and the two of us continued until he fell into a fit of laughter.

"Guess what?" Collin asked as he bent close to me.

"What?"

"Last night I saw Abby," Collin said, his eyes bright and shiny.

Dad turned from the stove so fast that he dropped the fork he was holding. He picked it up and walked over to Collin. "You did? Where did you see her?" he asked.

"She came right into the house and slept next to me all night long."

"Sounds like a wonderful dream," Dad said, and ruffled his hand through Collin's hair. Collin squirmed away from him.

"It wasn't a dream," he insisted, his happy mood vanished. "She's been visiting me at night. She sings me a lullaby when I can't sleep."

"You're pretty lucky she came to see you," I told him.

"It was even more special than those other people who saw her, because she stayed with me," he said. "She didn't run away. She really loves me. I just don't know why she didn't stay here and left again."

I leaned my head against the window next to the kitchen table. It was cool on my forehead, and I pulled back, blowing the glass to fog it up. I took my finger and drew a heart.

Collin smiled and drew his own heart encircling mine, reminding me how important family is.

56

Collin wasn't the only one who believed he'd seen Abby.

The Miracle Seekers kept a constant watch in our field for glimpses of her. They claimed she appeared more and more out of the blackness that leaked like ink through the field, but I wasn't buying it. It was always one person at a time who claimed to have spotted Abby, the rest left wondering how they could have missed her.

"How gullible are these people? Don't they find it odd that she's never been spotted by two people at the same time?" I told Dad before he left for work. He fought with Mom about the circles almost every day, but they'd gotten so big, it was next to impossible for him to put a stop to them anymore. "I mean, that's kind of a red flag that maybe these people are making it up."

"We're trying to believe in something right now," he said.

"But a ghost version of Abby?" I asked, my voice rising from frustration. "Abby isn't a ghost. This has to stop, Dad. It has to end. These people are ridiculous."

And they were. Especially since those who claimed to see her affirmed that she didn't just come at night, but during the day, too, in places that didn't even connect to our field.

"I was walking out of Calloos Pizzeria with my order and there she was," Jeannine Wilson said. "I spotted her across the street, bent over tying her shoe. I figured it was one of the high school girls, but when she stood, it was Abby. I yelled to her, but she moved too fast. I would've chased after her, but I had boxes of pizza in my hands."

"She was outside my bathroom window," Mr. Miller said. "I got out of the shower and glanced outside. She was cutting through my backyard. She climbed right over the chain-link fence, dropped down on the other side, and slipped through some bushes." He shook his head, as if he'd done something wrong. "I have no idea what she was doing there."

More people gathered in the field to try to catch a glimpse of my sister. Abby became some kind of urban legend. She was like the little girl in the story who appeared on the side of the road asking for a ride. When the man in the truck returned her to the house where she told him she lived, her parents said that she died over a year ago, and sure enough, she'd vanished from the front seat.

Abby sightings were the stories people told each other, like the ones we used to whisper around campfires or under blankets during sleepovers, the thrill of anticipation and fear running through us. But while people hung on to the idea that they really were seeing my sister as a ghost, I felt like she was moving further and further away. As everyone was looking for a ghost of Abby, I was terrified they were forgetting to find the real version of her.

57

Homecoming snuck up and tackled me before I could escape. I considered hiding when Tessa pulled into the driveway, but she'd track me down and drag me out like some Neanderthal caveman if she needed to.

I smoothed my sweaty hands on my dress. Correction, Abby's dress. It had hung in her closet forgotten after she went missing, the plastic bag around it and the price tag dangling from the back zipper. It had waited for her on a satin hanger that she had talked Mom into buying. The dress was pale yellow, like the glow under your chin when you hold a dandelion to it. It was strapless and dipped low in the front, different from anything I'd ever wear.

I tried it on last night because it was my only option. I didn't own anything nice enough for the dance, and I wasn't about to ask Mom to take me to the mall to get something to wear. The idea of Mom functioning anywhere beyond our house these days was a joke, so I didn't really have a choice but to wear it.

I'd waited until Collin was glued to some TV show, Dad was at work, and Mom was out in the field.

I'd slipped it on, jammed my feet into her shoes, and pretended for just a moment that I'd stepped into Abby's life.

I pushed that thought aside. Wasn't it this type of pretending that had ruined everything?

I'd practically ripped the dress off and hung it back up in the closet among Abby's other dresses, shirts, and pants that waited for her to come back and wear them again.

But with only thirty minutes until Tessa picked me up and no other options, that dress was going to have to work. I put it on in the downstairs bathroom so no one would see that I borrowed it.

I stood in front of the mirror, and felt like an impostor once again. Who did I think I was? What right did I have to wear my sister's dress to a dance she could no longer go to? And how was this any different than thinking it was okay to kiss her boyfriend? You don't just take things that don't belong to you, but that was exactly what I'd done and what I was about to do again. I reached back to unzip the dress. I needed to take it off. This wasn't right. Not the dress or going to the dance. But before I could, a horn blared from outside.

Tessa was here.

I ran barefoot to the car, out of my house before my parents found me in Abby's dress. I'd written a note earlier that I placed on the kitchen table for them to find when I was gone.

Abby's dress skimmed the ground and stirred up a fog of dust around the bottom. I was shorter than her and the dress wasn't quite the same on me.

Nothing was quite the same.

Tessa rolled down the window and whistled as I ran to the car. "Looking good, girl."

I put my finger to my lips and hoped she'd get the hint.

"Let's go," I said as I stepped into the car.

"What's the hurry? You're acting as if you robbed a bank."

"More like my sister's closet," I said. "This is her dress."

Tessa turned to me, and I waited for her to tell me I was crazy. Because really, who wears their missing sister's dress to a dance? The dress her sister didn't get to wear.

But Tessa didn't.

"It looks great on you," she said.

Her words made me feel even worse. I shouldn't look good in Abby's dress.

"There's only one problem," she said and reached over toward my armpit. She grabbed a tag that I hadn't even noticed and pulled it off in one quick yank. "There, you're ready."

I didn't like the finality of pulling off the tag. Of wearing something for the first time that didn't belong to me.

"Right now," I said as I buckled my seat belt, "I'd be happy to be just about anywhere other than this dance."

"Come on, Rhylee, tonight is going to be fun. Wait and see. You'll have a good time."

I wasn't sure that I wanted to. If I deserved to. I'd stolen Abby's boyfriend, her dress; could I steal her good time, too? What else would I take from her?

Tessa drove to Jarrett's house and honked the horn two times. When the lights above the front door flashed, she laid her hand on the horn and continued to announce her arrival.

"Uh, I think he knows you're here," I said.

"That's obvious, but Jarrett is worse than a girl. He'll take another ten minutes to get ready," Tessa complained. "If I keep beeping, he'll hurry so his mom doesn't get pissed."

I fluffed the fabric of my dress around me. It was as if I was sitting on a cloud, the skirt floating.

Jarrett came outside, his suit jacket flapping behind him half on and half off, and instead of opening the back door, he threw open the passenger side door. I held up my hand.

"Sorry, this seat is taken."

"No worries, I'll fit. I'd rather be here with you ladies." He slid in, the bones of his hips poking me as he pushed me against Tessa. "Nothing wrong with getting close to each other."

He laid the top half of his body against me in order to kiss Tessa. I grabbed a handful of the yellow dress fabric and yanked it out from under him. He positioned himself so he wasn't quite squashing me and ran his hands through his spiky black hair. I couldn't help but laugh at the baby blue suit he had put on with black and white two-tone shoes. As obnoxious as he was, Jarrett and Tessa were made for each other.

The ride went by way too fast. Before I knew it, we were at the high school.

"I don't know if I can do this," I told them when Tessa parked the car in the overflow lot by the football field. I played with the white sparkly bracelet I'd found in Abby's jewelry box. What was I thinking, agreeing to go to a dance that my sister couldn't go to in a dress she might never wear?

"Tough. I didn't want to shave my legs, but I did so I wouldn't hear Jarrett bitch about it later. We all have to do things we don't want to do."

"She's right," Jarrett said. "I like a woman with smooth legs." He reached over me again and tried to run his hand up Tessa's leg.

I stretched my body to the right and opened the passenger side door. Jarrett fell out.

"Hey, watch the merchandise," he joked before he walked over to talk to a group of guys standing around a truck.

"Tessa, really. I can't do this," I repeated. "I shouldn't be here. This was supposed to be Abby's dance."

What made me think it was okay to do this? I didn't go to dances or wear fancy dresses and makeup. Abby was the one who loved that kind of thing.

"Please, just take me home," I said, my words getting caught in my throat as I fought back tears.

"You can have a little fun," Tessa said and pointed at Abby's shoes on the floor of the car. "Put those on and let's give it a shot. If you're uncomfortable, we'll leave. I promise."

In the distance, people headed into the school. Couples held hands and groups of my classmates walked, laughed, and joked with one another. Three faint red dots glowed and then dimmed by the corner of the parking lot; the last cigarettes snuck before entering the gym.

I turned one of the shoes over, the bottoms black and scuffed, which was odd; I'd thought they were new shoes bought with the dress. I ran my fingers over the scratched soles and wondered when Abby had worn them. I slipped them on and before I could resist, Tessa grabbed my hand and yanked me out of the car and into the dance.

"Let's do this," she said, and reluctantly, I followed.

58

The dance theme was fire and ice. Lights shone down in a blue haze and cast a gray hue on everyone's faces, making them look like zombies. The corners had red strobe lights that flashed into the air, on and off.

The football team won last night, so everyone was in a good mood. The players strutted around and a good-size crowd of people jumped to the music on the dance floor. I could picture Abby among them. She had this way of dancing with giant movements that seemed to take over the space. She'd be right there in the middle of it with a huge smile on her face, not caring what anyone thought of her at all. I turned away from the dance floor, missing her.

Jarrett wandered over to the food table, where cookies in the shape of snowflakes and suns sat, and stuffed his face. Tessa grabbed my hand and tried to get me to the dance floor. I shook my head. I was here; she needed to be happy with that.

257

I found a table along one of the walls and planted myself in a chair, glad to be off my feet. I could count on one hand the number of times I'd worn heels. Tessa stayed near me, but moved to the music by herself. I rolled my eyes when a particularly fast song came on and she shook her head all around, her hair flashing in the lights so that it looked as if she was a part of the fire theme.

We stayed like that for a while, me sitting and Tessa rocking out until Jarrett came back and Tessa gave up dancing to make out with him. So much for sticking by me at the dance.

I wandered away from the spit fest that was now occurring and slipped through the crowd, not wanting to watch the two of them sucking face. I stood on the edge of the dance floor while everyone moved with the music. My classmates were dressed as fancy versions of themselves.

Someone grabbed my hand and yanked me into the crowd. It was one of Abby's teammates. She pulled me into the group she was dancing with. I slid through bodies slick with sweat that moved against me, threatening to swallow me up. I fell into the dark pulsating core. Those around me moved to the music, not caring who they bumped into, so I did the same. I danced with everyone the way Abby would have. I threw my arms up and moved with the crowd. I closed my eyes and the strobe lights darkened and brightened against my eyelids. The bass pumped deep into my chest so I wasn't sure if my heart was beating or if it was the music that kept me alive.

I allowed myself to be swept up in the group until a hand grabbed mine and pulled me out.

The person pulled me through the crowd, and it wasn't until we broke through that I saw it was Tommy.

My history teacher, Mr. Scott, stood guard near the door that led outside. His cell phone screen lit his face and he repeated the rules that he must have said a million times tonight without looking up. "No touching, no yelling, no running around, or you'll go back inside."

I couldn't make a scene. I couldn't do that to Tommy, so I let him pull me through.

He shoved his hands into the pockets of his black pants and looked at the ground. He wore a white dress shirt with the navy-blue tie he wore when he played the piano at weddings. His hair was slicked back and his sneakers were still in their perpetual state of being untied.

"Tessa told me you were coming tonight," he said. "I thought maybe we could talk. Maybe we—"

He was about to say more but paused as he noticed my dress. He reached out and touched a section of it. The fabric slipped through his fingers.

"Abby was supposed to wear this," he said. "She showed it to me after she bought it because she was so excited."

I was uncomfortable. Self-conscious. How could I explain to him why I was wearing Abby's dress? Why I'd tried it on?

"And you had her tennis shoes that day you were running," Tommy said. His voice was heavy with sadness.

We stood against the brick wall, our faces hidden in the

shadows. Inside, the music pulsed so deep that you could feel the beat in the ground, thumping through you. Red lights lit one corner of the courtyard. He took a step toward me, so I took a step back, the bottom of my dress swishing against my legs.

"At first I didn't know it was you," Tommy said. "On the dance floor, before. Maybe it was the lights or the music, but I thought . . ." He trailed off as if looking for the right words. Someone far off in the grass laughed. There was a flash of light, a match struck before a hand concealed it. "I thought you were Abby."

I touched the satin, cool in my sweaty hands. "I'll never be Abby."

But wasn't that what I was doing? Dressing like my sister? Going to the dance she was supposed to go to? I focused on my sister's shoes; clumps of dirt stuck to the heels. I had stepped into her life again, just like I had when I tried to make Tommy mine. I had taken so much away from Abby, and here I was doing it again.

"Why would you think I want you to be her?" Tommy asked, but wasn't the answer obvious? Abby had had Tommy.

"Everyone wants Abby," I told him.

Tommy ran his hand through his hair and paced back and forth, frustrated.

"I don't," he said, and my heart ached for what could never happen between us.

A large group of kids came out, laughing and pushing each other. The door stayed open, held by a boy who couldn't decide if he was going in or out. I knew that feeling. What it felt like to stand in between, not fitting on either side.

The outside door swung open again, and Tessa stepped out. She scanned the yard and stopped when she found me. She looked from me to Tommy, turned around, and headed back inside. She was giving me the chance to be with him, but she had it all wrong. I couldn't be with him.

I stepped away from Tommy and slipped through the doors before he could stop me.

59

I hid out in the bathroom for about half an hour, and when I came out, Tessa was back at the table with Jarrett, trying to get him to slow dance.

"I need to leave," I told the two of them. "Can we go?"

"What about Tommy?" Tessa asked. "I saw the two of you together."

"There is no Tommy," I said in a voice that made it very clear I wasn't going to talk about him.

"Yeah, sure, okay, let's go," Tessa said as she stood up. "We're ready, right?"

Jarrett nodded and followed the two of us out of the dance. I walked fast. I wanted to get out of there before Tommy found me again. I needed to stay away from him.

On the ride home, Tessa didn't mention anything about seeing us outside, and I wasn't about to volunteer any information. Instead, I turned the radio up loud enough to drown out any conversation we might have wanted to have.

When we got to my house, Tessa stepped out of the car and hugged me.

"I'm glad you came tonight," she said. "You know you can call me if you want to talk."

"Thanks for the ride," I said, not revealing anything else. I waved to Jarrett before heading inside.

I didn't see the Miracle Seekers at first. The group usually stayed in the field, so when one of them stepped out on our front walk, I jumped in surprise.

She stood in front of me in a sweater that went to her knees, her arms crossed.

"Sorry," I said. "I wasn't expecting anyone to be here." I reached into my purse for the house key. Since people now camped out in our fields, my parents had decided to keep the doors locked.

She took a step toward me and her sweater fell open. She wore a shirt with Abby's picture. Someone had taken an old photo from the sports section of our paper of her grinning and holding a medal and made piles of shirts for those searching for her. I didn't have to see the back of the shirt to know that the words "Homeward Bound" were written in bold purple letters.

"It must be nice to be able to go out and have fun when your sister isn't able to," she said.

"Excuse me?" I asked, stunned. I wasn't sure I heard her correctly. Usually the Miracle Seekers talked to my family with faces of concern and sadness, but this lady was looking at me with anger. I took a few steps closer to my door, now clutching the key I was holding tight in my fist in case I needed to use it. She made me nervous.

She moved forward so that she was right in front of me and blocked my path.

"You dressing up and having fun with your friends," she said, "when Abby can't. I sure wouldn't do something like that."

I stared at this woman, this stranger who knew nothing about my family beyond what she saw on the news or heard through gossip. This woman who had taken over my yard with her foolish optimism and acted as if my life was her business. I thought about the dance and how fun had nothing to do with it, but here she was judging me, as if I didn't already feel incredibly guilty for going.

"Screw you," I spat out with an anger I'd buried deep inside. I pushed her out of my way. She stumbled and threw her arms out, trying to gain her balance.

I didn't wait to see if she righted herself or fell. I jammed my key into the door and locked it behind me.

I went straight to Abby's room, kicked off her shoes, climbed onto the bed, and crawled under the sheets. I didn't even bother to take off her dress. I sobbed into her pillow until my eyes were swollen and aching.

That night I slept deeper than I had since Abby first disappeared. I swore I could smell her in the sheets, and it felt as if she was there with me.

60

Dad found me in the morning, cocooned under a pile of blankets, Abby's dress tangled around my legs.

"We need to talk," he said in a stern voice, and I was pretty sure he'd spoken to the Miracle Seeker who'd intercepted me at the door when I came home from the dance.

I followed him to the kitchen and poured the last of the box of cereal. It was stale and mostly crumbs, but I needed something to do with my hands, a way to keep my mouth shut.

Dad opened the curtains that covered the sliding door to our backyard, and for a second I was afraid that the woman would be out there. But only bright sunlight flooded the room.

"What happened last night? One of the women in the circle, she said her name was Mrs. Butler, stopped me when I went out to get the paper and told me you pushed her. Is this true?"

"Yeah," I told him. If he wanted the truth, I was going to give it to him. For once.

"First the woman at Otis's Diner and now this. What would possess you to do something like that?" He stared at me as if he didn't even recognize me.

I thought about apologizing, stepping down, but I didn't want to. The way that woman treated me wasn't fair. "Because of the way she was talking to me, like I did something bad. I went out last night to a school dance. Something pretty much everyone at my school did. I was just trying to get back to normal. She has no right to judge me. None at all."

"You're right. What she said wasn't appropriate, but that doesn't mean you can respond by pushing her. You do understand these people are here for your sister, don't you?" Dad asked.

"Abby is my sister. *Mine.* They act like they own her, but they don't. Not at all. This is happening to me, to you, to *our* family."

Dad sighed and rubbed his eyes. "I'll talk to her. This is hard for all of us, and she shouldn't have said what she said, but we raised you to be respectful."

Outside, Mom pulled into our driveway and stepped out of the car with boxes of doughnuts. She walked over to the group and passed them around to everyone.

"Mom shouldn't be out there. She cares about everyone in the field more than she does about her own family."

"That's not true—" Dad said, but it was. It couldn't be healthy. Mom blended in so well with the people outside that she was a part of them. Ever since that tiny step forward, the

266

crop circles and Miracle Seekers had made her go a hundred steps back. She'd become a Miracle Seeker herself. She was so obsessed with those circles that she couldn't even see what was going on with her own family. Just the other day Collin wore pajama bottoms to school because he didn't have any clean pants. There was a pile of bills on the dining room table that were overdue, and I'd thrown away almost everything in our fridge last week because the food was rotten. We were a mess, and Mom refused to see that.

"Those people aren't right, Dad."

He shook his head. "They aren't hurting anyone."

"What about Mom? They're hurting her. She stands out there waiting for Abby to come home. Mom's looking for this ghost version of Abby, when she should be with us. Instead, she's in our field with a bunch of strangers."

"Your mother is trying to make sense of this, just like us."

"How can she, when she's pretty much forgotten the other three people in her family who are still here, because she's too busy with everyone outside filling her head with that bullshit? Abby might be gone, but we're still here and she doesn't even care."

"It's her way, Rhylee."

"Her way of what?"

Dad paused. "Grieving."

The clock in our kitchen ticked away the minutes and the voices outside rose and fell in peaks, valleys, growing loud, and then soft.

"We're grieving too," I finally said. "And right now Abby isn't the only one that I feel like I've lost."

61

"Did you hear about what happened when we left the dance on Saturday? Everyone is talking about the fight between Tommy and Kyle," Tessa said as soon as I got to school Monday morning.

"Tommy got in a fight?" I asked.

"I guess the two of them went at it in the middle of the dance floor. Mr. Ralston pulled them apart before much could happen, but people said that Kyle went nuts screaming at Tommy. He didn't mention it to you?"

"We don't really talk anymore," I said and hoped that would be enough to shut Tessa up. But things were never that easy.

"I saw the two of you were outside together at the dance," Tess pointed out.

"It wasn't like that," I said. I stayed on my knees in front of my locker and pretended to search through my books and papers. It was a lot easier to speak to the scratched metal and pile of books inside than to look at Tessa's face.

"The two of you were outside together in the dark. You're really going to try to tell me that isn't something?"

The bell rang, and I had no choice but to stand up. People slammed lockers around me and headed toward their classes. A book bag swung into me, and I almost became a casualty in the mad dash to avoid a tardy slip.

"Really, nothing happened."

"It's okay to spend time with Tommy," Tessa said. "No one says that there is anything wrong with talking to a person. You're allowed to be around him."

"I wish it were that simple."

"It is," she told me, and I couldn't believe we were arguing about whether it was okay to like my missing sister's boyfriend. Tessa had always supported me, but this, this seemed like too much.

"And what do I tell my sister when she returns?" I asked. "Sorry, Abby, I've been getting pretty close with your boyfriend while you disappeared."

"You can't stop living," Tessa said. "You're still here."

"But she isn't," I told her. "And until she is, I can't betray her." *Again*, I thought.

Tessa nodded as if she understood, but my words felt sour on my tongue.

The two of us headed to class, and the irony of worrying about betraying Abby made me sick. Can you betray a person a second time? Especially when the initial betrayal was enough to destroy them?

62

I ditched sixth period and called the suicide hotline again. Tessa's words spun in my head. There was no way I could ever be with Tommy. How could I after what we'd done?

"Are you in immediate danger?" a woman's voice asked.

"No," I said. "I need someone to talk to."

"This is a great place do to that. I'm Laura. What's your name?"

"Abby," I said again without thinking, then felt ashamed to take something of my sister's once again.

"What's on your mind, Abby?" she asked, and there was a rustling, as if she was eating something from a bag. I pictured her lounging on the chair wherever the hotline was located, her feet up on her desk, popping almonds into her mouth.

"I can't stop thinking about what I did." I decided to take the confessional route. Laura might not be a priest, but it sure felt good to burden someone else with my sins. I was afraid that if I carried these secrets around by myself much longer, I might collapse under their weight.

"What did you do? Was it something that could put you in danger?"

"It wasn't something I did to myself. It was my sister. I hurt her so bad she hasn't returned. I don't think she'll ever return."

"Did you hurt her physically?" Laura asked.

"No, no," I quickly said so she wouldn't try to trace my call and send the police for me. "I did something to her that I don't think she can ever forgive."

"I'm sure she doesn't feel that way."

"She can't feel anything," I said, my voice rising as I felt the bitter sting of my guilt. "She's gone, and I'm the one who should have disappeared."

"Oh, honey, nothing in this world is worth disappearing for."

I pressed the change return button repeatedly while scanning the area to make sure no one walked by. "I don't know what I'm allowed to feel anymore. It all seems wrong no matter what I choose."

"What do you want to feel?"

"Love," I said and thought about Tommy.

"Why don't you think you feel it?" Laura asked.

"I'm not allowed."

"Everyone is allowed to feel love," she answered, but she was wrong. There is no way that someone gets to love after what I did. Not a chance.

Of course she was going to tell me I was allowed to love; her job was to fill my head with positive thoughts and warm fuzzies so I didn't want to off myself, but she didn't know. How could she understand that it was impossible to love someone when loving them was what drove away the only other person you could possibly love more?

"Yeah, maybe you're right," I said to please her and make sure she believed I was okay. "Listen, I have to go. But thanks for listening."

I hung up the phone before she could say anything more. Maybe in her world you could feel love, but in mine, the love I felt was an impossible curse.

63

I stayed in the library until the bell rang for the end of the school day. I followed the crowd out the door to the buses, which was where Tommy caught up with me.

It was no use running from him; I'd make a scene doing that, so I slowed down, and he seized his chance to fall into step beside me.

"I need to talk to you," he said. I couldn't see his face—he had a hoodie pulled up over his head—but I could hear the urgency in his voice.

"We can't," I told him and fought to keep my voice firm, even though I was crumbling inside.

"Please, Rhylee," he begged. "This is important."

I relented and nodded. I reached out and touched his hoodie. "You don't have to hide from me. Tessa told me what happened."

"I don't want you to see me like this," he said, but pulled down the hood.

His left eye was puffy and swollen almost completely shut. A mess of yellow and purple tinged the edges and his face held a kaleidoscope of bruises.

"Oh my god," I breathed as I took in what Kyle had done to him.

"That's why I wanted to talk to you. I need to say good-bye."

"Good-bye?"

"I'm leaving," he said, his voice dull and empty.

"What are you talking about?" I asked in a voice loud enough that a few of my classmates turned around and stared at us. I lowered my voice. "Okay, we can talk, but not here. Where's your truck?"

He gestured to the right of the parking lot and the two of us headed toward it together. He unlocked the passenger door and grabbed a bunch of papers and junk from the front seat. "It's messy in here, sorry."

"I can handle it." I climbed in and pushed a few crumpled bags away with my feet. The truck smelled different from Tommy. A mixture of smoke and fresh grass. I remembered the last time I was in his truck, on the way home from the bonfire. Things were so different now. That night seemed like a dream.

"I'm sorry if I upset you at the dance," he said as he pulled out of the parking lot.

"I shouldn't have gone. It was a stupid idea."

"I don't know why I went either."

"No one knows what's right anymore," I said.

"That's why I have to get out of here for a while."

"What do you mean?"

"I need to get away. No one wants me here. My aunt said I could stay with her, which is a good thing. She's in upstate New York, so maybe I can work with a piano teacher, look into auditioning at some colleges in the city," he said, and it was as if the bottom dropped out from under me.

"You belong here," I told him, unable to hide the fear in my voice. Tommy couldn't leave; I wouldn't survive if both he and Abby were gone. And I was selfish enough to say it.

He gripped the steering wheel so tightly that his knuckles turned white. "They won't stop until they've gotten their revenge for what they think I did to Abby."

"You didn't do anything."

"But everyone thinks I did. They'll destroy me."

I wanted to tell him he was wrong. That people weren't like that, but Tommy was right; this was only the beginning. They wouldn't stop until Abby came home.

"I'll tell the truth." I pled with him, willing to do anything if it meant keeping him here. "About the two of us and what Abby saw. I'll let them know that you were with me the whole time. I'll make things right."

"It would only make it worse. Think about what they'll do to you if they find out you were a part of this. I won't let that happen."

"Maybe we should run away together," I said, only half joking.

"Remember when we tried to do that? What were we, in fourth or fifth grade?" Tommy smiled at the memory.

"I was mad at my parents because they wouldn't let me get my ears pierced."

"And you insisted on packing that giant blue suitcase that I had to carry."

"It was full of very important items," I said. I unrolled the window and let the air wrap itself around us.

"Oh yeah, you're right. We needed to bring your favorite books and a bathing suit."

"You never know when you might need to cool off. And don't forget I also packed the cookies you ate before we were even a few blocks from my house."

"Too bad you had to use the bathroom and we needed to turn around and come back."

"I guess I didn't plan for everything," I said and laughed, my body now relaxed. "I was so mad that our parents didn't even notice we had left."

"Now they'll be glad if I left," Tommy said, and reality shook me once again. The mood darkened in the truck.

"That's not true," I said, but I was lying. Mom didn't talk about Tommy to me, but she blamed him; everyone did. I'd heard her talk about him with the people in the circles, his name drifting through the open window.

"Believe me, it would be better for everyone if I was gone," he said.

"Not for me," I said, my words a betrayal of my sister and my promise.

"I have to get out of here," Tommy said.

"Don't leave me," I told him, unable to keep the fear out of my voice. "I've lost so much already. I can't lose you."

"You won't," Tommy said.

"Please," I begged.

Tommy didn't answer right away, but finally he sighed. "Okay, I'll stay for now. Until we find Abby. But I can't make any promises."

"I've made enough promises for the both of us," I said, and wished that wasn't true.

When he turned onto our street, I saw a large crowd of people in my yard.

"Do you go out there? To the circles?" Tommy asked.

"My mom keeps trying to get me to, but Tessa and I think they're a bit nuts."

"Yeah," Tommy said in a way that I couldn't tell if he was agreeing with me or not.

"You can park at your place. I'll walk the rest of the way."

"I don't mind dropping you off," Tommy said.

"I do," I said, the meaning of my words obvious.

I told myself it was because of the woman who yelled at me the night of the dance. If she flipped when I went to homecoming, what would she do if I showed up with Tommy? Would anyone understand why we were together in the truck? I didn't even know how to view it myself. But what I did know was that once again, I was a coward, unable to face the truth, especially when Tommy was willing to stay here for me and needed it the most.

277

64

Mom came into the kitchen that evening as I washed the dishes. They'd been sitting in dirty dishwater since yesterday, and we were out of silverware. The way Mom was these days, she probably hadn't even noticed them piled in the sink.

"I can do that," she said as she walked behind me.

Instead, I lifted my hands out of the water and pointed toward the towels. "You can dry."

She grabbed a towel and took each plate as I passed it to her. I could smell her rose-scented hand lotion. It was a smell I was familiar with, but hadn't been reminded of for weeks. I wasn't sure if it was because I hadn't been this close to her in such a long time or if she had stopped wearing it.

I dunked a plate underwater and scrubbed it.

"You should think about coming outside," Mom said. "Tomorrow night we're doing a prayer vigil."

"I've told you this before. There's nothing there for me." I picked at a piece of dried-on egg with my fingernail. I sounded like a broken record. I wished that we could just be together here instead of listening to her talk about the circles once again. It seemed as if those people invaded everything, stealing Mom away with their nonsense and pointless vigil.

She went on as if I hadn't spoken. "I can feel your sister when I'm out there. We all can. It's like she's at the edge of the woods waiting for us to find her," she said.

The truth in her words shocked me, and I dropped the plate I was holding. It shattered around my feet.

"I'm sorry," I said.

I bent down and picked up the pieces, holding them in my hands. A jagged section cut into my palm. I let go of it and a thin line of blood appeared.

A wave of dizziness washed over me. Mom pressed a cool wet towel into my palm. It was nice to have her take care of me, a feeling that seemed foreign to me now after we had been so consumed by bringing Abby home.

"Hold it tight, and don't let go. You need to put pressure against it. Go sit at the table, and I'll clean this up."

I didn't argue. I was woozy. I never could look at blood, mine or anybody else's. I wasn't even able to watch a TV character get a shot without feeling as if I was going to pass out.

Mom cleaned up the dish with a little broom and joined me at the table. My hand throbbed, but I didn't care, because Mom was here and for this brief moment, she was my old mom. I'd forgotten how much I missed just being with her.

"Would you at least think about coming outside?" she asked, and placed a hand on my arm. I caught the scent of her again, and it reminded me of what life was like before. I breathed her in and yearned for what we used to have.

"I'll think about it," I said. And maybe going outside would change things. Maybe it would be a good thing. I pressed the cloth harder into my hand, and the pain bit into my palm.

65

Collin was sitting on the front porch swing when I got home from school the next day. He broke into a run and met me as I got off the bus.

"Mom said I could go out into the fields tonight if you went out too. Will you do it? Please? Please?"

He tugged on my book bag and made it fall off my shoulder. I searched the yard for Mom, so I could tell her exactly how I felt about this little plan. Leave it to her to rope my brother into all of this. She knew there was no way I'd say no to Collin.

"You really want to be outside at night? There are bugs, and it's wet and cold. It's so much more comfortable inside."

"No, no way! Please say yes."

I remembered how he'd woken me in the middle of the night crying over Abby. He wasn't getting much attention, and it wouldn't be that big a deal to go outside for one night if it helped make him feel better.

"I'll go out for a little bit," I told him. "But don't think that I'm going to do this all the time."

"Yay!" He yelled and ran up the driveway, no doubt to find Mom so she could celebrate the victory.

I told him we had to wait until after dinner, and as soon as we cleared the dishes, he was waiting at the door.

Collin raced into the field, but I moved slowly, still skeptical about these people and their belief that they were doing the right thing to help bring Abby back.

I expected everyone to be in small groups in the backyard, kind of like high school where we sat in our cliques, not daring to cross over into a section that wasn't your territory, but it wasn't like that at all. It was one big group, as if they had become friends or family. Adults talked to teammates of my sister, neighbors sat next to teachers from my school, and the few classmates who were there seemed to be friends with one another.

I dragged Collin to Mom first. She was with our neighbor Karin, the one who suggested the circles had to do with Abby in the first place. The two of them were deep in conversation.

A woman with a pile of blankets tucked under one arm walked over to me and placed her hand on my shoulder.

"You must miss you sister very much," she said.

"Of course I do," I replied, immediately defensive, because is there any other way to feel?

"When I think about how much I miss her, I have to stop because it could never be as much as your family does."

I tilted my head to get a better look at this woman. Was she for real?

"How do you know Abby?" I asked.

"The same way most of these people do. She's a part of our town. I might not have known her personally, but I can feel the loss."

"Right," I said, wondering if the loss she felt hurt as much as the one I did.

She hiked the blankets higher and gave me one last smile. "Well, I wanted you to know that we're praying real hard for your family."

"Thanks," I mumbled and turned to Mom.

"Honey, you're here. Karin and I were just talking about how important these circles are."

"Oh, yes," Karin said. "I don't know what I'd do without them."

Um, how about go home and live your life, I thought to myself, because so far, the Miracle Seekers were pretty much exactly what I thought they'd be: a bunch of fakes who clung to Abby's disappearance to fill some hole in their own empty lives.

I didn't bother to answer her. Instead I turned to Mom. "I'm taking Collin over to Mary Grace, but we need to talk later."

She put on a fake smile and turned back to Karin. She knew exactly what I wanted to talk to her about, and I had a feeling she'd spend the night stuck to someone's side so the opportunity wouldn't happen.

I helped Collin spread out the blanket we had brought from inside and the two of us sat next to Mary Grace.

"Hi," I said, and wondered how I'd gotten to the point where I was outside sitting with her. She was surprisingly nice to me, considering the last time we'd spoken I wasn't exactly the most pleasant person in the world.

"I'm glad you're out here."

"Yeah, well, I didn't have much of a choice. It was either this or stay inside with Hound Dog. Since he stinks and needs a bath, coming out here won."

"I totally get your decision. I remember when he got sprayed by a skunk, and it took forever for you guys to get the stink off of him," she said. Her face grew serious. "Seriously, though, it's good to see you."

"Rhylee said we can come out here every night," Collin told her, settling onto the blanket I'd spread out next to Mary Grace.

"I said nothing of the sort," I told him.

"We'll see about that," he said and sounded exactly like Mom. He lay on his back and studied the sky. Stars peeked out among the inky blue backdrop, and he traced a path between each with his finger.

I pulled bits of grass out of the ground as a group of people came to stand by Mom and Karin. One of them rang a large cowbell.

"We're going to welcome in the evening with a song," he said, and those around me quieted down. The ladies drew together and sang something full of words about "god's glory" and "saving love."

The group passed around purple candles. I took one and

when Mary Grace lit her candle from the candle of a man sitting near us, I reached mine out and watched the flame catch. Collin stuck his candle in front of my face, and I helped him light it.

I stared at the flickering center as the sky grew darker and night fell.

"Why does everyone sing?" I asked Mary Grace.

"For Abby," she said.

"Abby doesn't like singing. She dropped out of choir freshmen year because she said it was boring."

"We don't sing because of the songs," Mary Grace said. She brought her candle close to her face. "It's so she can hear us. If she's out there somewhere, maybe she'll hear our voices and come home."

I almost laughed out loud at the ridiculousness of her response. Mary Grace was smart; she had to know that no amount of singing was going to bring Abby home. I turned to her to tell her as much, but what I saw made me keep my words to myself. She was holding her candle with both hands, staring into the flame that lit up the tears that ran down her face.

"I know this is all kind of stupid," she said, whispering the words that moments ago I'd been thinking.

"It's not," I told her, because I got it. I understood her sadness, because I felt it too. And maybe the circles were bullshit, but what we were missing wasn't.

66

When I got home from school the next day, I found Collin digging around in the guest room closet. We never had anyone stay over and use the room, so it had basically become a place to dump any random junk we had. Collin pulled out gift boxes, mittens that had no mates, and sports equipment I didn't even know we owned. He created a pile on the floor of so much stuff, you'd think the closet went on forever.

"What are you trying to find?" I asked him when a winter boot flew across the room and nearly hit me.

"My sleeping bag," he said.

"What for?" I asked, way too skeptical of his plans.

"The circles," he said, confirming what I already knew.

"Collin, last night was a one-time thing—"

"I don't care," he interrupted. "I'm going out there. You and Mom can't stop me."

"There isn't anything out there for us," I said, but he wasn't about to reason with me. Instead, he turned and began to dig through the closet again.

I sighed and pushed him aside. "Let me look. I think they're up top on the shelf, and you're not going to be able to reach them." I stood on my tiptoes and rooted around until my hand touched something soft and squishy. "Bingo!"

I pulled out a sleeping bag and dropped it down. We both stared at it, neither one of us making a move to touch it.

It was Abby's sleeping bag.

We each had our own color and Abby's was purple. I'd always been jealous Mom had let Abby pick her sleeping bag first and she got such a pretty color, while I was stuck with red.

Her bag well-worn from family campouts and sleepovers, especially the ones where we only ventured as far as the family room. It used to be a tradition to bring them out when a storm rolled in. We'd lie in our sleeping bags on the living room floor, open the curtains on our huge front windows, and watch the lightning flash across the sky. The four of us would fall asleep like that, lined up in a row listening to the weather rage outside, and wake to the bright sun filtering in. Mom acted as if we slept there to watch the storms, but she wasn't fooling us. They spooked her and she didn't want to sleep alone. We only did it when Dad was at work.

We stopped when Abby joined the cross-country team freshman year. We'd overslept one morning after an October storm shook most of the leaves off our trees. The team had stood outside, their hoodies zipped up and running in place to keep warm.

"Abby," Dad had said, still in his work uniform. "Your crew is on our driveway waiting for you."

She had scrambled up from her sleeping bag.

He'd opened the front door and waved. "Morning, everyone. Abby is just waking up. Do you want some breakfast while you wait? I bet you could give up a day of running for some of my blueberry pancakes."

Abby had pushed Dad aside, embarrassed, and waved the team away. "Go ahead without me. I'll catch up."

She'd closed the door before Dad could entice them in again with his pancakes and stomped up the steps.

We never slept in the living room after that. Abby had refused during the next storm, and it didn't feel the same to sleep beside Mom and Collin, so I'd stopped doing it too.

But tonight I stretched my hands back up to the top shelf and found Collin's green sleeping bag. I tossed it to him.

"Does this mean we can go outside?" Collin asked and jumped from one foot to the other, excited at the possibility.

"One more night," I told him.

"Yes!" he said, and made his way down the steps and toward the front door before I could get another word in. I reached into the closet to find my sleeping bag, but then thought better of it. Instead, I bent down, grabbed Abby's sleeping bag, and followed Collin.

67

It was nice to see Collin happy and excited about something, even if it was the circles. So as crazy as it sounded, I agreed to go outside for the third night in a row. I figured if spending a few hours out there helped him, I could grin and bear it.

I spent the time last night with Mary Grace again. The two of us traded stories about Abby. We told each other things about my sister that the other had never heard. And when you talked in the dark, it was easier to tell things we couldn't say to anyone else.

I told Mary Grace about how Abby would spread butter on Mom's meat loaf, a practice we found disgusting but one Abby assured us was delicious. Or how she left her tennis shoes in the hallway after a run and would have to find them from whatever hiding spot Hound Dog decided to drop them in after having a good chew.

Mary Grace shared the time she let Abby drive her parents' van before she got her license and she scratched it on a curb in the parking lot. She told her parents she did it so Abby wouldn't get in trouble. Or about the time when Abby tried to drink a whole gallon of milk after she heard it was impossible. Two-thirds of the way through, she found out the hard way why people couldn't do it.

I liked being with Mary Grace. Together, we brought parts of my sister back to life. If we were talking about her, it was as if she was still there, and we needed her with us so badly.

"Do you remember the duck eggs in the woods?" she asked.

I did, pale yellow and sitting in a nest of feathers. When I was younger, before there was Tommy, Abby and Mary Grace didn't allow me in on their secret adventures, even though I'd begged them. They'd run into the woods together, sometimes with me trailing after them, but they were always too fast. I'd fall behind and watch them disappear into the trees. I'd stand guard at the entrance until they reappeared, sweaty and flushed, laughing together.

The duck eggs, though, were a secret I became a part of. Abby and Mary Grace burst out of the woods one day, breathless. "Rhylee, come with us," Abby said.

At first, I suspected they were playing some trick on me, but Abby grabbed my hand and pulled me forward. "Hurry. You have to be quick or you'll miss it."

I blindly followed the two of them. They led me in twists and turns to some secret place.

"Where are we going?" I asked, surprised they were letting me join in.

"We need to be quiet or we won't be able to look," Abby said and pushed away branches and made her own path. We walked like this for about five minutes without breathing a word. Suddenly, Abby stopped. "Rhylee, look."

I turned to where she pointed and between the branches, near the edge of the riverbank, was a nest with seven fat eggs in it.

"It's her nest and that's the dad," Mary Grace said and pointed to a duck swimming in the water with another duck near the nest.

"When are they going to hatch?" I asked and kept my eye on the mother.

"Soon, I think. We've been visiting for about a week and she's always on the nest. Any day now there's going to be babies. We'll come back."

On the way home, and I couldn't stop thinking about those seven eggs and the fuzzy chicks that would hatch from them.

Abby and Mary Grace took me back every day. We made sure not to stay long if the mother was on the nest. She'd shift back and forth nervously and was bothered by our presence.

Until one day we got to the pond and she wasn't there.

Instead, there was only her nest with a single egg split in half. A long jagged crack down the center, the rest of the nest empty, the pond still.

"Abby, what do you think happened? Why are the eggs gone?" I'd asked.

She was scared. She walked around the nest and there were feathers all over. I thought about the coyotes we could hear howling at night.

"Do you think something—"

"Stop it," she interrupted. "Don't even say it." She'd turned and run away, leaving Mary Grace and me alone.

I shook my head, trying to get rid of the images of that day. We'd never talked about what happened to the eggs.

Just like we hadn't talked about what had happened with Tommy. She'd run away. And I'd never followed her.

Mary Grace poked me. "Earth to Rhylee. Are you still here?"

"Yeah, I'm here. I remember the eggs," I said.

"What do you think?" she asked.

"Think?"

"About them. Did they hatch? Or did something get to them?" She moved closer to my sleeping bag; the two of us huddled together.

"Of course they hatched," I said, because you couldn't think any other way. "And the mom took her babies away to an even bigger place so they could swim without bumping into one another."

"Me too," Mary Grace said. "I'm sure they survived."

68

A few days later, Tessa waited for me outside in the line of buses. From the way she stood with her hands on her hips, she wasn't looking for a casual conversation.

She took one long look at me as if I was a cow and she was appraising me for auction. "You look like crap."

"Don't even start with me," I grumbled. "I'm exhausted. I was outside in the field last night."

She placed both her hands on my shoulders so we were facing each other. "You, my friend, have turned cuckoo."

She walked around me, inspecting my head.

"What the heck are you doing?"

"Checking for a hole where they sucked your brains out. They've brainwashed you. I can't believe you're buying into the circles."

"Believe me, I'm not. Those people are still as crazy as they ever were. But if it helps Collin, I'm willing to do that,"

I told her. What I didn't tell her is that it helps me too.

"There are a million other things you can do to help your brother."

"Being out there isn't so bad. I usually spend the time talking with Mary Grace."

Tessa rolled her eyes. "Mary Grace? I thought she drove you nuts."

"She's not that bad. I actually kind of like her now."

"Whatever, do what you want, but it seems to me that your life is on pause right now."

"Shouldn't it be? My sister is missing."

"You're right, *she's* missing. But you aren't. Think about what you lose in the meantime. Do you really want to continue to spend the hours of your life suspended, waiting for Abby to return?"

"I can't let her go," I said.

"No one is asking for that. I miss her too, Rhylee. But I also miss you."

"I'm right here," I argued. I'd always been here.

"You're different," she said. "You're not the same anymore."

"How can I not be? My sister is missing."

"You don't think you've disappeared? What's the use of being here if you act as if you're gone too?" Tessa said. "You've let go of everything that you were, so it's almost as if you're a ghost too. We can't stop living. None of us."

And maybe she was right. Maybe I was gone. Maybe I was losing myself, little by little, until there was nothing left.

69

I wrote texts that I didn't send to Tessa. Words I wanted to say, explanations I tried to create, and excuses for the way I was acting. But I deleted them all, because nothing sounded right, especially when there was a hint of truth in her words and I didn't know what it meant. Was I losing myself? Was that even possible when I wasn't sure I ever knew who I was to begin with? I'd always been Abby's sister and that was enough. So now that she was gone, what did that make me? Who did I want to be?

I continued to take Collin outside to the circles, and the secrets Mary Grace and I traded grew darker, as if we needed each other to unleash those worries that were swirling around in our heads. I felt bad that I was confiding in her instead of Tessa, but she understood what I was going through.

"This morning I tried to remember what Abby looked like, but I couldn't picture her eyes," Mary Grace said. "It was as if her face was there, but her eyes were empty spaces. I couldn't even remember what color they were."

"A bluish-gray," I answered because I could see them clearly. Her eyes matched mine, and sometimes when I was looking in the mirror, I imagined it was Abby looking back at me. "And she had a tiny mole on her left cheek."

"You're right," Mary Grace said.

"Sometimes," I confessed, "I run downstairs because I think I hear the doorbell. I've thrown the front door open and there's nothing but the wind out there. The other day I stood in front of the open door for more than a half hour. I was convinced Abby had rung the bell and was out there."

"I call her phone to listen to her voice mail and look for her when I watch TV," Mary Grace said, understanding what I was talking about. "I search faces in the crowds on the news, thinking I'm going to find her."

"I haven't moved her stuff off the sink in the bathroom," I said. "Her towel is still hanging where she left it before we went to the bonfire and the cap is off on her lotion."

"Do you think—" Mary Grace started, and stopped. I didn't say anything because I knew, I just knew, this was it. We'd arrived at the place we'd been working to cross, and I needed her to step over it first.

She did.

"Do you think she's coming back?" Mary Grace asked.

"My mom does," I answered, even though that wasn't the response she was looking for.

"What about you?"

I felt the familiar sting of remorse before I answered. This conversation. These questions were because of me, and now, here was Mary Grace asking if I thought my own sister was going to return.

"I could hear her voice in my head when she first disappeared," I said. "It was so clear, but it's fading. It's like how I can't remember things about her. How I've forgotten what she sounds like, what she likes, who she was."

"I'm scared I'm not going to see her again," Mary Grace said. She filled in the spaces I left open. The real words I couldn't say yet.

Someone sang near us and more voices joined in. It was a song I'd heard Tessa sing before, the words from a musical that she was once in.

"Day by day, right?" I told Mary Grace.

"It's the only way to survive until she comes home," she agreed. And the two of us focused on the song because we didn't dare mention any of the fears we held deeper inside.

70

The next evening, the entire cross-country team was at the circles. They stayed for hours, some of them falling asleep, heads resting in one another's laps, music softly playing from a speaker someone brought. We talked about Abby, but we didn't focus on her the entire time. We also talked about other things, things that really weren't important but had once felt very important. We gossiped about certain classmates and complained about our teachers. We told one another funny stories and made plans for the following weekend.

As the sky grew darker, the team left, until it was only Mary Grace and me, the way it had been for the last few days. I told her about the time when Abby, Tommy, and I took Collin to the county fair and how Collin was stuck on top of the Ferris wheel with Tommy.

"It was one of the ones where the cage that you're in

swings around. Tommy spun it so fast that I swear you could hear them both screaming from miles away. I don't know who was more scared."

I remembered Abby and me at the bottom trying to record the two of them on her phone.

"I've never seen any two people more inseparable than you and Tommy," Mary Grace said.

"We *used* to be inseparable," I told her.

"Abby told me that Tommy was going to break up with her. Did you know that?"

"She what?" I asked, taken aback.

"He was different. She kept saying that something was going on."

I considered acting as if I had no clue what she was talking about, but it would've been a lie, and my lies were beginning to add up so high that they'd all topple down soon.

"It was because of me," I said. "I was the reason Tommy was going to break up with my sister."

And there, in the hours that come after the sky grows dark, that I told her what I hadn't been able to admit to anyone else.

"I kissed Tommy."

It was the first time I'd said the words to anyone. They came sliding out as if it was meant to be known.

I played with the zipper on my sleeping bag and waited for her to tell me how awful I was. For the sting of those words to finally get the reaction I deserved. But it never came.

"I'm not surprised. You two have always been close friends," she said, as if what I'd told her made perfect sense, as if it were only natural that Tommy and I would be together.

"No," I said, knowing I needed to correct her, but wishing I could leave it at that. Absolution doesn't work unless you dive all the way in, and the hardest part was still to come. "I don't mean . . . recently. I kissed him before Abby disappeared."

There was a silence before Mary Grace asked, "When they were together?"

"The night she disappeared," I whispered.

I paused and didn't say anything. Off to the right a group was singing and I swear that off in the distance, softly, so softly, I could hear Tommy playing the piano, the notes sliding over the night like a faint breeze.

"I'm the reason she's gone," I said, the words thick and substantial. "Tommy was going to break up with her that night. We kissed and Abby saw us. I'm the reason she ran into the woods."

My eyes stung with tears, and I willed myself not to cry, because I didn't deserve to feel bad about what I had done. But it was no use. Something in my chest was broken and it all fell out. Everything I'd kept hidden deep down seeped up like when you knock a glass over at the dinner table and it spreads out all over.

When we were little, Abby and I used to curl up and lie back to back. We'd pretend we were connected, that we were one person, pressed against each other. I moved onto my side and pulled my knees to my chest. I shut my eyes tight and imagined Abby next to me. "And I wasn't even sorry I'd done it."

There it was. Everything. Out on the table. Exposed.

I waited again for Mary Grace to snap at me, to recoil in disgust. To shun me.

It didn't happen.

"Tommy's always liked you," Mary Grace finally said.

"What?" I asked. I could hardly believe that was her answer to my secret. That after everything . . . there was no shouting, no accusations, no shame.

"If we're telling secrets, I guess this one is worth a million." She paused, and then sat up, as if preparing herself for what she was about to reveal. "Abby was jealous of the way Tommy felt about you, even after they were together."

"That's ridiculous," I said, and it was. Abby had everything. Why would she be jealous of me?

"She told me once that she was afraid he'd realize he was with the wrong person and leave her."

That couldn't be true. Mary Grace had to be lying. Abby had never shown any indication that she was worried about my relationship with Tommy. But then I remembered Abby's words in the woods that night.

I always knew, she had said tearfully.

And there was the time when Tommy had come over to give Abby some notes she'd missed in class, but she wasn't home when he got to our house. Instead of heading back home, he'd sat on the porch steps with me. We were doing impersonations of people at our school and cracking up. It had been like old times, when we were still close. Tommy had me laughing so hard, I was bent over to catch my breath when Abby walked up.

"What's so funny?" she had asked, her hand on her hip.

"Nothing, just stupid stuff," I'd said, but when I'd looked at Tommy, the two of us fell into another fit of laughter.

"Really?" she'd asked.

"Your sister is hilarious," Tommy had said. He'd stood and grabbed my hand, pulling me up too. "Here's the papers. I'd better get going."

"You don't want to stay?" Abby had asked, pouting.

"I told my mom I'd help take some boxes into our shed. I need to get it done before it's dark," he'd said, and then turned to me and grinned. "I don't think I've laughed this hard in months. You're hilarious, Rhylee."

I'd taken a bow as Tommy waved good-bye to the two of us.

"He never laughs like that with me."

"What?"

"Tommy . . . the way he is with you. It's different." She had given me a look I couldn't quite place.

"What do you mean?"

"Nothing, it's stupid. Forget it. I need to go inside and study."

"Tommy's my friend," I'd said. I'd been angry. She had no right to get mad at me. "I'm allowed to talk to him. He was my friend long before you two were together."

"I know," Abby had said and sighed. "But sometimes it seems like he'd rather be with you than me."

"Believe me," I'd said, my voice low and serious. I'd remembered the night I had pushed him away. I'd pictured him kissing my sister. "You have nothing to worry about."

"I'm not worrying," Abby had said. Her voice had had a bit of an edge to it, as if she was angry that I'd have to reassure her of this.

"Abby used to say that it seemed so easy between the two of you. She worried about that," Mary Grace said.

"And then it happened," I said. "In the worst possible way."

"It's not your fault, Rhylee."

"How can it not be?" I remembered the look on Abby's face when she saw us. There was no way I could say that I hadn't caused that.

"You didn't know what was going to happen."

"No, but if it wasn't for us . . ."

"You can't think that way. No one caused Abby to disappear. It was an accident."

"Sometimes I believe that if I can find her, I can fix everything. I can tell her that it was a mistake, and Tommy and I will never, ever be together again. But most of all, I'd tell her how sorry I am."

"Are you?"

I turned to her. "Of course I'm sorry."

"But for what? Kissing Tommy? When she knew someday it would happen? When we all knew?" I couldn't see her face, but Mary Grace's voice got lower. "She didn't have to run away. She didn't have to run away from us."

Her words struck me hard in the chest. I'd never thought about it that way. About how maybe Abby had been just as much of a coward as me.

I gazed at the star-flecked sky and wished it was okay to believe Mary Grace.

71

I stayed outside all night with Mary Grace and the rest of the Miracle Seekers, and as soon as the light began to show in the sky I texted Tessa to call me.

"Seriously?" she grumbled when I picked up. "This is way too early to be awake, let alone trying to make conversation."

"Sorry, I needed to talk to you before you left for school. It's important."

Tessa yawned. "What's up?"

"Is there any way you could get your mom's car today? And then maybe cut school with me?"

"Whoa, rebel," she said. "Now you have my attention. What for?"

I thought about what she'd said about living and about what Mary Grace had said about Abby making the choice to run. We all made choices; those of us who chose to stay and those of us who ran.

What would it mean to move on? What would it feel like to live outside the shadow of my sister?

"I was thinking we could go somewhere. Somewhere far away. Somewhere Abby isn't the focus of everyone's attention," I said, and to Tessa's credit, she didn't argue with me.

"I've got this. Let me shower, and I'll be over in about an hour."

"Thanks," I told her, relieved that she understood.

I got dressed and made sure Collin was ready to catch the bus. When Tessa pulled up, I gave Mom a hug good-bye.

"I'm going to hang with Tessa after school," I told her in case she wondered where I was, which was silly. Mom was so consumed with these circles and the people inside of them that I could probably run away to Mexico and she wouldn't notice I was gone.

I climbed into the passenger seat and Tessa handed me a bag from my favorite doughnut shop.

"Here you go, vanilla custard with sprinkles," Tessa said and pointed at a cup of hot chocolate. This was the breakfast we used to grab together when Tessa had the car. Our morning sugar rush, she'd joke.

"You're wonderful," I said and sank my teeth into the glazed doughnut.

"Of course I am. That's why you love me," Tessa said. "Did you call in sick?"

"Yep, we're set." I faked a cough. "I have a very bad sore throat today, so I need to stay home."

"Perfect! Now let's road trip the hell out of today!"

I couldn't help but laugh. As guilty as I felt to admit it, it was nice to be with Tessa and just be ourselves. "Where are we heading?" I asked.

"That's for me to know and you to find out," she said, and I was okay with that. Life had been so much about doing what I thought I was supposed to be doing, that it was nice not to have to make a choice for once. So I settled into my seat and watched the streets that were so familiar to me disappear as Tessa did exactly what I'd asked her to do, drive us far far away from Coffinberry.

72

I must have fallen asleep, because it only felt like seconds later that the car was stopping and Tessa was declaring that we'd reach our destination.

I stretched and glanced at the clock. "I slept for two hours?"

"You needed it," she said. "I can't imagine you get the best sleep outside in those circles."

I didn't bother to argue with her, especially since she was probably right. I felt a million times better after that nap. My head wasn't foggy, and the world was clearer.

"Where are we?" Tessa had parked in a big parking lot packed with cars, so it was impossible to tell.

"Our future," she said. "We've fast-forwarded two years so you can see what's waiting for you.

I laughed. "I slept for a long time, but I don't think I slept that long."

She got out of the car, so I did the same.

"Trust me, this is where you want to be. And if it's not, we'll go somewhere else tomorrow until we figure out the perfect place for you."

She grabbed my hand and gave me a gentle pull. I followed her, curious about where we had ended up. She took me through the parking lot, along a sidewalk.

"Okay, keep your eyes on the ground until I tell you to," she said.

"Really?"

"Come on, Rhylee."

"Fine." I relented and let her lead me around the corner. We walked for a few minutes, and then she stopped.

"All right, open your eyes," she said, and when I did, a giant stone gate stood in front of me. It was the entrance way to a long path lined by old brick buildings. Boys and girls were all over the place, most with backpacks slung over their shoulders.

"We're at a college?"

"Not just any college, Westing College. One of your dream colleges!"

And she was right. I recognized the buildings from the brochures I pored over. We had a student who went there visit our study hall one day and talk with the class. The school sounded amazing. Tessa loved their musical theater department, and I thought the art therapy program sounded interesting. The girl talked about all the work-study programs they had to make it affordable, and the cost wasn't crazy expensive. The school actually seemed within my reach. But it was what they didn't have that had caught my attention: a strong athletic program, which meant that it was a school Abby would never consider. A school where I could go and be my own person.

"So here's the deal," Tessa said. "I'm going to go check out the theater department. Hopefully, they let me sit in on a few classes. And I think you should do the same. Sign up for a tour or walk around. Talk to some people about their majors. Walk through the art building. Figure out what the heck it is you want to do."

"Wait? Showing up here and taking a tour, is that the answer to figuring out my life?" I joked.

"Yep, I fully expect that you have a major figured out and a plan for your life," Tessa said.

"If I had only known it was that easy," I said.

"Don't be so serious. Have fun. You don't have to decide anything now, just check out college life." She paused and gestured toward a group of boys across the street. She let out a low whistle to show her appreciation. "And when I say college life, I mean *all* of it. Check it out from top to bottom."

"You're too much," I said, but laughed.

"We'll plan to meet up in a few hours. Give this a chance."

"I will," I said, but this was all a bit crazy to me. Westing College was the last place I had expected Tessa to take me today.

"Remember, you're still here. You've got to make the most of that." She opened the giant bag she was carrying and pulled a backpack out of it. "Here, put this on your shoulder. Now you look like an official college student."

"You're too much," I said, but slipped my arms through it.

"Perfect!" She waved her phone in the air. "Go explore. I'll text you in a little bit."

And like that, she was off as if we really were living our future and had simply made plans to meet after our classes. She headed down the path and the funny thing was, I could see our future happening for the first time in a long time. My future. All of this seemed more real than I could have ever imagined.

73

Across from the front gates was a small downtown area with a coffee shop, bookstore, post office, and bars lining the brick-paved road, so I headed toward that.

I ducked into the coffee shop first. I was starving. The doughnut felt like a lifetime ago. I ordered a Mediterranean bagel, with feta and fire-roasted red peppers. Foods that never existed in our house because Abby was such a boring eater.

"What do you want to drink?" the girl asked. She had thick dark curls and her nose was pierced. She chewed loudly on a piece of gum while she waited for my answer.

"How about a chai tea with almond milk," I said; the combination sounded foreign and exotic.

"You got it. Grab a seat and someone will bring it out when we're done."

I picked a booth right next to the window so I could see outside. The sidewalk was full of students. They walked in groups or alone; some talked on their phones, while others moved their heads to whatever song was playing through their headphones. Life moved on, people passed by, and not one of them noticed me.

And for once, I wasn't the sister of Abby the cross-country star or the girl whose sister disappeared. I didn't have to try to be like my sister or live the life I thought she should be living.

Here, I was nobody.

And it felt amazing.

I paged through a newspaper that was on the table. *The Westing Post*. It said it was student-produced under the title and each article had the author's name and graduation year on it. Many of them also included the author's major, but not all of them. It was the ones that didn't have the major that I read. These students wrote about rallies going on around campus, a project that was being done in a history class, and an opinion piece about the value of taking a public speaking course. I studied each of them. I tried to find hints of indecisiveness between the lines, but their words were strong and confident. Nothing in them told me they worried that they didn't know what they wanted to do yet. They didn't sound confused or lost. And maybe that wasn't the case at all. Maybe instead, it was freeing. They had the whole world in front of them and a lifetime to decide what to do.

I glanced around the coffee shop and wondered how many people here knew what they wanted to do. And for those that did, when did they decide? Was it something their parents had forced on them? Did they follow in the footsteps of someone else? Did their teachers push them toward something? Or were they like me and never felt they had the chance to even think about it, because their lives were spent living in the shadow of others? How many of them looked deep inside of themselves and chose what they loved? And were they happy with their decision? It was impossible to tell, but maybe that was the way it was with a lot of things. If there was anything I'd learned in the last few months, it's that you can never be certain of a single thing.

I finished my lunch and headed back to the front gate and the path Tessa had disappeared down earlier. I pretended I went here. There wasn't a soul who knew my story, so I created my own. I walked along the path as if I belonged. Students passed on either side and not one of them noticed me. I followed a group of girls into a building and took a seat behind them in a large lecture hall. The seats began to fill and there must have been over a hundred people in one single class.

A boy slipped into the seat next to me.

I waited for him to call me out, to tell me I didn't belong here, but instead, he pointed at his textbook.

"Did you do the reading last night?"

I shook my head and he nodded.

"Same here. I swear, Dr. Kohlings gives us more work than any of my other classes combined."

"Tell me about it," I agreed.

"Guess we'll have to just wing it. I won't tell if you won't," he said and winked at me.

"Deal," I said as a bubble of nervous excitement began to

form in my stomach. Was this boy flirting with me? A college student? But as quickly as the idea came, I pushed it back down. What would he think if he knew the truth about me and what I did to my own sister? And how was it fair that I was here and Abby wasn't?

You're allowed to live, I thought to myself, Tessa's words a mantra. But if that was the truth, why was it so hard to believe it?

A man I presumed to be Dr. Kohlings walked into the room and began to talk about an experiment that must have been a part of last night's reading. Something about rats being trained to do specific things in order to get a reward, even if it meant they'd harm themselves. Was that what it had been like with Tommy? Did I go after him even when if it would ruin everything? But what was the alternative? To be in the control group and never experience what it was I wanted? What would life have been like then? There was no right answer to this, only the consequences.

"So, I was wondering," the boy next to me whispered when class was over. "Since we both didn't do the homework, it might help us actually do the work if we had a way to remind each other."

"Remind each other?" I asked.

"Like if you texted me to see if I got it done, or I could text you," he talked fast and fidgeted.

"Are you asking me for my phone number?"

"Maybe . . . well, yeah," he said. "If that's okay. I mean, if you're dating someone, it's cool. Forget I said anything."

"No, no, I'm most definitely not dating anyone," I said.

"How about I give you mine," he said, his eyes lighting up. "That way, if you don't want to talk, no worries. I won't make it awkward."

I surrendered my phone to him and he typed in his number.

"I'm Dylan," he said. "In case you want to know who you're talking to."

I paused. Abby's name dangled on the tip of my tongue, because she's the one who caught boys' attention and got phone numbers. But that wasn't who I was. That wasn't who I was supposed to be. And maybe my world could be different.

"I'm Rhylee," I said and smiled.

"Rhylee," he repeated, and I liked the way my name sounded. "Hopefully, I'll get to talk with you soon."

He slipped out of the seats and followed the crowd out of the room. I stayed where I was until everyone was gone. The lecture hall stood empty. A room so big you could fit my graduating class in it, but I didn't feel alone. In fact, for the first time in forever, I felt as if I actually belonged. And not because I was Abby's sister, but because I was Rhylee.

74

Tessa didn't ask me how my day went, so I didn't say anything. I kept it deep inside of me so I wouldn't lose the magic that the day had held. When she dropped me off at my house, I reached across the front seat and gave her a hug that was so much like the infamous hugs she always gave me.

"What's that for?" she asked, surprised. She knew that wasn't my usual style.

"Today," I told her. "Thank you."

"It was pretty great, wasn't it?"

"The best," I said as I got out of the car.

Tessa leaned out her window. "You're pretty awesome, Rhylee. Don't forget that."

"I won't," I said and waved. Tessa blew me a kiss, and I laughed. The sound still felt unnatural, but I liked it.

I headed toward my house, where I lived surrounded by everything that was so familiar. But my view of the world had changed. I'd moved out of my sister's shadow, if only for a minute, but it was that taste of freedom that I held on to and the thought that maybe one day I really could get out of here.

Today no one knew my sister or what I did.

I could leave and live my own life.

I could be myself.

75

That evening I stayed away from the fields. Instead, I opened my desk drawer and pulled out the two pieces of the picture I had found in Abby's notebook. I lined our faces back up next to each other and carefully placed a piece of tape down the middle to put them back together to make us whole.

The image was complete again, but you could still see the tears around the edges. It didn't fit perfectly together, but did it ever? Did we ever? And did we need to?

Abby was my sister, and I loved her, but we still had our flaws. We both made mistakes, we both fought, we both resented part of each other, but the important thing is that we also loved each other.

"I miss you," I whispered to the image. The pain of her loss consumed me. The void she had left behind was the size of the world.

"And I miss us," I said. "I miss us so bad."

But what did "us" mean?

I wasn't exactly sure of the answer, but what I did understand was that Abby and I were never meant to be the same person and I needed to figure out how to stand on my own. I wasn't my sister. I wasn't defined by her. And I didn't need to be. You could exist alongside a person without being that person. And maybe that could be enough.

76

The next morning, I'd just gotten out of the shower when I heard a rush of voices outside. I pulled back the window and saw everyone from the circle racing toward the woods.

The bathroom was hot with steam around me, and yet goose bumps appeared all over my skin.

I went to Abby's room and looked at our field. The Miracle Seekers were frantic, most running toward the edge of the woods, their belongings scattered as if a tornado had blown through. Mom and Collin were in the middle of the group, the two of them moving with the same urgency toward whatever caused the commotion.

I threw on some clothes and got myself out of there as fast as I could.

"What's going on?" I asked a neighbor who stood on the edge of the crowd.

"It's your sister. We saw her. She was beyond the trees over there."

"What are you talking about?" I turned to look where she pointed. I couldn't spot Mom anymore. Had she gone into the cluster of trees that guarded the edge of the field?

"She's here," my neighbor said. "We saw her before she went into the woods."

I searched the crowd again for Mom and instead found Collin. He was still in his Spider-Man pajamas and sat on Mary Grace, sobbing. As I got closer, I saw that his lip was bleeding. Mary Grace held a tissue against it as tears ran down Collin's cheeks.

"What happened here? Is he okay?"

"He tripped and fell when everyone was running. It doesn't look too serious; he's a bit shaken up, though."

"Where's my mom? Why isn't she with him?"

"She ran into the woods with the others."

Anger flashed through me. How could Mom let this happen? Did she really think it was okay to leave Collin here alone?

"Hey, buddy." I got down on his level. "You're being really brave right now."

He wrapped his arms around my neck and buried his face in my shoulder. I stroked his hair, trying to calm not only him but myself. This was ridiculous. The town was going mad and no one seemed to be the voice of reason.

Collin clung to me until his sobs turned into sniffles. He pulled his face away so he was facing me. "I saw her, Rhylee. She was here. Why did she run from me?"

"I don't know. I don't know what's going on." I untangled myself from Collin and held out to him one of the tissues Mary Grace passed to me. "How about you keep this against your lip to stop the bleeding?"

He placed it against his lip and looked up, his eyes two giant watery orbs.

"Do you think you're okay? Can you wait here so I can go and see if I can find Mom?"

He shook his head and his eyes filled back up with tears. "Don't leave me."

"How about you come with me?" I asked and bent down so he could climb onto my back, even though he was too old for that. The two of us hiked into the tress, Collin only letting go of his death grip around my neck to knock branches away from his face. We headed toward the voices.

We found everyone in the clearing where our bonfire had been the night Abby disappeared. The group didn't seem as frantic as the one outside of the woods. Instead, they sat around the burned wood and ashes, most people on logs but some right on the ground. They faced outward, everyone's back turned to the center.

As Collin and I stepped into the circle, a woman stood and shouted at us. "Oh my god, it's Abby. She's here!"

The group turned toward us. Collin climbed off my back and people rushed at me.

"Abby!" A woman said and sobbed.

A gray-haired woman moved toward me with her arms outstretched, as if she planned to embrace me. I took a few steps back and held out my hands to stop her, but she wrapped me into a hug. Her breath was hot on my neck.

People gathered around the two of us and reached out to touch me, as if they needed to make sure I was real. I broke free from them and tried to separate myself from the group.

"No, I'm Rhylee. Not Abby," I said and shook my head. It didn't even occur to me to try and pretend for them. I wasn't Abby. I wasn't.

A few stayed near me as if to make sure I was telling the truth, but most sat back down. I spotted Mom and stormed over to her.

"What are you doing here?" I yelled. I didn't care who saw me or what kind of scene I caused. "You left Collin in the field sobbing. He fell and cut his lip. He was bleeding."

Mom inspected his lip. "You're okay now, right? I had to follow everyone."

"It was your sister," a man prompted, and I shot him a disgusted look.

"That was not my sister," I said. "She's not out here."

"I don't get it," a woman yelled in frustration. "Why does Abby keep doing this to us? Doesn't she understand how much we want to see her? That we're waiting for her to return?"

"It not right," another woman agreed. "Her running away from us. How can she hurt us like this?"

"Are you kidding me?" I shouted at the group as they argued about the unfairness of this all. "Abby isn't doing this. You're not seeing her. How can you be mad at someone who isn't even here?"

I tried to make them understand what I was saying, but it fell on deaf ears. Mom had already tuned out, and her eyes scanned the woods again. In fact, everyone had gone back to looking for a ghost that seemed more real to them than the lives they'd forgotten about.

77

Dad was getting out of his car when we all came out of the woods. Collin stayed close to my side, unnerved by everything that had happened, but when he saw Dad, he broke out into a run toward him.

"Hey, buddy," Dad said and hugged him. It wasn't until Collin pulled back that Dad noticed the blood all over him. "What's this blood from? Did something happen?"

Instead of responding, Collin broke out into sobs. He tried to tell Dad what had happened, but couldn't get the words out.

"Is he okay?" Dad asked me, and I shrugged.

"Physically, yeah, but those people are out of control. They all ran into the woods thinking they saw Abby. Mom followed too and left Collin all alone. Mary Grace found him on the ground; he had fallen and cut his lip open. It was bleeding all over, and Mom wasn't even here to take care of him."

Collin stuck his bottom lip out for Dad to inspect and wiped his nose with his sleeve.

"They saw Abby in the woods," he told Dad. "Why can't I see her?"

"That wasn't your sister. They made a mistake," Dad told him as he scanned the crowd of people. He found Mom and gestured to her to come over.

"What a morning, huh?" she asked.

"You could look at it that way," Dad replied. "Rhylee said you left Collin behind to run off into the woods. Is that true?"

"There was an Abby sighting. I had to go check it out. Collin was fine," Mom said.

"You call this fine?" Dad asked and pointed to Collin's bloodied shirt. "Your son was hurt and left alone. This is where I draw the line. I let these people stay in our yard, I didn't say a word when you went outside to join them. But this—this is too much. Collin is not to go out into the circles anymore."

"He's okay," Mom said at the same time Collin spoke up.

"That's not fair. I didn't do anything wrong," Collin said and another round of fresh tears began.

"That's the way it's going to be," Dad told him and looked Mom straight in the eyes. "That's the way you're going to make sure it is. No more encouraging him."

"If he wants to go outside—" Mom began, but Dad cut her off.

"Collin is not to hang out in them anymore. If that's too hard for everyone to understand, I'll make sure the circles simply get cut down, so it's no longer a problem."

"Will, the circles are good," Mom insisted.

"I didn't say you can't go out there, but I don't want my son out there. This isn't up for debate."

"This isn't fair. I'm not hurting anyone. I should be allowed in the circles," Collin argued.

"End of discussion," Dad said. "Or those circles will be gone by tomorrow."

Collin stormed away to the house and slammed the door so loud that we could hear it from where we stood across the yard.

"I meant what I said. I don't want Collin spending time out here anymore," Dad told Mom, but I wasn't sure she heard. Her eyes were focused on the patch of trees where Abby had been spotted, and I was pretty sure she was lost again in a world where real and make-believe merged.

78

Mary Grace was unusually quiet in school that day. She stared off in the distance with unfocused eyes.

When she wiped her sleeve across her eyes, I could tell something was going on.

"Is everything okay?"

She nodded, but she wasn't fooling me.

I put my hand on top of her arm and squeezed gently. "You're not okay," I said. I raised my hand and asked Mrs. Tetonis if we could go to the bathroom. As soon as the classroom door closed behind us, I turned to Mary Grace. "What's up?"

"It's stupid. It's so stupid," she said, and sank onto the floor, her back against a locker. I sat next to her.

"I'm sure it's not, if it's getting you upset," I said, and the irony didn't miss me. Here was the person who only weeks ago I couldn't stand. She'd oozed sympathy and all I'd wanted her to do was get the hell away from me. Now I was the one trying to help her. I understood the frustration she must have had with me when I refused to let her in. "It might help to talk about it."

Her eyes turned bright and wild. For a minute, I thought she was going to get up and run away. Instead, she said, "I'm so pissed off."

"At me?" I asked, confused. I tried to think if I had done anything to make her feel that way.

"No, Abby. I keep thinking about why she hasn't chosen me. What did I do wrong?"

"What are you talking about?"

"She's appeared to everyone but me. I've stayed up the last few nights hoping she'd run by. I don't get it. My mom has seen her. Complete strangers have seen her. Doesn't Abby know how bad I want her back? Doesn't she care?"

Mary Grace pulled her legs to her chest and wrapped her arms around them. She rested her head on her knees and her body shook with her sobs. You could probably fill an ocean with the amount of tears we'd cried over my sister. I stretched my feet out in front of me and stared at the lockers as I spoke.

"You can't be mad at her. It's not her fault she's gone," I said and thought back to my conversation with the Miracle Seekers in the woods. "That person they're seeing, she's not Abby."

"You don't know that for sure. What if it is? It's like what I said about her face. I can't remember what she looks like. What if she's standing right in front of me and I don't even know it's her?"

"It's the opposite for me. I'm afraid of seeing this vision of her and then knowing for sure it's not really her."

Mary Grace lifted her head. "I want to see her so bad."

"So do I, but not this way."

Mary Grace gave me the weakest of smiles and wiped at her eyes. "This ghost is what's been keeping me going. I search through the trees in every yard, look toward the woods and at sidewalks across the street."

"There isn't a moment that goes by when I'm not hoping she'll appear," I said, and wished there was a way to rewind our lives so we were back to the days when "missing" and "vanished" weren't even words in our vocabulary.

"It's my fault," she said.

"What do you mean? You didn't cause this."

"Not Abby. The circles. The way everyone is waiting for her to return," she said, but that didn't help. She wasn't making any sense.

"How are you to blame?"

"I have to tell you something, but I'm not sure what you're going to say."

When someone starts a sentence like that, you know it's going to be bad news. But Mary Grace didn't judge me when I told her about kissing Tommy, so how could I judge her?

"You can tell me," I said.

She took a deep breath and let it out before she spoke again. "I made the circles in your yard."

"You *what?*" I didn't know what I expected her to say, but I sure didn't think it would be anything like that.

The rest of her words came out in a rush. "The whole cross-country team did. The field where she'd run was overgrown and full of weeds. It killed us to see that. If Abby came home, we wanted it to be ready for her. So we cut it."

"How?" I asked, not quite believing her. "Those circles were huge. It would've taken hours."

"Some of the guys brought push mowers, because we didn't want to wake anyone. It was a tribute for her. Or at least, that's what we thought when we were doing it. The plan was to tell everyone what we'd done, but then the news came and reported on it and the police were looking for suspects, so we went along with everyone because suddenly it was a big deal."

"The cross-country team made the circles?" I asked, not willing to believe her confession.

Mary Grace looked like she was about to cry. "I swear, I wanted to say something, but the team promised to keep their mouths shut so we wouldn't get in trouble. We didn't think it would turn out this way. We honestly didn't know what to do."

"So you went along with everyone and let us believe they were made by my sister?"

"I wanted to believe they had something to do with her. We all did. I wanted to see your sister so badly. I began to fool myself, too."

"But the circles meant nothing," I said, and was surprised at how much it hurt to realize that the circles weren't, in fact, connected to Abby. "All those people out there every night, Collin, my *mom* . . . and they were just a hoax."

"But that's the thing, Rhylee. They started as a hoax, but it changed. They *did* mean something. Maybe your sister didn't make them, but the circles united us. They gave us hope."

"And now," I said slowly as the realization set in, "that hope is gone."

79

I didn't go back to class. I raced down the hall, my anger at her growing by the second. How could she do something like that? Those circles were our connection to Abby and now I find out it wasn't even real. How would Mom feel? And Collin? It would crush him.

I kicked a locker out of frustration; the noise echoed down the hallway. I yelped in surprise at the pain and tears gathered in my eyes. This was impossible. All of it.

I'd been so stupid to sit in that field and pretend we were connected. Pretend that Abby was closer to us because we were there. All of those things I confessed to Mary Grace in the dark, when she was the one who had fooled us to begin with by creating the circles.

Tears blinded me as I pulled out my phone and texted Tommy. I needed him, and I didn't care how it looked or what I was supposed to do or not do.

He rounded the corner less than two minutes later.

"Are you okay?" he asked. He reached out for me, but I pulled back. After weeks of avoiding any sort of contact, I still didn't feel right about him touching me. No matter how I was feeling.

Hurt flashed across his face, but was quickly covered by concern. "What's wrong?"

"What isn't wrong?" I asked and laughed, because it was the truth. How did I even begin to list everything? "I have no idea what's right anymore."

"I don't think any of us do," he said.

Before I could say anything more, the bell rang, and my classmates spilled out into the hallway.

"Hey, man," Kyle said, coming toward us. Two of his friends stood on either side like bookends, and all three of them looked at Tommy with disgust. "I told you nicely to stay away from Rhylee, but it looks like you didn't hear me."

Tommy stepped in front of me so I was hidden behind him. Protected. Other kids gathered around, as if sensing that something was going to happen.

"You can tell me whatever you want," Tommy said. "But I'm not going to listen to any of your bullshit."

"Kyle, really, it's fine," I said, trying to make peace between the two of them. "We're only talking."

It didn't work. He spoke to Tommy as if I wasn't even there. "You're not wanted here. In fact, you're not wanted anywhere."

"Go to your class," Tommy told me. "I'll take care of this."

"I'm not going anywhere," I told him. I was terrified, but if I left him, Kyle would do something worse than the black eye. I just knew it.

"Don't worry, I'll be fine."

"Listen to him," Kyle said. "It's better if you leave right now."

No. No more running away. No more being so stupid.

"I'm staying here," I said and crossed my arms over my chest. I tried to look tough, even though I was terrified.

Tommy shifted from foot to foot. He did not want me to stay, but I'd already backed away from so many other things and let him take the blame that I wasn't going to leave him alone now.

"Suit yourself," Kyle said. "If you want to watch me kick Tommy's ass, so be it. This is a school. Not a place for killers."

Tommy stiffened. He tried to let go of my hand, but I held on tighter.

"Forget about it," I whispered, but he couldn't. He broke free from my grasp and stepped up to Kyle so the two of them were almost touching chests.

"What did you say?" Tommy asked, his voice low and hard.

"You heard me. No one wants you here. Killer."

Kyle's fists went up, and I squeezed my eyes shut. There was a sickening crunch and Tommy groaned. When I opened my eyes, blood streamed out of his nose.

Kyle took another swing at Tommy, but Tommy ducked and landed a punch of his own. Kyle moved quickly, though, and drove his fist into Tommy's stomach. Tommy bent over and Kyle took the opportunity to push him to the ground. Tommy grabbed Kyle's ankle and yanked him down too. The two rolled around on the floor, a mess of hands, legs, and blood. Kyle got on top of Tommy and pinned him so that he was unable to fight back.

"Stop it!" I screamed as Kyle hit Tommy over and over again.

The crowd of students around us grew, and people held their phones out to record the fight as others cheered it on. And I hated them. Every single one of them.

Mr. Ralston and Mr. Scott pushed their way through the group, finally making it to the two boys.

"Break it up, both of you," Mr. Ralston said, but they wouldn't stop. Tommy wiggled out from under Kyle and curled up in a ball, and Kyle just kept hitting him.

"Please stop them," I yelled. "He's going to kill him!"

They were finally able to pull the two of them apart.

Tommy slowly sat up, his face covered in blood. He looked around at everyone, dazed.

Kyle coughed and wiped his mouth with the back of his hand. "Did you see the way he was hitting me?" he asked Mr. Scott. "He's psycho. No wonder the police think he killed Abby."

"Kyle's right," one of his friends said. "Tommy went after him. We were trying to go to class."

A few other boys nodded to confirm the story. I was amazed by how bold their lies were.

Tommy stood and backed away from everyone with his hands in the air. "I was only protecting myself."

"We'll discuss this in my office," Mr. Ralston said, and then faced the group of students gathered around. "I need all of you to go back to class. I'll take care of this. Mr. Scott, please escort Kyle to the bathroom to wash off. He can come to the office afterward to give his statement."

"Thanks," Kyle said. "I'm a little shaken up by all of this."

"Tommy didn't start it," I said, unable to contain myself. He was not going to take the fall for this. "You have it wrong."

"I need you go to go back to class too. I'm sure your parents wouldn't like it if they knew who you were hanging out with at school."

I tried to catch Tommy's eye, but he refused to look at me. His shirt was covered in blood and his left eye was starting to swell shut. I wanted to reach out and touch him, let him know it would be okay, but that was impossible. None of this was okay. Not at all. And no one was going to do a damn thing about it.

"No," I said, my voice sounding a lot stronger than I felt.

"Excuse me?" Mr. Scott asked.

"Miss Tower," Mr. Ralston warned, but I was done listening to him. He'd made it painfully clear whose side he was on, and I wasn't going to stand for it anymore.

"Tommy didn't do anything. He's innocent," I told the two of them and then faced the crowd. "You're the ones who should be ashamed of yourselves for what you've done to him."

"If he's so innocent, then why is he the police's number one suspect? You can't deny the obvious," Mike Connors, a football player in my grade, said. The group of students around us laughed.

"It's because of me!" I shouted to all of them, and there was no turning back. "It's because of me."

"Rhylee, no—" Tommy started, but I spoke over him.

"Do you want to know why my sister ran into the woods that night? It wasn't Tommy's fault. It was mine. I kissed him, and Abby saw it. She found the two of us together. That's why Tommy went into the woods. That's why he was muddy. He was trying to bring my sister back, because *I* betrayed her. So if you want to target someone, blame me. I did this. I made my sister disappear!" My voice broke as I battled the sobs that threatened to escape. I broke down, and I didn't care who the hell saw me.

Both Tommy and Mr. Ralston made their way to me, but I was done. I'd confessed. I ran past them before they could stop me, my feet flying across the floor as if I were Abby, racing to the finish line.

80

I ran all the way home, where I found Dad outside talking to Officer Scarano. They were next to his police cruiser, using it like a shield from the people in the field, who seemed to have moved a little bit closer, as if trying to figure out what was going on.

"What are you doing here?" I asked, because I was tired of not asking and not knowing.

"Afternoon, Rhylee," Officer Scarano said, ignoring my question. He turned back to Dad. "I'll talk with you tomorrow. We'll keep you up to date on everything."

"I appreciate that," Dad said and shook his hand.

Officer Scarano nodded at me once more before he left, but didn't make eye contact.

"Why was he here?" I asked Dad when the police car pulled away, kicking up gravel.

"He was checking in."

Dad headed inside, and I followed him. He was hiding something from me and after the day I'd had, I was done being nice to people. I was done with lies. Mine, and everyone else's. "What did he say?"

"He didn't have anything new to report," Dad said. He headed up the steps. "And I need to get ready for work now. I was already running late before he showed up."

"Why won't you talk to me about this?"

"There isn't anything to say."

"Stop, Dad. Please. Just stop!" He did. He turned to look at me, a little surprised. "We never talk anymore. If Abby did return, she wouldn't know where the hell she was. This isn't our home anymore. She'd never recognize this place; how could she when it feels so empty and cold?"

"That's enough," Dad said, and it really was. All of this was way too much. It was time to stop pretending. He paused and didn't say anything for a moment. Then he nodded.

"No, you're right," he said and his voice faltered. I wondered if he was going to cry. I'd never seen Dad cry.

"What's going on?" I asked.

Dad was quite for a moment. "The police think it's time we face the truth about what was found by the river."

His words hit me hard. Dad took a deep breath and let it out in one long sigh. My family had never, ever spoken those words out loud to one another. The policemen had talked in circles around what they had found at the river, both the shoe and the shoe prints, and what they might mean, but we'd never dared to connect the dots.

"They believe we should consider the facts," he said.

"I don't want to look at the facts," I told him, my body growing cold.

"None of us do," Dad said, his voice breaking again.

"Why now?" I asked him, fighting back my own tears.

"There haven't been any of leads or clues about what might have happened to Abby except what was found in the water. If there was some sign that said she could be somewhere else, the police would follow up on it, but there's nothing. They spoke to Johnson again and believe the river is the only place they can find answers. They plan to dredge the lake again and look for . . ." Dad's voice trailed off, and he didn't say it, but he didn't need to. I could finish the sentence with words I never thought we'd say.

"How can we just let go of hope?" I asked. "Won't that mean we're giving up on her?"

"It's been impossible to think of anything other than Abby coming home safely," he said, his voice thick with the same sorrow and regret. "I couldn't face any other possible truths, but I think we need to now."

I wanted to be mad at him. I wanted to yell and rage and strike out, but how could I? What he was saying made sense. I was an expert about not wanting to speak the truth—and how much damage that caused.

81

I didn't go back out to the circles. I couldn't. Everything I believed in wasn't true. Instead, I searched the house for my own sneakers. I was done wearing Abby's shoes.

I took off down the driveway and kept my eyes on the sky. The day had been filled with inconstant weather, and there was talk on the news that we'd finally get rain, providing relief to the drought that had plagued us for weeks. The sky grumbled and groaned echoes of thunder from the distance, moving closer to our house.

I ran with the clouds that raced in over our field and the wind that whipped around me so I had to strain to push forward.

I ran faster than I'd ever run before and left the crowd in the field.

I moved away from a family that was so busy trying to hold on to one person that they forgot about who was still there.

I ran and ran and ran, but it wasn't far enough. I couldn't lose myself in the pain.

Dad's words echoed in my mind. He'd mentioned Johnson. What had happened when the police talked to him again? Was he what made them so sure that the lake was where my sister was? I needed to get some answers, and Johnson was the one who might be able to give them to me.

I made it to the square, half expecting to find him waiting for me. Of course, it wasn't that simple. He wasn't there. I moved quickly, half running, half walking down the sidewalk. I dodged people as if they were an obstacle course. A friend of Mom's recognized me and waved. I could tell by the way she stopped in the middle of the sidewalk that she wanted me to slow down and talk, but I rushed past with a smile and a quick apology.

I finally found Johnson heading out of town, going back to the woods. A piece of blue ribbon tied around the edge of his cart flapped in the wind.

"Johnson," I yelled. He turned and I held my hands in the air, as if I were surrendering. I had nothing to hide. He was the only possibility for help, and I wanted him to see that I was there, open, free, and offering whatever I could to him. "I don't know what else to do. I feel as if what happened to my sister was my fault. I drove her away that night, and I need to make it better."

His shoulders lifted as he took a deep breath. "I can't help you."

"You were in the woods. She ran in your direction."

"Don't you know when to stop? There are some things not worth knowing."

"Like what?"

"You don't want to know." He turned from me and pushed his cart again.

I ran in front of him. "What do you mean? You can't just say something like that and then not finish it."

"Ask your father, little girl. I have no business saying anything else. You need to leave me alone."

I fell to the ground. I couldn't leave him alone. My knees gave out, and my jeans scraped against the concrete as the pressure of it all pulled me down. The sobs came fast and heavy. I missed Abby with an ache so strong that it scared me.

"Listen, you need to be quiet or half the town is going to be here circling the two of us. Come on, girl."

I swallowed and tried to silence everything that was swirling inside. "Please, I need to know the truth."

"I didn't see anything; that's what I told the police, and it's the truth. But I heard something. A scream. I don't mean when you kids are partying in the woods; I hear that all night long. This was different. It was high-pitched and long. It seemed to surround me; it went on and on. Then it stopped."

"What do you mean?" I asked, even though I wasn't sure I wanted to know.

Johnson paused. "I've heard that kind of scream before. In the war. It's primal. It's about survival."

I understood what he was telling me, even though I didn't want to believe him. My heart throbbed. I felt like I was dying inside, but I stood up and stuck out my hand like I'd seen Dad do all the times we used to meet up with Johnson. "Thank you for letting me know."

He shook it, but didn't let go. Instead, he wrapped his rough fingers around mine. It seemed he was finally ready to confess too. "That's not the only thing I heard. There was a splash. A loud one. Usually I'll find a rotted-out tree trunk or a huge branch in the water. This time, when I went to check, there was nothing. At least in the water."

"But the shore . . . ," I said, still holding his hand.

"The shore," he repeated, and I was sure he was picturing the bank the way I'd seen it with the searchers. The footprints along the edge that slid into the water. He squeezed my hand and let go.

I felt numb. "Thank you," I told him, the words automatic on my lips.

"It's not easy to lose people. I couldn't tell you how many men I lost in combat, but what I do know is that it never got any easier."

His words definitely didn't help either. They pierced my chest. "No, sir, it doesn't," I said.

"You're a brave girl," he told me, and I sucked my breath in. Was I?

I could tell from the sadness in his eyes that in his mind, my sister wasn't going to return.

"I have to be," I said.

I left him there. I had found what I'd been searching for.

82

The rain caught up to me as I ran away from the center of town. Small drops at first, until the sky opened and poured.

I was soaked in a matter of minutes. I turned to head home. Lightning flashed in the sky and a few cars drove past. Their wipers made rapid movements to fight off the rain, and the water warped the faces of the drivers who peered out at me.

I ran through the grass on the edge of the road so a car wouldn't hit me, my feet squishing in the puddles of mud.

I stopped when I reached our field.

For the first time since the circles had appeared, the field was empty. There were no people, no candles, no singing, and no hope. The rain had driven them away. Now it was nothing but an empty field with the faint reminder of circles within circles carved into the grass. They were almost gone now that the grass had grown back, filling the empty spaces. The field looked a lot like our field again.

A normal field.

A field that didn't hold some kind of meaning or symbolism for our town.

A field that reminded me a lot of my old life.

My house was a blur in the distance; the lights in the windows were fuzzy in the slanting rain. Mom was probably in front of the computer, Collin in some tunnel deep in his sheets, and Dad at work.

Instead of joining them inside, I walked to the barn where the tools were kept. My clothes clung to me, my hair stuck against my face, and I was freezing. My hands shook as I picked up one of the tools. It was an old blade attached to a wooden stick. Dad called it a sickle and used it to create paths in the woods for Collin and his friends to explore. It was a bit rusty, but when I brought it down against a bale of hay, it cut right through.

I took it into the field.

I couldn't keep pretending Abby was going to return. It was time to stop believing the impossible. The police, Johnson, and Dad had all confirmed it. Abby wasn't coming home.

My body hummed with anticipation. As much as my family didn't want to admit it, we needed to move forward.

"Abby is gone!" I yelled into the storm. "She's gone and she isn't coming back!"

I brought the blade down against the middle of one of the circles.

"But we're still here! We're still living!"

I sliced again.

"And it's not my fault!"

I repeated this over and over as I sliced, the sickle moving back and forth.

It took me more than an hour to destroy the field.

I worked to cut the grass shorter and shorter, destroying any semblance of the circles that linked our town.

I hacked at the weeds, grass, and flowers in each of the centers, making it all the same length so you couldn't see any sort of shape.

I went from circle to circle doing the same thing. I chopped down everything until the field was only that, a field.

And the circles were gone.

I didn't stop. When the grass was sliced to the ground, I continued to cut. I hacked away at the field and the dirt and tried to uncover what used to lie beneath it.

I cut deeper and deeper and searched for the world that should've existed.

I cut until the field was nothing like what it used to be, until it was nothing but raw open earth.

Then I threw the blade down and headed toward my family.

83

My entire body ached so bad that it was almost impossible to climb the steps of our front porch. I kicked off my shoes and pulled off my wet socks. I was a mess of mud, sweat, rain, and tears.

Mom watched from the window. When she saw me, the curtain fell and she was gone.

What was she thinking, now that I'd destroyed the fields?

Our front porch was full of stuff from the Miracle Seekers: sleeping bags, baskets, lanterns, and other items that they must have stashed there when the skies opened. I pictured all of them coming back when the rain stopped and what they would think about the hacked-up field. Would they even return if the field didn't exist anymore? Was the field what had kept everyone together, or had it been something more?

To my surprise, Mom opened the front door and stood

with a towel. "I figured you'd need one of these."

I took it and wrapped it around my shoulders, the warmth welcome on my cold skin.

"I'm a mess," I said.

"I think," she said slowly, as if deliberating over each and every word, "we're all a bit of a mess."

"I can't keep living like this. *We* can't keep living like this."

"I know," she said and her voice was tired. Resigned.

"I miss who we used to be. We haven't just lost Abby. We've lost one another."

I waited for her to deny everything, to make up some excuse or say something about the circles, but she didn't. Instead, she looked ashamed. "I don't even know how I let this happen."

"We need to remember who we were. Please," I said, and it hurt that I was begging Mom to pay attention to me. But I needed her. I really did.

"We will," she said. "I promise."

I had to believe her. I needed to hold on to the belief that things would change.

I gestured toward the field. "I'm sorry I destroyed everything."

She shook her head. "We should've mowed down those fields when the circles first appeared."

"Not just the fields," I told her. "Everything. I did something awful."

"No, you didn't," Mom said, but she didn't understand.

"Tommy isn't the one you should blame for the night Abby disappeared. I am." I forced myself to meet her eyes. My sister deserved that. I wouldn't be a coward anymore. "When we were at the bonfire, Abby found Tommy and me together. We were kissing. She saw us, got upset, and ran into the woods. We chased after her, but she wouldn't listen."

"What are you talking about?" Mom asked. She reached out and brushed away a piece of hair that stuck to my wet face.

"She was so upset, and it's my fault. I did this to her. All this time you've been blaming Tommy, but it was me."

"Why didn't you tell me?" Mom asked, and I imagined the disappointment that I was so afraid was there. But I faced it.

"I was scared. I made her leave. How could I ever tell you and Dad that?"

"Oh, honey, you didn't make her leave," Mom said gently. "It was an accident."

"Abby isn't coming back," I said, and I wasn't sure if I was asking a question or making a statement. "What the police found at the river . . ."

"There's a good chance she isn't," Mom finished, so I didn't have to say anymore. It was the first time we'd acknowledged it to each other. The first time we'd tested out those words, and they felt strange and out of place, but also, they felt necessary.

Mom wrapped her arms around me, ignoring how dirty and wet I was. She tightened her grip and held on tight. "We can't forget who we are; Abby wouldn't want that."

"I feel like she's everywhere." I buried myself into Mom's

warmth. I smelled her. The familiar scent that seemed to be missing all this time. It made me remember how we used to be. I closed my eyes and tried to picture our lives before we lost Abby. I smelled all of us and summers sitting together on the porch, winters around the family room table, and life. Our life that was and the life I still had. The world I knew was still here, changed, but mine, and I clung to Mom and I clung to life.

84

I took a shower and changed into dry clothes. When I walked back downstairs, Mom was in the kitchen stirring something on the stove.

"I thought I'd make us some dinner."

I pulled the lid off a pot and a red sauce bubbled up.

"You're making actual food? That isn't delivery or from a box?"

"Hey, I can cook," Mom said defensively, one hand on her hip. "Maybe I took a break for a while, but it's about time to serve food to you and Collin that doesn't sit on the shelf for months."

Mom was right; it was nice to have something that wasn't from a can, and to eat it around the table together like we used to. Collin was so excited to have something this good for dinner that he had three helpings. I took my time, simply glad to be with my family.

After I did the dishes, I pulled on a hoodie and found

Mom in the living room. She was reading a magazine with the TV on low. Collin played on the floor with a bunch of his action heroes. The computer screen was dark.

"I need to go and talk to Tommy," I told her, and instead of fighting me like she usually did, she nodded.

The rain had stopped, but it was damp outside. The air was cool, the chill of fall settling in. The field sat raw, opened, and destroyed. I walked down the road slowly, not quite sure what I was going to say, but I had to see him.

He sat in his truck bed. Sparks blazed for a moment as he lit one match after another, letting each burn until he flicked it into the air and the flame fizzled out.

I climbed up with him. He moved over on the plaid blanket he'd spread out to make room for me, as if he'd been expecting me to join him.

I fought back tears as I took in what Kyle had done. Tommy's face was a mess. His eyes swollen, cheek battered and bruised. His lip was split and scabbed over.

"You didn't deserve this," I said. I reached out and gently touched a spot on his cheek that wasn't wounded.

"You can't change the way people think," he said.

"I couldn't walk away from you. Kyle was so angry, and what kind of person would—"

"It's okay, you don't have to explain," Tommy said. "Thank you. For everything."

"I told my mom the truth about that night. She said we'll have to talk to the police, but it wasn't our fault. What happened to Abby was an accident."

"She's right. We couldn't have predicted any of this."

Mom had said that no one had that kind of power, and it was true. We couldn't take things away, and we couldn't bring them back. No matter how much we searched or sat in the fields and wished for my sister to return, we'd never be able to make that happen. It was a cruel twist of fate the universe had played on us.

"How'd we get to this point?" I asked. I thought about everything between Tommy and me, from the night I didn't kiss him to the night that I did.

And here I was again with Tommy. My Tommy. The boy I grew up with and loved. The boy whose hands I'd clasped when I was young, the two of us shrieking as we jumped into the freezing cold swimming pool together. The boy who'd protected me on the playground when the other boys took my lunch box, and wrapped his T-shirt around my arm to stop it from bleeding when the dog down the street bit me. This was the boy who'd captured my heart and still held it. The boy I had to let go.

"I think if you want to go to New York, you should," I told him.

"I don't want to leave you alone," he said.

But I wasn't alone. I thought about Westing College and the day I'd spent there where I was able to be myself and nothing else. I thought about my future and where it might take me. What a world beyond my sister's shadow could mean.

"I'll be fine. I'm strong," I told him. "I'm Rhylee."

"You'll always be Rhylee," he said.

I let his words fill me and the two of us sat in the silence and instead of being afraid of what wasn't said in those moments, I felt at peace.

"She isn't coming home," I finally said.

Tommy nodded.

"I miss her so bad," I said.

"So do I," he answered softly.

"But we're still here," I told him.

His hand found mine, and I wrapped my fingers around his. The two of us sat there with nothing between us. Everything we wanted to say, everything we felt and our fears, right in front of us.

I thought about what I'd lost and what I still had.

I squeezed his hand and I was not Abby.

I was Rhylee and I was living and it was okay.

Author's Note

Rhylee called the suicide hotline as a way to cope with her sister's disappearance. If you are experiencing your own feelings of hopelessness or despair, know that there are people willing to listen and help. You are important.

National Suicide Prevention Lifeline

1-800-273-8255

suicidepreventionlifeline.org (to chat with someone online)

Acknowledgments

Writing often feels like a solitary thing, but the truth is, the help and support an author has is amazing. The list of people I could thank for helping to get this book on the shelves is pretty close to the size of the world. I may not be able to thank everyone individually, but you'd better believe that I've felt your love and encouragement.

This book started years ago as a tiny spark of a short story that demanded to be more. I couldn't shake it, the characters lingering inside of me and haunting my thoughts. Slowly, slowly, the story of Rhylee, Abby, and Tommy unfolded. So thank you to the NEOMFA Writing Program, specifically Prof. Rahman's Fiction Workshop class, where I first introduced the short story "Circles Within Circles." Your feedback, conversation, and ideas about that first version began to shape it into the book that it is now.

Thank you to my ever amazing, fabulous, and dedicated agent, Natalie Lakosil, who never, ever gave up on this book. You rock!

A thousand thanks to my editor, Alyson Heller. I can't even tell you how incredibly lucky I feel to have been able to work with you on this book. The story is so much better because of your insights, ideas, and enthusiasm. I'd like to "raise a glass" to you because you are "passionately smashing every expectation" for what an editor should be.

I am so appreciative of everything the brilliant team at Simon Pulse has done. Thank you to Regina Flath for designing the amazing cover, along with Rebecca Vitkus, Katherine Devendorf, Catherine Hayden, Carolyn Swerdloff, Steve Scott, and Faye Bi. Each and every one of you has put your magic touch on this book, and it's all the better for it.

The bond between sisters is one of the most important, loving, and complex relationships I've ever known. Thank you, Amanda, for being an incredible sister, best friend, and Auntie. We may have fought sometimes (okay, a lot of times!) growing up, but I want you to know I'm so lucky to have you in my life. Here's to years of stealing each other's clothes, visits from Michael Jackson and the Easter Bunny, crimping our Barbies' hair, The Shell Shop and Jensen Beach, Bobkittens, 303C Girls, Harborview, late-night Taco Bell, Wednesday visits, riding the choo-choo around the mall, and bowls of bone broth with Nonny!

Once upon a time, I met my Writing Soul Sister, Elle LaMarca, and life has never been the same. You're an amazing crit partner, cheerleader, and fellow Marnie-hater. WSS Book Tour, here we come! You bring the lipstick, and I'll bring the coffee!

Beta partners are the bomb-diggity, and I am eternally grateful for all my readers. Thank you to Nancy Skinner, Christina Lee, Marissa Marangoni, Colleen Clayton, Lisa Nowak, and Taryn Albright . . . you all rock!

Connecting with my readers is hands down my favorite part of writing. Thank you to all the book lovers out there. . . . I write for you.

A shout-out to what fueled this book: coffee, gummy candy, and some good old fashioned crying music (specifically, Coldplay, The National, Damien Rice, The Civil Wars, and The Swell Season...the melancholy in your words played on repeat as I wrote and revised this book). Thank you to Barnes and Noble in Mentor, Panera in Willoughby and Mentor, and the Willoughby Starbucks for providing a place to escape to when I needed to camp out somewhere and focus on nothing but writing. The amount of coffee I consumed writing this book may very well be able to fill an ocean.

Thank you to my family and friends who provide never-ending love and support for me to chase after my dreams. My colleagues (a special high-five to Jenny Hunter and librarian extraordinaire and future dog-walker Jodi Rzeszotarski) and students inspire me every day to want to write, write, write, and I'm so honored to have you are all on this journey with me. Especially to the NaNoWriMo Crew and Thursday Afternoon Writers' Club; Sarah Estvanko, Fatima Martinez, Alexis Beckwith, David Vesey, Megan Carlson, Autumn Graham, and Chelsea Marino. You're all the next generation of writers, and I can't wait to see what amazing words you create!

And always, always, always, to Nolan . . . you will always be my greatest adventure and the best story I ever get to witness.